ALSO BY LAURA DAVE

The First Husband
The Divorce Party
London Is the Best City in America

Eight Hundred Grapes

A Novel

Laura Dave

SIMON & SCHUSTER

New York London Toronto Sydney New Delhi

Simon & Schuster
1230 Avenue of the Americas
New York, NY 10020

First Simon & Schuster hardcover edition June 2015

SIMON & SCHUSTER and colophon are registered trademarks of Simon & Schuster, Inc.

For information about special discounts for bulk purchases, please contact Simon & Schuster Special Sales at 1-866-506-1949 or business@simonandschuster.com.

The Simon & Schuster Speakers Bureau can bring authors to your live event. For more information or to book an event contact the Simon & Schuster Speakers Bureau at 1-866-248-3049 or visit our website at www.simonspeakers.com.

Interior design by Ellen R. Sasahara

Manufactured in the United States of America

1 3 5 7 9 10 8 6 4 2

Library of Congress Cataloging-in-Publication Data

Dave, Laura.
  Eight hundred grapes : a novel / Laura Dave. — First Simon & Schuster hardcover edition.
     pages ; cm
  "Simon & Schuster fiction original hardcover."
  ISBN 978-1-4767-8925-5 (hardcover) — ISBN 978-1-4767-8928-6 (softcover) — ISBN 978-1-4767-8929-3 (ebook) 1. Families—Fiction. 2. Vineyards—California—Fiction. 3. Domestic fiction. I. Title. II. Title: Eight hundred grapes.
  PS3604.A938A616 2015
  813'.6—dc23

2014034389

ISBN 978-1-4767-8925-5
ISBN 978-1-4767-8929-3 (ebook)

J.
Without you, there probably wouldn't be a novel . . .
There certainly wouldn't be such great wine

You have to grow about eight hundred grapes to get just one bottle of wine. If that isn't an argument to finish the bottle, I don't know what is.

—*Anonymous*

Part 1

The Grapes

Sebastopol, California. Six months ago

*M*y father has this great story about the day he met my mother, a story he never gets sick of telling. It was a snowy December morning and he was hurrying into his co-worker's yellow Volkswagen bug parked in front of Lincoln Center, holding two cups of coffee and a massive slew of newspapers. (His first wine, Block 14—the only wine in his very first vintage—had gotten a small mention in the *Wall Street Journal*.) And between the excitement of the article and the steaming coffee, Daniel Bradley Ford didn't notice that there were two yellow bugs parked in front of Lincoln Center. That his East Coast distributor was not the one huddling for warmth in the yellow bug's driver's seat. But, instead, his future wife, Jenny.

He had gotten into the wrong car to find the most gorgeous woman he'd ever seen, wearing blue mittens and a matching beret. Her long, blond curls seeping out from beneath. Her cello taking up the whole backseat.

The legend goes—and knowing my parents I almost believe it—that my mother didn't scream. She didn't ask who my father was or what he was doing in her car. She offered one of her magical smiles and said, "I was wondering what took you so long."

Then she reached out her hand for the cup of coffee he was ready to give her.

Synchronization, my father would say. This was a very big word for him. Synchronization: The coordination of events to operate in union. A conductor managing to keep his orchestra in time. The impossible meeting of light reflection and time exposure that leads to a perfect photograph. Two yellow bugs parked in front of Lincoln Center at the same time, the love of your life in one of them.

Not fate, my father would add. Don't confuse it with fate. Fate suggests no agency. Synchronization is all about agency. It involves all systems running in a state where different parts of the system are almost, if not precisely, ready.

For my father, it was the basis of how he approached his work: first as a scientist, then as a winemaker. He was one of the first biodynamic winemakers in America, certainly in his little corner of it. He considered not just the grapes themselves, but—as he liked to espouse—the ecological, social, and economic systems that needed to be synchronized in order to properly grow them. My father said that doing it any other way was lazy.

As for me, I had trouble seeing the role synchronization played in my own life. The role it was supposed to play. Until it went and destroyed my blessedly ignorant, willfully optimistic life, in a way I couldn't ignore unless I ran from it.

So, on that fateful Friday, I did just that. I ran from it.

With only the clothes on my back and a hastily packed suitcase, I drove from sunny Southern California—the place that had been my home for the last fourteen years—to the small town in Northern California on the edge of the Russian River Valley. The place that'd been my home for my entire life until then.

Nine hours, five rest-spot stops, two terrible milkshakey coffee drinks (one vanilla, one strawberry), and a roll of Rolos later, I arrived in Sonoma County. I should have felt relief, but as I passed the familiar sign for Sebastopol—its wiry hills visible behind it—I caught a glimpse of myself in the rearview. My hair was falling out of its bun, my eyes were deeply unsettled, and I couldn't escape the feeling that I was about to walk into a new kind of hell.

So I turned around and started driving the nine hours back to Los Angeles.

But it was getting late, and I hadn't eaten (save the Rolos), and the rain was coming down hard, and I was so tired I couldn't think. So I pulled off Highway 12, getting off at the exit for downtown Santa Rosa, knowing where I was going before I admitted it to myself.

The Brothers' Tavern was something of a Sonoma County institution. The original owners—and brothers—had opened the doors seventy-eight years ago with the idea that it would be the place in the county that was open late, and the place that served the best beer. The subsequent owners had stuck with the plan, taking the bar and grill to another level, brewing award-winning beer on site that drew people from all over the state.

Of course, the current owners of The Brothers' Tavern were my brothers. Finn and Bobby Ford. And the jig would be up as soon as they saw me. They would see it on my face. What I had been through.

But when I walked into the bar, Finn was the only one standing there. No Bobby. Bobby was always there on the weekends, so this was the first confusing thing.

The fact that my father wasn't sitting on the corner bar stool having a drink with them was the second.

My father came by every Friday—the only way to start his weekend, he liked to say, was to have a drink with his boys. My heart dropped in disappointment, realizing that this was really why I had shown up, despite the ramifications. So that my father would have a drink with his girl, jig up or not.

But it was only Finn standing behind the bar, looking at me like he didn't recognize me. And, for a minute, I wondered if he didn't. My hair was in a disheveled bun, my smile fake and forced. And it was late. Maybe I looked like another straggler, trying to get a drink before he closed down for the night.

To his credit, Finn didn't call me out on any of this. He walked past the other customers, who stared at me as I took a seat at the end of the bar—the one close to the fireplace. My father's seat.

I sat down, ignoring their pseudo-casual glances, Finn drilling them with looks so they'd stop staring. This was Finn, the perpetual big brother. He was ready to protect me even before he knew what he was protecting me from.

He offered a big smile. "What are you doing here?"

"Took a drive."

"A nine-hour drive?" he said.

I shrugged. "Got carried away."

"Clearly." He paused. "No speeding ticket?"

"No, Finn," I said, knowing Finn thought I was an awful driver. Like running-out-of-gas-while-getting-a-speeding-ticket awful. It's hard to lose that reputation. Even if it only happened once.

"Glad to hear that, at least," Finn said, sincerely.

Then he nodded, trying to decide how hard to push, keeping his eyes on me.

Finn was my good brother. They both were pretty good, but Finn was the truly good one in my book, even if he wasn't the good one in anyone else's. Bobby was more ostensibly impressive: The captain of the high school football team, a local legend, a successful venture capitalist with a full life in San Francisco. A beautiful town house, beautiful cars, beautiful family. He was five minutes younger than Finn, but in every other way he seemed to always come in first.

Bobby had bought the bar as a hobby and to give Finn something to do. Finn believed less in employment. He owned the bar so he could drink for free and so he could keep taking photographs. Finn was a great photographer, but he seemed to only work—weddings, family portraits—when the mood struck him. He was a little like my father in that way, adhering to a code of purity that only he understood.

"I missed Dad?"

"He didn't come in tonight." Finn shrugged, as if to say, *Don't ask me.* "We can call him. He'll come now, if he knows you're here."

I shook my head, keeping my eyes down, afraid to meet Finn's eyes. Finn looked so much like my father. Both of them had these dark eyes, with matching piles of dark hair. They were handsome guys, all American. The only obvious difference was that Finn liked to keep that mane of hair under a backward baseball cap. Usually a Chargers cap.

It made it hard to tell him what was going on without feeling like I was about to disappoint my father too.

Finn cleared his throat. "So they don't know you're here? Mom and Dad?"

"No, and I'd appreciate if you don't tell them, you know, the circumstances. It wasn't planned, obviously."

"Obviously."

He paused, like he wanted to say something else, but thought better of it. "They'll be happy to see you," he said. "That you came. Whatever the reason. None of us thought you were coming home for the harvest, you know?"

The harvest of the grapes—the most important five weeks in my father's year. I'd arrived home under duress the very weekend he always held most sacred—the last weekend of the harvest. Every year I came home for it. We all did. We returned to the family house: The brothers slept in their old rooms, I slept in mine. Our various spouses and partners and children filled up the rest of the house. And all of us joined my father to harvest the final vines, to drink the first sips of wine. We all stayed for the harvest party. But this year was supposed to be different. For a variety of reasons, I wasn't supposed to be there.

Finn, realizing his error in raising this, shifted from foot to foot. "What do you want to drink?" he said.

I pointed at the entire bar behind him. The bourbon and scotch and whisky were like Christmas presents.

Finn smiled. He put a glass of bourbon in front of me, and a glass of red wine. "What you think you want," he said, pointing to the first. "What you'll actually take more than two sips of."

"Thank you," I said.

"My pleasure."

I sipped at the bourbon. Then I turned, almost immediately, to the wine.

Finn put the bottle on the table so I could see what he had poured. It was a dark and grippy Pinot Noir. The Last Straw Vineyard. B-Minor 2003 Vintage. One of the wines from our father's vineyard. My favorite wine from our father's vineyard, mine and Bobby's. One thing we had in common.

"This is a great bottle," I said. "You should take it away and save some for Bobby."

Finn nodded, tightly. Like there was something he didn't want to say, not out loud.

Then, just as quickly, he softened.

"You hungry?" Finn said. "I could get the kitchen to fix you something."

"They're not closed?"

Finn leaned against the countertop. "Not for you," he said.

It was the nicest thing he could have said, and I gave him a smile so he knew how much I appreciated it. Then he walked back toward the kitchen, taking a sip from the bourbon as he went.

I sat taller on the bar stool, more aware of the looks I was getting, now that Finn was moving away.

Finn turned back for just a second. "Hey, Georgia . . ." he said.

"Yeah?"

"You know that you're still wearing your wedding dress, yes?" he said.

I looked down at the sprawling lace, dirty from the five-hundred-mile drive and the run across The Brothers' Tavern parking lot. And what looked, sadly, like a lost Rolo.

I touched the soft skirt. "I do," I said.

He nodded and turned back toward the kitchen. "All right, then," he said. "One grilled cheese coming up."

The Last Straw

*S*ynchronization. Systems operating with all their parts in synchrony, said to be synchronous, or in sync. The interrelationship of things that might normally exist separately.

In physics: It's called simultaneity. In music: rhythm.

In your life: epic failure.

I pulled up to the driveway to my parents' house after midnight, woozy and exhausted. I immediately regretted that I hadn't taken Finn up on his offer to crash at his place in Healdsburg and to return tomorrow to face my parents. When I was more appropriately dressed. Though, after the day I'd had, I wanted the twin bed I had grown up sleeping in, complete with its flannel sheets and heart-shaped pillows.

As I took the left turn into the driveway, I passed the small wooden sign for THE LAST STRAW, EST. 1979, carved by hand. The vineyard spread out on both sides of me, twenty acres of vines sweeping by on either side of the car. The vines were rich and meaty with grapes and wildflowers, cushioning my parents' sweet yellow Craftsman straight ahead, up the hill.

It was a lovely house, comforting with its large shutters, flowers on the windowsills, a bright red door. Bay windows lined the back, running the whole length of the house, leading out to the original ten acres of vineyard. And to a small two-room cottage at the back of the property—the winemaker's cottage—where my father did his work every day.

I shut the ignition and stared out the car window at my parents' house. Every room was dark but their bedroom. It worried me that they were still awake, but more likely than not it was just my mother who was awake, reading in bed. She wouldn't hear me come in. She wouldn't be listening for it.

I stepped out of the car and headed for the front door, grabbing the spare key from the flowerpot. I let myself in. If I was going to wake them, if they were going to hear me, this was the moment. The red door squeaked when it opened. It was a lesson every child of the Ford family had learned the hard way the first time they attempted to sneak into the house after curfew.

I closed the door. And the house remained silent.

I smiled, standing there in the dark foyer, a small victory. It was the first still moment of the day, and I took it in, surrounded by the familiar smells: a mix of freesia and lemon—what my mother cleaned with—and the night jasmine from the windows my mother always left open, letting in a nice breeze. It was the kind of breeze that you couldn't find anywhere in Los Angeles. Which made Los Angeles feel a million blessed miles away.

I walked into the kitchen, leaving all of the lights off, running my hand along the wooden countertop and along the farm table. The remnants of dinner—plates, two glasses, and a bottle of wine—were waiting by the sink.

I decided to make myself useful and started gathering up dishes when I saw it through the window. It was next to the hot tub—taking up the patio and the yard. A large tent. Sailcloth white. It was the tent I was getting married under in eight days. Since it was after midnight, did it count as seven days? Los Angeles came screaming back.

Literally. My cell phone rang, piercing the darkness.

I picked up, on reflex, not wanting the phone to wake my sleeping parents, not wanting to scare them.

"Don't hang up," he said.

It was Ben. His voice through the phone line shook me.

"Then stop calling."

"I cannot."

I loved how Ben spoke. It was an opening statement about who he was: calm, sincere. British. I was a sucker for an accent, which was why I always listed the other qualities first. It was a way to keep my credibility. We had spoken on the phone for over a month before we ever laid eyes on each other. Ben, an architect, had lived in New York at the time. I was a real estate lawyer, my firm working on one of his projects in Los Angeles, a modern office building downtown. That was how we fell in love, on the phone, talking about the least sexy things in the world. Permits. And billing. And then, everything that mattered.

"You need to let me walk you through this, Georgia," he said. "I'm not saying there is a good explanation. I'm saying it's not what you think."

"No, thanks."

"This is madness. I love you. You know I love you. I'm not involved with Michelle, not since before I knew you. But Maddie . . ."

I hung up the phone.

Hearing the name Maddie was too real. She had a name. Ten hours before this phone call, she hadn't existed. Now she had a name.

Ten hours before this phone call, I'd been happy. I'd been late, but happy. I ran into Stella's Bridal Shop in Silver Lake twenty minutes late for my final dress fitting. It was a fitting for my wedding dress, which Stella had made entirely in her five-hundred-square-foot shop: a trumpet dress made with silky white Chantilly lace, draped Spanish tulle, soft sleeves.

I loved the dress—the way it hugged my hips, mermaid-style, the way it softened my shoulders—and I found myself smiling when Stella (after forgiving me for being twenty minutes late) asked me to shimmy across the floor in my satin heels and find my way to the pedestal, so she could do the hem.

I went to the pedestal by the window, striking a bit of a pose. Stella smiled, and egged me on. *Put your hands on your hips*, she said, enjoying the happy stares we were getting from people walking down the street.

Then I saw my fiancé walking down the street.

Ben was walking down the street with a woman I didn't know. And not just any woman. She was the most beautiful woman I'd ever seen, with long red hair, a stunning smile. A matching version of the woman—redheaded and tiny, four or five years old—was by the woman's side. But the woman outside the bridal shop window was the one who caught my eye.

I recognized her from somewhere, but it would take me a minute to place the where. Stella would actually place her for me. My fiancé was the side note.

And that wasn't the biggest problem.

The biggest problem was what happened when I knocked on the window, failing to get Ben's attention.

I was excited for him to turn around. I was excited to see Ben's face—his strong jaw and cheekbones, a dimple that made no sense. I figured there was a reasonable explanation for what he was doing there with the woman. We'd spent that morning in bed together, in our home together, eating peach French toast. Laughing, getting naked. We were getting married in eight days. We were madly in love.

But Ben didn't hear me. He kept walking, toward Sunset Junction. The woman was happily walking by his side, her mini-me by hers.

The woman leaned into him, into my fiancé, putting her hand on the small of his back, like it belonged there. And it jerked me forward, and out onto the street, wearing my un-hemmed wedding dress.

I gripped the lace in my hands, making sure the un-hemmed part didn't hit the dirty street. Stella ran out into the street after me.

"Ben!" I called his name.

Ben turned around. As did the woman. And her little girl.

And then I knew how I recognized the woman, holding her daughter's hand, as Stella said her name. Michelle Carter. The famous British actress. On the cover of so many American magazines. Close up she was light and lean, like a leaf. Like a pickle.

Ben looked at me. The woman looked at me. The little girl looked at Ben.

"Daddy," she said.

Let me stop there.

With what Maddie said.

To Ben.

Let me stop there before Stella bent down and bustled as much of the lace as she could—my eyes holding on the little girl, the beautiful little girl, her eyes holding on mine. People stopping on the street, staring at Michelle, pointing.

Ben was moving toward me, completely panicked. Three words coming out of his mouth, but maybe not the words you'd think. Not: *I am sorry.* Not: *It isn't true.* Not: *I can explain.*

Just this. As though it was all he could see. And if it was, does that count for anything?

"You look beautiful," he said.

~

Ten hours later, I took off my satin heels and headed up the stairs, holding my dress so I wouldn't slip, moving quickly to the safety of my room.

My phone rang again, vibrating through the house.

"Don't hang up," Ben said.

"Didn't we just do this?"

"You answered, didn't you? A part of you wants to hear what I have to say."

He wasn't wrong. There was a way to turn off the phone. I hadn't done it. I hadn't been able to. Part of me wanted Ben to tell me a story that would make this all okay, that would make him familiar again.

I sat down on the staircase, my dress billowing out to the sides.

"You need to understand, I didn't even know about Maddie until a couple of months ago . . ." he said.

"Your daughter?"

He paused. "Yes. My daughter."

"How old is she, Ben?"

"Maddie is four and a *half*."

He emphasized the half and I knew why. We had been together for five years. The half meant she was conceived before me, before us.

"I obviously wasn't going to keep this a secret forever, but it's complicated with Michelle," he said. "And I wanted to smooth that part of this out before I dragged you into it."

"Complicated how?"

He paused. "That's complicated."

I stood up again. I'd had enough—enough of Ben's non-explanation, enough of my heart pounding in my throat.

"Look, I just don't want you to do anything rash. We're getting married in a week."

"I'm not so sure about that, at the moment."

He got quiet. "That's what I mean by rash," he said.

He sounded devastated. And the problem was that it reminded me of the first time I'd spoken to him. My law firm had just signed Ben as a client and I called to introduce myself shortly after his bike was stolen. I didn't know this about him yet, but Ben had owned that bike for ten years. It was less his preferred mode of transportation and more . . . an appendage. And still, by the end of our conversation, he was joking, happy. His bike, and his sorrow, a thing of the past. Because of me, he said. And, even now, there was a huge part of me that wanted to make him feel that good again.

"Where are you?" he said. "Let me come talk to you in person."

I was at the top of the stairs. Maybe because Ben asked where I was, I looked around. My bedroom was to the left—the door wide open. My parents' bedroom was to the right.

And coming out of my parents' bedroom was a large man. Two hundred and fifty pounds large. With hair and skin I didn't recognize. In a towel.

My mother, in a matching towel, stood close to him.

This man, who was not my father.

I dropped the phone. "Oh my God!" I screamed at the top of my lungs.

"Oh my God!" my mother screamed back.

The man moved away, backward, toward my parents' bedroom, which he apparently knew all too well.

Then, as if thinking better of it, he reached out his hand. "Henry," he said.

I was stuck in place, right at the top of the stairs. I reached, as though it made sense, for this man's hand.

My mother covered her mouth in abject horror. I thought it was her disgrace at being caught. But then she reached for me, touching my cheek with the front of her hand, then with the back.

"What did you do to your wedding dress?" she asked.

Regarding Henry

*I*f I were keeping count—and who was keeping count?—it wasn't shaping up to be the best day of my life.

I sat in the dining room with my mother, the two of us dressed in sweatshirts and jeans, my dress hanging on the door, the silence between us aggressive.

Henry was gone. My mother had said good-bye to him on the front steps while I waited for him to walk away. It was like what my mother had done to me my senior year of high school, when I was dating tattooed and mean Lou Emmett. But in a gross reverse.

My mother poured herself a cup of coffee, avoiding my eyes. I wasn't going to be the first to speak. Normally, I'd reach across the table, make this conversation easier for her, but I couldn't do that this time. My mother was going to have to do that—she'd have to figure out herself how she was going to explain this.

Instead, I stared at the wall above her head, lined with photographs, all the photographs that made up my parents' life together—beginning when they were young, at this vineyard, and even before that. One of my favorite photographs was of my mother, still a cellist with the New York Philharmonic, smiling at the camera, her cello resting against her long black dress. The woman sitting here now looking remarkably like the photograph of herself then. She had the same long curls, wide cheeks, a nose that didn't quite fit. She was still not wearing a drop of makeup, still not needing any.

Next to that photograph of her was one of me playing softball. I'd been a complete tomboy growing up (care of trying to keep up with Bobby and Finn). I'd pretty much lived in a T-shirt and sneakers, my hair perpetually in a ponytail. But there was no denying how similar we used to look: my curls the darker version of her curls, my nose tilted like her nose, my eyes dark green like my father's but shaped like hers.

My mother used to say that I was the spitting image of her, cloaked in my father's coloring. That was until I moved to Los Angeles and transformed in the way Los Angeles seems to transform people: a little bit at a time until you don't recognize yourself anymore. With all the gorgeous women strolling through yoga class and into parties, I found myself paying attention to all sorts of things that I hadn't historically.

Maybe it would have been the same thing if I'd left Sebastopol for New York or Chicago, but for me, at eighteen, it was Los Angeles that I left for, so it was Los Angeles where I learned some fundamental lessons that growing up in a house full of men and farmers had forgotten to teach me about how to look and feel sexy.

You could see the transformation on the wall. My mother joked that I'd morphed from the darker version of her into the glam, movie star version—which, I assured her, a walk down Abbot Kinney among the real movie stars would prove untrue. Though, in truth, I did look different and I took a certain amount of pride in that.

The Southern California sun had lightened my hair, I'd slipped off ten pounds, and I'd started to dress as though I had *some* idea of how to. Under my friend Suzannah's supervision (and insistence), I'd spent more money on a pair of shoes than on a month's rent. I tried to return them the next day—in guilt and nausea—but the store had a strict no-return policy. So I'd kept them. And loved them. In fairness to myself, these had been magic shoes: slinky stiletto heels that made your legs look endless. In further fairness, the shoes had outlasted that apartment and all the ones that had come since.

Whenever I'd come home for a visit, my mother would always say how stylish I looked. But I knew she judged my evolution from ponytails to pencil skirts. My mother thought style should be effortless and easy. She took to touching my straightened hair, saying, "Shiny." She commented on new items of clothing with a whistle and a shifty grin: "Look at that Los Angeles armor."

And it was always first thing in the morning—when I was freshly awake and racing downstairs for her walnut and cherry waffles, the same way I'd done as a child—that she would touch my skin and say, "Gorgeous."

The disjunct left me feeling somewhat alone in navigating my two homes. Sonoma County was blue jeans and fleece pullovers and practical field boots. Los Angeles was slingbacks and blue jeans distressed to the tune of $275. I wavered between the two worlds, neither feeling like it fit exactly right. I was self-conscious about my lifestyle in Los Angeles—a lifestyle on which I felt I had a tenuous hold at best. And when I came home, the put-together version of me who seemed to have it all together felt myself judging, in a way I never used to, how unrefined and rural local life was. I didn't like being judgmental in that way, but I was having trouble stopping myself. I was still trying to find the balance.

I lowered my gaze from the photographs, looked down. My mother caught my eyes, held them. Then she crossed her arms over her chest. "Don't stand there in judgment of me," she said.

It didn't seem wise to tell her I was sitting in judgment.

"There was a naked man coming out of your bedroom, Mom," I said. "Who wasn't Dad."

"Well, who shows up at midnight unannounced?" She shook her head. "It's our fault for not redecorating your room. You think nothing here is supposed to change."

"I think you're not supposed to be shtupping someone who isn't Dad."

"Well, I'm not shtupping him."

I looked at her, confused. "What?"

She shrugged. "Henry is impotent, if you must know."

I covered my ears. "I must not know. I must go back in time and know anything but that."

"I'm sorry," she said, holding up her hands in surrender. "I'm just saying . . . I'm just trying to explain to you that things are more complicated than they seem."

Complicated. That was Ben's word too. The problem was that they were both using it passively. When the truth was that they had made things complicated. Actively. That was the important part they each were leaving out.

"Where's Dad?"

"Dad and I are taking a little time apart," she said. "He's been staying in the winemaker's cottage for the last couple of weeks. Not that he doesn't do that every year during the harvest."

There was an edge to how she said that, which I chose to ignore.

"Because of Henry?" I asked.

"Because we're taking time apart," she said.

I looked through the bay windows to the lantern-lit vineyard, the lantern-lit path that led to the winemaker's cottage. My father was asleep in one of the two bedrooms inside. When I was a little girl, I'd beg to sleep in the other room and go out with him first thing in the morning to help pick the first grapes before school. I told him that when I was older my brothers and I were going to take over the land for him—to keep his legacy running. I meant it. Running the vineyard was what I had wanted more than anything when I was a little girl. Now I had left him there alone. Each in our own way, we all had.

"How could you not have told me what was going on?" I asked.

My mother reached for her coffee. "We were waiting until after your wedding. We didn't want to ruin it for you."

I met her eyes. Apparently Ben and I had done that all ourselves.

"I've tried not to burden Finn and Bobby with this either. They both have their hands full with other things."

I thought back to the bar—Finn acting weird when Bobby came up. Bobby nowhere to be seen. "With what things?" I said.

She shook her head. "I can't get into all of that right now. They should be allowed to be here to offer their side."

How had we gotten to the place where everyone in the family was on different sides? I had been home for the last harvest, I had been home another time since—everyone had seemed fine. Now though? I felt like I was going to cry. And Ben—usually my first call when I felt this way, the one person who could help me find perspective on this—was the reason I had none.

My mother cleared her throat, seeing an opportunity to change the subject. "Are you going to tell me what happened?" she said.

I shook my head.

"Did he do something unforgivable?"

"What kind of question is that?"

She leaned in. "A bad one, probably. What's a good one? Tell me and I'll ask."

Ever since I'd left the bridal shop, I'd envisioned sitting at this table with my mother and my father, talking it out. The way we had when I'd needed to figure out what college to go to, how to pay for law school, how to get over a thousand broken hearts. Now my concern was that the three of us were never going to be sitting here again.

"Georgia . . ."

I looked up.

"Did you do something unforgivable?"

"Stop using that word. No."

"Well, is there someone else?"

Normally, my mother was the first to think adultery went into the unforgivable category.

"Yes, there is. And she's four-and-a-half years old."

My mother looked confused.

"He has a daughter. That he's kept from me."

She went silent, the calm before her impending storm. My mother couldn't stand dishonesty. She was wisecracking and irritable and stubborn. But, beyond all that, she was remarkably genuine. And she demanded the same of the people she loved.

She reached for her coffee. "I'm sure Ben has an explanation for this," she said.

"You can't be serious," I said. "I just told you that Ben has a child with someone, and he didn't choose to share that information. I found out at my dress fitting when I saw him walking down the street with the mother of his child."

"I understand. It's awful. Particularly that he didn't tell you." She paused. "I'm just putting it out there that he may have an explanation for keeping this to himself."

This was what she had to offer me? Pre-Henry, my mother would have demanded blood from Ben. She would have stormed around the dining room talking about values, the way she'd done when my best friend in high school had used her parents' restaurant to throw herself an open-bar birthday party. Even when I explained how that had happened, she had said there was no explanation. You either were truthful or you weren't, and that defined you.

Where was that mother now, screaming about Ben's lie of omission? Why couldn't she take on that role so I could find my way to the other one—the one where I got to find sympathy for Ben in her outsized protection of me. That was the mother I knew.

I stood up. "I can't deal with this right now. I'm going to bed."

"Then go."

I headed for the door, completely exhausted and ready for the night to be done.

"Henry is an old friend," my mother called out after me. "We knew each other back in New York. And he recently was named the conductor of the San Francisco Symphony."

I turned around, but stayed in the doorway.

She shrugged. "He's only been out here a few months, but it's been nice. Just . . . to be a part of that world again."

Part of that world. She looked defeated saying the words and remembering it—who she used to be, *how* she used to be. It made me want to convince her that she was still a part of it: She had been the music teacher in town for decades. But that wasn't the same thing. And what was the point in trying to convince her it was, anyway? As if anyone could convince you of the one thing you didn't want to see.

"What does that have to do with you and Dad?" I said instead.

She looked up at me.

"I'm not talking about Dad. I'm talking about you and me. You have always tried to take care of everyone in this family, just like I have. As opposed to figuring out what you want. Not what you're supposed to want, but what you truly want."

I started to laugh. I couldn't help it.

"You can't seriously think you're in a good position to offer me advice on my romantic life at the moment."

She met my eyes. "I think I'm in a great position, actually," she said. "No one sees what an incomparable person you are more than I do. Except, perhaps, Ben."

She paused. And then she said it simply. "Be careful what you give up."

I crossed my arms over my chest, trying—in spite of myself—to hear what she wasn't saying. "Because you can't get it back?"

She stood up, walking past me in the doorway.

"No." She squeezed my shoulder. "Because, eventually, you get it back any way you can."

I waited for her to disappear up the stairs before heading that way myself. But before my mother was gone, she called out a final good night. "For what it's worth, I'm glad you're home."

That made one of us.

The Contract

I woke up to the sound of a Bach cello sonata, the sun heaping through the windows, joining the music in an intense wake-up call. It was how I woke up most every morning as a kid—my father wanting us to get up with the sun, my mother reserving the first half hour of each day to practice, to keep her hand in.

I used to love the sound of her cello, the warm tones greeting me. Post-midnight run-in, though, her cello had another connotation, images of a naked Henry running through my head, dancing along with the music.

I rummaged through my suitcase, searching for a decent pair of jeans and a sweater, lamenting how little clothing I'd brought from Los Angeles. Nothing to battle the early morning fog, nothing to battle the late afternoon heat. The only shoes I had with me were a pair of ballet flats. My favorite boots left behind, my favorite everything left behind.

In my rush to get out of the house before my mother finished playing, I almost missed the note she had left on the countertop: "Coffee on. Banana muffins in fridge. Made yesterday, but delicious."

I took a cup of coffee and a muffin, and headed down the hill to the winemaker's cottage to find my father.

It was just after 9 A.M.—a gorgeous time in the vineyard. The sky was intensely blue, the early morning fog starting to burn off, letting in the sun, the morning heat. I passed through the gardens that served as cover crop, their wildflowers snaking between the vines, the land all purples and greens.

I stopped to study the vines, touching the shoots, feeling it come over me. It was a feeling that I only knew when I was back in the vineyard. A potent mix of happiness and excitement and something I couldn't name except to say that being back in Sebastopol, back at my parents' house, was like seeing a lost love again.

Until I was fourteen, I couldn't get enough of the vineyard. I'd followed my father around to do the most mundane tasks: to trellis the vines, study the grapes, make teas to feed the soil. My father would dig into the compost, and I would join in, just to be a part of it. Before school, after school, we discussed vines and vintages. My father would even take me down to the wine cave and give me a taste of the racked wine, a taste of the wine still waiting to be racked. He never said it, but he was thrilled I wanted to be a part of it.

Then came the day I wanted nothing to do with *any* part of it.

The same vineyard, the same fifty acres that had brought me so much joy, became suffocating as opposed to freeing.

It coincided with two awful harvests in a row. The first harvest had gone awry due to weather, the rain forcing the grapes off the vines long before they were ready. The second had been the result of rolling forest fires, the smoke drying out the Sebastopol air, searing the vineyard. After years of everything going fairly smoothly, the two bad vintages—the only two my parents ever had in succession since early on, since before I remembered—had threatened to put us out of business.

It was still hard to think about how awful those winters were. My parents had tried to shield us from how scared they were about losing everything they had built together. But late at night, after we were supposed to be asleep, I'd hear them talking quietly in the kitchen, a pot of coffee between them. It would have been better if they had screamed it out loud as opposed to what it felt like, sitting on the other side of the door, thinking about all the ways I couldn't fix it for them, thinking about all the ways our family's life was about to fall apart.

I started going into San Francisco every chance I had. One night I convinced my father to take me to see an art exhibit of light installations. The truck broke down on the way and we took a cab the rest of the way into the city. Afterward, we walked the streets downtown, past the Ferry Building and the pier, up into the ritzy hills of Pacific Heights. We passed a small jazz club, a ninety-year-old woman singing Gershwin. If that sounds ridiculously romantic, it was. And I was completely hooked. I loved the noises of the city, people fighting and laughing in the streets. The old woman singing Gershwin. It'd be easy to say that it was the energy of the city that pulled me in, but it wasn't. It was the noises. Suddenly, it felt like everything I had known before then had been too quiet. My parents' sadness, the vineyard, Sonoma County itself.

I spent the next summer staying with my cousin who ran a law office downtown. She was beautiful and elegant and she took me under her wing, introducing me to city living: coffee shops and skyscrapers, streets and bookstores, fancy shoes and cigarettes at parties. She even gave me an internship at her law firm.

She warned me that it would be boring, but it was a relief. Law was specific. It was concrete. The soil and fruit and wind and sun and sky didn't have to cooperate for work to go well. After years of watching my father struggle at the mercy of the weather patterns, that type of control felt empowering.

When the vineyard worked, it was beautiful. But two years of fallow crops were decimating. And they were especially decimating when I realized they weren't the first. After I left for college, I learned that my parents had narrowly escaped previous disasters, previous moments when it had seemed the only option was throwing in the towel.

My chosen path was far less unpredictable, which felt like a good thing, a different thing.

Maybe that was just childhood? You hurry up, pick the opposite path, try to make childhood end. Then, as an adult, you have no idea why you were running away. What, exactly, you needed so desperately to get away from.

~

When I arrived at the winemaker's cottage, the front door was open, but no one was inside.

"Dad?" I said.

There was no answer.

I nudged the door open and walked in, taking a seat in the small living room. I knew my father was probably somewhere in the vineyard, but I'd be better off waiting for him to take his normal morning break after they finished picking. That was how it worked. They'd pick grapes from 2 A.M. until 10 A.M.—when the land was cooler, night lamps guiding their way. Most winemakers left this to the vineyard manager to oversee, but my father liked to be involved in the picking himself.

I didn't want to try to find him out in the vineyard, or by the receiving table, watching the grapes come in off the vines, sorting through them, picking which ones would last. I didn't want to interrupt. Maybe I wasn't anxious for a confrontation.

The point is that I didn't plan on snooping. I planned on sitting, all the windows open, the late morning sun streaming in, an entire banana muffin and cooling coffee waiting to be enjoyed.

But I put everything down on the coffee table too quickly—and I spilled the coffee. All over the table. All over a heavy pile of files.

Files labeled: MURRAY GRANT WINES SALES FOLIO.

There were no napkins, so I picked up the wet files, wiping them against my T-shirt. I was trying to dry them off, though I doubted it mattered. My father hated Murray Grant Wines. He wasn't alone. Most of the small winemakers in Sonoma County did. They hated them not only because of the quality of their mediocre production, but because they treated winemaking like a business. It was a business, of course. It was just also supposed to be something else.

So I assumed the papers were a dumb mailer, my father keeping up on what Murray Grant Wines was doing. He had to keep up with them. They were one of the biggest wine producers in Napa Valley, shipping five million cases of wine annually.

Direct competition, of course, to my father's five thousand.

But then, as I rubbed the second file clean, I came across a series of contracts. They were lengthy and specific contracts that couldn't say what they seemed to say. Except that I was a real estate lawyer and worked on far more complicated deals. And I knew they were saying exactly what they seemed to say.

The Last Straw Vineyard. Ownership Transfer. To Murray Grant Wines.

My pulse started to throb in my ears, drowning out my ability to slow down, figure out what I was reading.

"No way!"

I looked up to see my brother Bobby in the doorway. He was standing there, wearing a dark blue suit, his tie slung back over his shoulder. The smile on his face, which on another day I would describe as charming, was more like a smirk.

I wondered if this was one of the reasons we had trouble getting along. Bobby had a penchant for showing up at the exact time that there was no one there to blame but him.

"What are you doing home? Aren't you getting married in, like, ten minutes?" he said. "I have two incredibly excited and very cute ring bearers who can't wait for the wedding."

I still hadn't said hello, the files in my hands. I held them up higher. "Did you know about this?"

His smile disappeared. "About what, exactly?" Bobby said.

He ran his hands through his blond curls, which matched our mother's—and which Bobby thought made him look angelic. What did make him look angelic were his ragged fingernails—Bobby biting them to stubs since we were little kids. It was my favorite part of him.

"Mom and Dad are selling the vineyard," he said, trying to sound casual, as if it was the most obvious thing in the world. As if we were talking about a car.

I sat back down and opened the files up, trying to ascertain where they were in the process. I was unhappy to see my father's signature already on the final page, notarized.

Along with the signature of someone named Jacob McCarthy.

Jacob McCarthy. CEO of Murray Grant Wines.

Bobby shrugged. "I guess Dad didn't want to bother you until after the wedding."

Then he leaned down over me, a little too close for comfort. I thought about swatting him with something. My muffin came into view.

"What happened to the contracts?" he said, biting his nails nervously.

I moved away from him.

"And why are you freaking out?" he said. "This is a good thing. Dad won't have to work again. Murray Grant made them the kind of offer that comes around once in a lifetime."

"Do you even hear yourself?"

"Do you even hear *yourself*?"

If looks could kill, I might have killed him. Right then. That was the thing about Bobby. He had always been logical and robotic about everything. His feelings were like something he practiced—he should be emotional about a wedding, shedding one calculated tear—but never embraced. It was why he was so good at business. It was why he was so bad at showing that he cared about anything else.

"Since when is that what they want, Bobby?"

"That's what *everyone* wants!"

Bobby drilled me with a look.

"You're yelling at the wrong person," he said.

"I'm not yelling."

"You are YELLING," he yelled.

"You are both yelling."

We turned toward the doorway to see my father. He stood there in jeans and a T-shirt, looking younger than he was, with a thick mound of hair, skin brown from the sun. He was holding a thermos and a glass jar of grapes, his hair sweaty against his face.

He looked toward me as I dropped the files on the table, back in their pile of wet coffee.

He clocked it, my tenseness. He didn't ask when I'd arrived home, and what I knew about what was happening here with my mother. My father knew what I knew. He was already thinking about how to make it better.

"Daddy," I said, which I hadn't called him since I was a little girl. "Please tell me it's not true."

He walked past Bobby, squeezing his shoulder hello, and sat down beside me, putting down his grapes.

He put his arms around me, kissed the top of my head.

Waiting for another minute, so I could possibly believe him.

"It's not true," he said.

The Secateurs

This is what your mother and I want to do," my father said. "Honestly."

We arrived on the northwest part of the property, the last twenty acres my father bought. These were the farthest vines from my parents' house. He'd bought them from a developer for too much money—the beautiful, slightly lusher land that he thought could make a Pinot that was slightly more fruity and light than what he was producing with the western light.

We knelt down in Block 8, and started clipping ripe grape clusters off their vines, picking at a rapid pace. These were the grapes that produced B-Minor—the wine that I loved, the wine that Bobby loved. These clones also helped to produce a wine called Opus 129, which I found to be sharp, too rigid—though it was among my father's most popular wines. How they were both made from the same grapes could be confusing, but it didn't confuse my father. That, he believed, was often how it happened. The grapes liked to do different things depending on how you fermented them, how you trusted them to ferment themselves.

Normally we wouldn't be picking midday. The grapes were at risk for fermenting in the sun, crushing in the bins. But my father had tested the Brix—the sugar in the grapes—and he didn't want to wait until tonight to get them off the vines.

That was where he had been, testing the Brix, when I'd found out that he was giving away his life, as he had known it.

"Murray Grant Wines . . ." he said, "made a generous offer."

"You hate them."

He smiled at me, his warm smile. "I don't hate anybody."

Then he motioned for me to keep moving. His hands wove through the clusters effortlessly, clipping in quick succession, dropping the clusters in a bucket. I was going at half-speed, not a fast enough speed for him, not when he wanted these grapes off the vine and somewhere cooler.

"All hands on deck, or we can have this conversation later."

"I want to have it now."

"Then keep up," he said.

I started moving faster, gently removing the grapes, careful of the heat coming off of them, careful not to add to it. Truthfully, my father didn't need the help. He had five men out in the vineyard helping already. He needed to be doing something that made him seem busy, though. My father needed to be busy so there was a chance I wouldn't notice how sad he was.

But I did notice. My father was sun-kissed and solid from spending a lifetime outside, doing work that he loved. And he was usually pretty happy doing it. His eyes and his bright smile made him seem perpetually young, Finn's big brother as opposed to his father. So the contrast was sharp. His eyes were dark. His skin tight and gaunt. I could see how much energy it was taking him just to smile.

He shrugged. "It all fell into place," he said. "I hadn't sought it out, but your mother had been wanting to make a change of some kind, to not be so locked to Northern California, and Jacob came along . . ."

"Who is he?"

"Murray and Sylvie's son," Bobby answered.

"I was asking Dad," I said.

"I can't answer?" he said.

Bobby gave me a look, perplexed as to why I was so pissed off at him—as to why, in his mind, I was demonstrating the version of myself that was more like Finn as opposed to the one that was more like him. The version that Bobby had embraced, who had put herself through law school and had become a lawyer, who was marrying a stand-up guy.

"Jacob is Murray and Sylvie's grandson," my father corrected.

Those were names I recognized. We had heard them often when we were growing up. They were the founders of Murray Grant Wines—or, actually, Murray's father was, but they were the ones that had taken it national—and then international. They'd put production in the millions. Their daughter, Melanie, was about ten years older than my parents, but she'd moved to New York and married a Wall Street guy when she was young. Big society wedding. Last name McCarthy, apparently. Son named Jacob.

Bobby, unfazed by all of this, kept working, pulling off clusters of grapes. He surveyed them as he dropped them into that silver bucket. The way my father had taught us, now second nature.

"Murray wanted to slow down, so Jacob moved to the Valley last year. He has taken over most of their operations, and he's doing a good job for them. He's smart and he's a nice guy."

"I don't doubt that," I said. I doubted it very much.

"What's your problem?" Bobby said, angry.

I ignored him. "I'm just not sure why you didn't talk to me first, Dad, before making such a big decision."

"It felt like the right decision to make for my family," he said.

"And we appreciate it, Dad," Bobby said.

I shot Bobby a dirty look.

Bobby met it with a look of his own. "What?" he said.

"How about Adler Wines, Dad?"

"How about Adler Wines?" He met my eyes, annoyed.

Adler was a small, biodynamic winery near Alexander Valley. The owners, Beth and Sasha, were friends of my parents'. They got bought out by Seville Wineries. The folks at Seville promised that they would keep production exactly as it had been. That devotion to biodynamics, to sustainable farming. At first, Adler retained the same level of quality. Its first year as a subsidiary of Seville, it had its best harvest. The grapes turned out richer and riper than usual, yielding the kind of fruit-forward, jammy wine that came from Sonoma County's warmest harvests. But the demand that harvest created made Seville greedy. They grew the company far too fast for any type of quality control. Then they put Adler Wines in every Whole Foods in the country. All it had in common with the original was the label.

"That's not going to happen here," my father said.

"How do you know?"

Bobby met my eyes. "What do you mean, how does he know? He knows!"

I wanted to empty out my bucket, all over Bobby's head.

"Jacob isn't turning The Last Straw Vineyard into a household name," my father said. "He wants The Last Straw as a showcase property, a model for his other wineries on sustainable practices."

"Until he doesn't," I said.

"Easy," he said.

My father didn't like to be pushed, especially by one of his children. Even if he knew I was correct. He knew it better than I did. Which might be why he stepped back and turned the focus on me.

"Is everything okay with Ben?" he asked.

I laughed, unsure how to answer that. Was I slightly on edge because my fiancé was a liar? Maybe. But did it discount what I was saying to my father?

I looked out at the vineyard, everything my father had spent his life building. I never felt more peaceful than when I was out there with him. It wasn't just about the grapes, the wine. It was about the land he had kept safe to make that wine. It was about the farm and the house and how proud he was of what he had built here. And it was about the people he was giving that to—the last people who would appreciate it.

And that wasn't even touching on the most tragic part of what my father seemed to be giving away. What my parents both seemed to be giving away—each other.

"Dad, it just seems like a bad time to be making a big decision."

My father met my eyes. It was the first acknowledgment between us about my mother and Henry.

He shook his head. "You're out of line, kid," he said.

My father looked angry, something he rarely was.

"Dad . . ." I said. I started to apologize, but my father was already up and moving in the direction of one of his workers.

"Keep it up over here. I'll be right back," he said.

But he wasn't coming back. He was going to help them load the final

33

grapes from their shift onto the receiving table. He was going to study those grapes to see what they had to tell him.

I watched him go, wanting to call out after him now that I knew what I wanted to say. Which was, I love you and I'm here for you. Who doesn't start with that?

"Nice," Bobby said, glaring. "You need to learn when to back off."

I looked down at the bucket of grapes, angry at myself. I had pushed my father too far because I didn't know how to push him in the way he needed pushing—toward my mother.

"Is this because he didn't ask you if you wanted the vineyard?"

I met Bobby's eyes, hurt that he thought I was thinking about myself as opposed to our family.

"'Cause you're moving to London with Ben. You can't do this thing long distance. I don't want it. I have Margaret and the kids. Margaret is talking about going back to work. And Finn . . ." Bobby shook his head.

"What is going on with you two?"

He wiped his hands, reached for the water. "You'll have to ask him."

"What does that mean?"

"It means you'll have to ask him." He shrugged. "He's acting like a dick. And he doesn't want to talk about it with me, which is probably my fault. I've been a little judgmental."

"About what?"

Bobby chugged his water. "All the women he's been messing around with."

"Finn always is dating someone."

"This is different. He's dating everyone."

Bobby put the water down.

"And he says he wants to move to New York to go work for his buddy Sam, who has a new restaurant. He's talking about selling me his share of the bar. I only bought the bar so he could run it. Now he's leaving me with it."

Bobby crinkled his forehead. He looked hurt that Finn was freezing him out—when they never froze each other out. Hurt that Finn would want to move away from him.

They were truly best friends—my good brother, my bad one. They always had been. I was the little sister they took care of in different ways: Bobby tutoring me in algebra, Finn sneaking me out for two-for-one pizza and a drive-in movie the night before the algebra test. But their relationship with each other was reciprocal, the two of them always sticking by each other's side. Until, apparently, now.

His cell phone rang. He reached into his pocket, a smile returning to his face.

"Hey, pal."

Then he held out the phone so I could see who it was. *Ben*, complete with a smiling photo, beckoning. Bobby put the phone back to his ear, happy to be talking to him.

Bobby loved Ben, though he loved him for the wrong reasons. He loved him for being an impressive architect, an upstanding member of society, a member of Soho House. All the things Bobby valued these days.

"You coming up?" Bobby said, into the phone.

I shook my head and whispered to Bobby, "Tell him I'm not here."

"Sure," Bobby said. "She's right here."

He handed the phone over.

Instead of putting the phone to my ear, I ended the call. And handed the phone right back to him.

Bobby looked down at the phone in his hands, confused.

"What the hell?" he said.

"Don't look at me like that. I wanted to finish our conversation."

"You could have told Ben that," Bobby said.

I felt my face start to turn red.

Bobby registered it. "Oh no." He paused. "Are you blowing this with him?"

"No, but thank you for the support."

"That's why the obsession with the vineyard. So you don't have to admit that you're blowing this with him." He shook his head. "Why am I the only one in this family that has a clue about being a grown-up?"

"Has it even occurred to you that you don't know everything that's going on with me? Let alone with Mom and Dad? If you did, you'd understand that selling the vineyard isn't about selling the vineyard."

He smirked, unimpressed. "Is that so?"

I looked at him confused. Did he know about Mom and Dad too?

"Bobby, they're running away from the thing they care the most about because it feels too hard to stay. We can't let them do that."

His phone rang again, Ben on the line again.

"Well, we're going to have to," he said. "Because it's already done."

Then he turned away and picked up.

Sebastopol, California. 1979

*T*he word the real estate agent used to describe the land was *bucolic*. *Bucolic*, Dan knew, was generous. The dirt was dusty, muddled. There were dozens of stumps he'd need to dig out by hand.

"*Tons* of possibilities here," she said.

Possibilities. Bucolic. Real estate speak. She was, after all, a real estate agent who was trying to convince him to buy ten acres of land in an area where no one was buying ten acres of land. Not for what he wanted it for. Not for making wine. They were doing that an hour east and south over the winding, trepidatious climb of CA-116, leading you to a different world, to Calistoga and St. Helena, the tony world of Napa Valley.

That was a world Dan had only visited, a world still rejoicing from their win in the Judgment of Paris a few years earlier. The victory had been a big deal in the wine world. Eleven judges, graded tastings, California wines rating best in each category. Beating out the French, beating out the world. A French judge had demanded her ballot back, but it was too late. She had already spoken. Napa Valley was the winner.

Sebastopol wasn't Napa Valley. It wasn't obvious for growing grapes—this wedge-shaped hunk of land separating the Russian River Valley from the Petaluma Gap, all sloping land and overgrown trees, winding roads like obstacle courses.

This was Western Sonoma County. It was rolling country, a land of apple orchards. This very acreage had been an apple orchard, the real estate agent told him. Now it was dehydrated, empty.

But he wasn't only looking at the land. He was looking at the rest of it. Sebastopol's prevalent but predictable weather patterns. Mornings always warm, especially when the fog burned off. Evenings always cold. The elevation here keeping the land above the coastal fog.

He had been a scientist by trade until he felt compelled to do something else, until he felt he had to be standing here. He had been standing on the top of the hill—the high point that looked over the acres—every morning this week. He had been standing here for two hours at a time, as he clocked how the sun came up, how the wind felt. He thought he could work with this. And, if he managed, he would be the first to succeed.

He would have to try. He couldn't afford a piece of land in Napa Valley. He could barely afford this land, in the middle of nowhere. But that wasn't the only reason. Maybe if he honored the land—if he honored the elements that made it the strange and unique way it was—he could make a different type of wine. He could do something worth doing.

The real estate agent was trying to be patient. She had been standing on the top of the hill with him every morning this week, standing over him as he reached down, his hands grabbing soil, studying it.

He knew if she had any other potential buyers, she wouldn't be here. She knew that he knew this.

He tried to ignore her, but she followed his eyes out to the empty land. She looked at his empty ring finger.

"Are you going to build a home here?" she asked.

"A vineyard."

"Really?" She tried to recover. She did a terrible job. "Very exciting!"

He was looking straight ahead.

"Are you a winemaker?"

"No."

She looked at him, perplexed. "Do you have someone to help you?"

He shook his head. "Not yet."

He was twenty-five years old. He had no family, no money, two classes so far in viticulture. Fourteen more classes to go.

He had no business doing what he was about to do.

"I'll take it," he said.

And he looked out at nothing. The beginning of his life.

Mr. McCarthy

fter we left the vineyard, I went back to the house and showered. When I got out, I checked my phone for the first time that day.

There were two messages from Suzannah in my office. Suzannah Calvin-Bernardi (Savannah-born, former homecoming queen, current spitfire), who in addition to being a co-associate at my law firm was one of my best friends in Los Angeles. She managed to make it all seem easy. She was raising a child and eight months pregnant with a second (both with her homecoming king), kicking all kinds of ass at work. Taking no bullshit from any of them. Her kid, her colleagues. Herself.

But in my attempt to get out of town as quickly as possible, I'd done something unlike myself. I'd saddled her with the case we were currently trying to close. I never saddled her with anything—never left a deal unsigned, worked late into the night so that she didn't have to—especially now that she was pregnant. Which made me scared to listen to her message. Her tone firm and fast.

"Hey . . . this is work Suzannah. Remember when you were stepping out of the office for your dress fitting? Call me when you get this. I hate you."

Then there was Suzannah's second message. Her tone soft and melodic.

"Hey . . . this is friend Suzannah. Remember when you were stepping out of the office for your dress fitting? Call me when you get this. I love you."

As I clicked over to phone her back, I got another call. I thought it was going to be Ben—who had left several messages of his own. But it was Thomas Nick, Ben's business partner.

Thomas was in London, setting up the office. He wanted everything to be up and running by the time he flew to the States for our wedding.

"Georgia," he said. "How's the move going?"

The move. I sat down on the edge of my bed and wrapped the towel more tightly around myself. Ben and I were moving today. In the chaos, I hadn't even considered that. All of our stuff was leaving our house in Silver Lake, heading in a van and then a plane to our new home in London, on the edge of Notting Hill. It was my dream house, situated on a pretty cobbled mews near Westbourne Grove, arguably the coolest street in London. The house was a knockout. It had lovely natural light, white bookshelves lining the living room, large windows throughout the kitchen. And maybe the greatest thing of all was the front door, a red door, reminding me of my parents' door.

"I'm standing in the town house now. It's lovely. Lovely but empty. You'll need to come in here and make it homey. It needs the Georgia touch, if you know what I'm saying."

Thomas was just being nice. Ben was the one who made things beautiful. He could take any room and turn it into a place no one wanted to leave. When he moved to Los Angeles, he moved our bed to the back room. It was a library that wasn't supposed to be a bedroom, but he knew how good it'd feel to wake up under the large bay window. Was it yesterday that I'd woken up there beside him? My heart hurt, thinking of it.

"Thomas, I'm in a bit of a rush."

"Sure thing, but I'm actually just trying to reach Ben. We have an issue with the Marlborough Project. I need a quick answer from him so I can handle it," he said. "Is he with you?"

"No."

He paused, my short answer confusing him. "Okay, do you have any idea where Ben might be?"

"Did you try the mother of his child?" I said. "Maybe he's with her?"

"The mother of his child?" he said.

The world slowed down to a crawl, hearing him repeat those words. And I realized how deranged I sounded.

Still, instead of explaining, I hung up the phone.

~

I always understood how deeply my father loved the vineyard, but I experienced it firsthand when my mother took Finn and Bobby to visit her parents, and I spent the week at home with my father. In biodynamic winemaking, you plant and root based on the position of the moon and the stars, and that week, I learned what that involved. I couldn't have been older than five, but he woke me at midnight and handed me a cup of hot chocolate, and I followed him as he planted and sowed and rooted. He was so focused on each and every step—as if what he did, what he didn't manage to do, was going to change everything. I had never seen anyone concentrate like that on anything. It was like watching love.

~

I threw on a T-shirt and jeans and got into my car. I headed down CA-116—the winding road that would take me from one world to the other, from Sonoma into the heart of Napa Valley.

Napa had the fixings of a big city. It had entertainment, fancy hotels. Fancier restaurants.

For my twenty-first birthday, I'd come home from college so the five of us could have lunch at the fanciest restaurant—up the road in Yountville. The French Laundry: named after the actual French laundry that had occupied the countryside house before the restaurant did. This restaurant, among the best in the world, served you nine courses and the best wine you'd ever tasted. We weren't just celebrating my birthday, that day. The French Laundry had recently added my father's wine to their extensive wine list. Block 14. Estate Pinot Noir. 1992. My father's favorite Pinot. It was still grown exclusively on those initial ten acres, and we were giddy seeing it on the menu, knowing people from all over the world would be drinking it. For two hundred and fifty dollars a bottle. My father ordered two bottles in the hopes it would help it stay on the menu.

As I passed The French Laundry, I shifted back to that special afternoon. Bobby had announced that he was going to ask Margaret to marry him. Finn had screamed that no matter how beautiful she was, he was crazy to get married when he was barely able to legally rent a car. Bobby then announced that Margaret was pregnant. The two bottles of wine hadn't helped anything.

Ben and I planned to take my family to the restaurant as a thank-you to my parents for hosting our wedding at their home. Was that one more thing that wasn't happening? First the thank-you meal, then the wedding?

I took a left off of Washington Street onto the side street housing Murray Grant Wines, parking in one of only two spaces available out front next to an old Honda.

I looked at the contract I'd swiped from the winemaker's cottage to make certain I was at the correct address. It didn't feel like I was. That was the thing about wine country in Northern California. It was a small world, but with two distinct factions. There was rural and peaceful Sonoma County in one corner, commercial Napa Valley in the other. Some would argue that the divide was diminishing—Sonoma County was industrializing their wine, the same way Napa Valley had, decades earlier. For now, the divide still existed, small Sonoma producers still the David to the Goliath of corporate conglomerates like Murray Grant.

But, surprisingly, the offices of Murray Grant Wines were hardly an evil, intimidating complex. This place looked as though it belonged in Sebastopol: the hidden second story at the back of a small courtyard, with vines lining the staircase, and red, yellow, and orange plants in every window. Bright green shutters. It looked less like a corporate office and more like an artist's apartment.

I knocked on the screen door, to which I got a distant reply of, "It's open."

I walked into the waiting area, which had no chairs, no sofa, just an empty receptionist desk, and a very nice painting of a pear behind it. For some reason, I kept staring at it. The pear. Its bright green hue pulled me in, slightly magical.

"It's mesmerizing, right?"

I turned to see a man in the doorway of the office, looking at the pear with his head tilted to one side. He was wearing jeans and one of those zipper cashmere sweaters with a tie sticking out from beneath it. He was good-looking, in a way, but nowhere near as good-looking as he thought he was, standing there in that brazen East Coast way that reminded me of some guys I'd met at law school. The Masters of the Universe guys. This guy carried their vibe. Brandishing a half smile.

"I haven't been able to figure out what it is about the painting, exactly. And I've tried," he said. "At first I thought it was because my mother painted it, but everyone seems to focus on it. So it must be something. There must be something there."

He turned from the painting and we made eye contact for the first time.

"It's you," he said.

"Excuse me?"

"The bride. From the bar."

That threw me. I looked at him, confused.

"I almost didn't recognize you because your hair was up in that bun." He paused. "Falling out of that bun . . ."

I reached up and touched my hair, which now cascaded over my shoulders, moving from its Los Angeles straight toward Sonoma curly. "What are you saying, exactly?"

He cocked his head. "It looks much better like this."

He motioned toward the top of his head—his own thick hair—as if he were waiting for me to return the compliment. Instead, I pulled on my T-shirt, wishing I had worn something more lawyerly. He didn't seem to notice, though. He was still stuck on my wedding dress.

"I was there when you came in last night at the small table by the fireplace . . ."

He made a triangle sign with his hand, trying to demonstrate. He pointed to the index finger to show where I was, and the opposite thumb to indicate himself.

"You know what? Reverse that. I was there with my girlfriend. She was talking about chia. She loves chia. She puts it on everything. Salad. Oatmeal. Pasta. Apparently it's good for you. Did you know that?"

I nodded, slimy chia a staple at trendy Los Angeles restaurants. Still, this was not the way I wanted this conversation to start. This guy, somehow, in control.

"Anyway, I didn't want to try the chia, so I was looking around the bar, and then you appeared. And now you're here. That's so weird. Don't you think that's so weird?"

"No," I said.

Though, honestly, I thought it was. Who was this person? What was he doing in my brothers' bar fifty minutes away from here? And why did it seem odd that he remembered me? After all, I was dressed slightly more formally than everyone else.

"Why did you walk out on your wedding?" he said.

I looked at him, completely taken aback. "I didn't walk out on my wedding."

"I did that once," he said. "Or, actually, I guess I had that done to me. If we are being precise about it."

I put my hands up, trying to halt this conversation. "I didn't walk out on my wedding, okay?"

He held up his hands in surrender. "Okay . . ." he said. "I get it. You didn't walk out on your wedding."

"Thank you."

"So why exactly were you in your wedding dress then?" he said, confused.

"I walked out on my final dress fitting. That's not the same thing."

He nodded, like he was contemplating that. "I guess that's different."

"It is."

"Right. For one thing, you aren't humiliating anyone on what is supposed to be the happiest day of his life. For another, you can get the deposits back. On most things."

"On all things," I said.

He paused. Then he tilted his head. "Well . . . probably not on that dress."

"Look, I'm actually just looking for Jacob McCarthy," I said.

He looked around the empty office, empty except for him. "Apparently I'm Jacob McCarthy."

I hated the way he said his full name, so proud of himself. I wished that Jacob McCarthy had an idea that I was a serious lawyer as opposed to someone he met in her wedding dress, not on her wedding day.

"What can I help you with?" he said.

"I want to talk to you about The Last Straw Vineyard."

He motioned toward his office. "Then come in," he said.

He stepped out of the way, so I could walk inside. I did so reluctantly, clutching the contract closer to my chest. The actual office—*his* actual office—was nice. It was designed with soft white couches and an enormous antique desk, and another painting—this one of a giant red tomato—behind his desk.

"Also my mother's," he said, pointing at the painting. "She has a thing for fruit."

"That's so nice for her."

He smiled, ignoring my tone, sitting on the edge of his desk. "What's your interest in The Last Straw? Besides the obvious?"

"What do you mean?"

He shrugged. "It's great wine."

I folded my arms across my chest, not letting that throw me. "It's my family's vineyard," I said. "And I'm concerned about the sale. We all are, quite frankly. Some of us just aren't aware of it yet."

"Georgia. Of course. The family resemblance, right around the mouth."

He motioned around his own mouth.

"You're definitely your father's daughter. It's nice to meet you. You have a great family. I love your family."

"You don't know them."

"I disagree."

Then he reached over for a glass jar on his desk, full of long pieces of licorice, and held the jar out to me.

"Are you serious?" I said.

"Why wouldn't I be serious? Licorice is the best candy there is, and, as an added bonus, it has been used since ancient times for a variety of medicinal purposes. Including the relieving of stress."

"Still going to pass," I said.

He took a piece out of the jar, then took a huge bite. "Your choice," he said. "Though not the right one."

"I'm not interested in this," I said. "Whatever you're trying to do here."

He smiled. "And what am I trying to do here?"

"I don't know. Charm me."

"Why would I want to do that?"

"Because you know this contract is rife with error and it's not too late for me to nullify it."

"You sound like a lawyer."

"I am. And I negotiate sales much larger than this on a daily basis."

"Well, you probably have one up on me, then . . ."

He pointed to his degrees on the wall, mounted in fancy frames. Proof that he was a jerk, those degrees in such fancy frames. Cornell University College of Agriculture, Cornell Law School.

"I went to law school, but I never practiced," he said.

"How about viticulture? Did you practice that?"

He smiled. "I can assure you, your father is getting a great deal."

"That's beside the point."

"What is the point?"

I was honest, as hard as it was to say it out loud to a stranger. "My father's going to regret it."

He looked at me. "You think so?" he said.

And, suddenly, it looked like he cared. His eyes went soft, and the smirk disappeared.

I nodded, meeting his eyes and trying to impart my true feelings about how much my father was going to regret this. "I do."

He nodded, like he'd heard that.

"Hmm. I don't," he said.

Then he started rummaging through papers on his desk, my hope of him being a reasonable and kind person deflating.

I pointed at him. "Escrow hasn't closed yet. You don't take possession until after the new year."

"I believe that was so someone could get married on the property," he said. "Isn't that next weekend?"

"Don't insult me."

"I'm not insulting you. I'm just letting you know that all the contingencies have been met. Your dad requested that we not transfer ownership until after your wedding. Until they're able to close up the house."

"I intend to contest this sale, Mr. McCarthy."

He shot me a look.

"No one's called me Mr. McCarthy. Like ever." He paused. "I don't like it."

Which was when my phone buzzed. Suzannah appeared on the screen with a text message.

Ben called me and told me what was going on!!

Where are you? Call me already, so I can tell you what to do. After I yell at you for sticking me with this case. (Still at work and furious btw.)

Jacob was staring at the phone. "Who is Ben? The jilted groom?"

I put my phone away. "I'm just here to talk about the sale," I said.

He laughed. "Then there's nothing to talk about," he said. "That isn't your business."

"My father's well-being is my business."

He nodded. "So you should know that the contract has been signed and notarized. His business is now . . . my business."

Then he smiled—a smug, assured-of-itself smile, his going-out-on-a-limb-for-no-one smile. Which was when I decided it. How much I couldn't stand him.

"Good of you to come by. Though I think we should probably end this conversation," he said.

"I couldn't agree more," I said as I headed out the door.

A Guy Named Mark and a Guy Named Jesse

When I got back to the house, the sun was setting over the vineyard. The magic hour, as my father would call it. So much of what my father did at the vineyard, he did after the sun was down. The magic hour, the time before he went to work, involved respecting where the vineyard had gotten to in the daylight. After dark, when the grapes were on the vines, he'd help pick. If they were off, he'd help care for the soil, or care for the wine.

My father also thought it was the magic hour for another reason. The sky turned an odd shade of yellow, which he swore it never had before he started working the land. He said it was reflected that way because of the land—how lush and vibrant the land had become.

I was too exhausted to get into it with anyone. But Finn was sitting at the kitchen counter, wearing his backward baseball cap and running shorts, looking like the little-boy version of himself, back from pitching practice. He was eating an enormous piece of my mother's famous lasagna, straight from the baking pan.

This was the big joke of the lasagna. We all loved it. Never once did it actually make it to the kitchen table for dinner. No matter how pissed we were at each other—all of us would sit at the counter and eat it as soon as my mother took it from the oven to cool. Burning our tongues on it.

She made the lasagna with olives and tomatoes from the vineyard, spinach, five cheeses, and something else she wouldn't ever confess to.

Finn swore he'd walked in once and seen her adding chocolate chips to the bottom layer of noodles. We had spent years, cumulatively, searching for a sign of them.

Finn looked up as I walked into the kitchen. "I was bribed," he said.

"I can see that."

He took a large bite as I climbed on the stool across from him and put the contract down on my lap. It was a reminder—as if I needed one—that if I didn't figure out what to do, this could be the last time I'd be sitting in this house with Finn, eating our mother's lasagna, staring out at a vineyard that we would soon have to say our family used to own.

Finn puffed his cheeks out and tried to cool the lasagna already in his mouth. Then he shoveled more inside. "Mom didn't want to be alone with you," he said. "She called in reinforcements."

"So she told you about her and Dad?"

He nodded. "She told me."

Finn handed over a fork. I dug into the middle of the large pan. Finn's look of sympathy turned to annoyance, always annoyance when I took lasagna from the middle of the pan, even though he liked the edges.

I stopped caring as soon as I took a bite. The gooey, cheesy mess, sweet and salty with the first taste. The tomatoes as sweet as strawberries, the whole-wheat noodles buttery tender. It reminded me how hungry I was. It reminded me that I had failed to eat anything all day. Licorice included.

"I already knew, really."

I stopped chewing and looked at him. "How?"

He shrugged. "Mom has no poker face. And when I showed up unexpectedly for dinner last week, she panicked. She said Dad was at the Science Buzz Café. But it wasn't Thursday. Then she made me chocolate cake."

"Great. I get a naked man, and you get cake."

"It was pretty good too," Finn said.

Then he motioned toward the vineyard, where our parents were walking together. They were walking the way they normally did, except there was distance between them. My father's hands were behind his back; my mother's hands by her side.

It hurt to watch them. I went in for another bite, but he knocked my fork out of the way.

"Slow down on the lasagna," he said. "Don't you have a wedding dress to fit into?"

I knew he didn't mean it. My mother's lasagna made him do crazy things. To make amends, he cut a small square, moved it toward my side of the pan.

"Make it last," he said.

"What are we going to do about Mom and Dad?"

"What can we do? I mean, it's their life."

"And ours."

We each took a bite, quietly. Then I moved the contract over, so he could see it for himself.

"It's been a great day for you, huh?"

"Why didn't you tell me?"

He shrugged. "It was Dad's information to share."

My head was spinning thinking about all the things people in this family knew. And the things that people were leaving out.

"He only told me to make sure I didn't want the vineyard, which I assured him I didn't."

"Why did no one ask me? What if I had wanted the vineyard?"

"You don't want the vineyard."

I was moving to London in twenty days and joining the new London office of my law firm. London, a city I had been a little in love with since the first time I'd visited for a friend's wedding after we'd graduated college. After the reception, I decided to walk the city, winding my way down the cobblestone streets outside Chelsea, heading toward Pimlico. I dreamed of walking those amazing streets late at night, lantern-lit streetlights leading the way toward a tiny bistro famous for their rosemary potatoes. I couldn't believe that bistro was about to be my neighborhood bistro, those streets about to be my streets. Even if my relationship was in shambles, I was excited for those things.

Finn shook his head. "Honestly, Dad knew you don't want the vineyard any more than I do," he said.

"That's not the point."

"It should be," Finn said. "Besides, you made me and Bobby sign a contract your second year in law school that said we'd never take over the vineyard. And we would stop each other from doing it. Remember that?"

I did remember. I remembered why I had wanted us to sign it. I'd been having a hard time in law school, and part of me had wanted to come home and quit. But that was what coming home felt like to me. Quitting. Giving up on my dreams to build a life away from here, a life that was more stable than a vineyard felt. And I hadn't wanted to give up. I hadn't wanted Finn and Bobby to give up either.

Finn shook his head. "Bobby still fucking has it, I'm sure . . ." he said.

I pointed my finger at him. "What was that? And what is this about you moving?"

He shook his head. "I think you should probably stay out of it," he said.

"I'd like to, but you both keep dropping hints, and it's making it pretty hard to ignore."

He stuck his fork in the lasagna, like he was putting a stake into the ground, blocking off his portion.

"Okay," he said. "I'll tell you. But I don't want your judgment."

"Of course."

"No, don't say of course. You won't mean it. Not when you hear the details. Because the details are going to make you think that you under-stand what I'm dealing with. And you don't understand what I'm dealing with."

"Why? What did you do?"

"Is that a good place to start?"

I put my fork down, moving the pan physically toward him like a peace offering.

"So I think it's best, for impartiality, if we just talk about it like we're talking about other people. People you don't know. People who aren't your brothers. A guy named Mark. And a guy named Jesse."

Did Finn see himself more like a Jesse or more like a Mark? I'd guess Jesse.

"I see what you're doing. Don't try to guess which one I am," he said.

"Any other players I need to know for your story?"

"Just Daisy," he said. Then he sighed, Finn actually sighed out loud. "Daisy is this woman that Jesse met when he was really young. Daisy. And he loved her since he was very young. But he's a guy. And guys are stupid. Sixteen-year-old guys are so stupid they don't know yet what stupid even means. So he decided he shouldn't have anything to do with her. He met someone else . . . Lana."

"Bobby is cheating on Margaret?"

"How did you get there?"

"It's obvious."

"Except you're wrong." He looked at me. "I'm Jesse. Bobby is Mark."

"And who is Lana?"

"Lana is Annabelle Lawrence."

I looked at him, confused. Annabelle Lawrence was a girl that Finn had dated in high school. She was short, with tons of freckles and a big laugh, the kind of laugh that made you want to be around her all the time. I cried when Finn broke up with her. And I remembered what he'd said. He'd said there were going to be many Annabelles. He hadn't been kidding.

Finn picked up his fork, taking two big bites in quick succession. "I can't help how I feel and I can't do anything about it. And that's not new."

"What is?"

"She has feelings for me too."

Which was when I knew what he was saying. I knew the people who were in love here and who were being kept apart. "Margaret."

He nodded. "Margaret. Me and Margaret."

My heart dropped. How had I not known this? How had it not occurred to me, ever? The summer before Bobby and Margaret had started dating, she had been at the house all the time. She and Finn had been lifeguards together at the Ives pool. She had been Finn's friend first, before she was Bobby's wife.

"Please don't look at me like that," he said.

"Finn, are you sleeping with her?"

Finn shook his head. "That's your question?"

"Hey."

We looked up, the sound of a voice shocking us. It was Bobby, standing in the kitchen doorway. Bobby, who, if he'd heard the end of our conversation, certainly seemed to have no idea it was about him.

He walked in, an overnight bag in his hand.

"Holy shit," he said. "Lasagna!"

He made a beeline for the table, not even dropping his bag as he reached for a bite. Finn leaned back, not fighting him.

It seemed fair: Something was going on between Margaret and Finn. Bobby should have as much of the lasagna as he wanted.

"What are you doing here?" Finn said.

Finn's tone was less than welcoming.

"Mom called for reinforcements," he said, slightly taken aback. "You too?"

"Yep," he said.

I looked up at Bobby. "So you know about Mom and Dad too?"

Bobby nodded, took another bite. "It's my second lasagna this week."

This was when Margaret walked in, a twin on each hip, Peter and Josh Ford, dressed in matching firefighter uniforms complete with enormous red pants, suspenders, and fireman hats. Margaret was that way: five foot ten, long, blond hair, beautiful. And able to carry matching five-year-old firefighters on each hip and make it look easy.

Margaret forced a smile. "If someone's drinking already, I want in," she said.

She moved toward the counter, coming over and giving me a kiss. "Say hello to your awesome aunt!" she said, shoving the twins in my direction.

The twins reached in for a hug, their fireman hardhats falling off. They were the hardest part of not living near home, these little versions of their father: blond curls, strong smiles, adorable little boys. I loved them from five hundred miles away, but it wasn't the same as seeing them more often than that, and I felt it when I squeezed them, thinking how that five hundred miles was about to get exponentially larger.

I wrapped my arms around the twins, nuzzling into them. "What are you guys wearing?"

"We're firefighters," Josh said.

Margaret touched the top of Josh's head. "A fireman came to the boys' kindergarten to do a presentation," she said. "It's their chosen career path for the week."

Peter looked at her with disdain. "You mean, forever."

Margaret touched his cheek. "Yes, love, I mean forever."

I nodded, letting them know that I believed them. But they were already squirming away, starting their fire truck engines and running out the back door to the vineyard to play, to get the kind of love only my mom could provide for them.

"I guess I should go too," Margaret said. "We'll catch up later?"

I nodded. "Sounds good, Margaret."

It did not sound good.

She looked over at Finn. "Hey, Finn," she said.

Finn looked up, right at her, but only after she looked away. "Hey," he said.

And it was impossible to ignore what was between them—like it was taking everything they had to avoid looking at each other at the same time.

The room was silent. Margaret followed the twins outside. Bobby moved toward the doorway awkwardly, standing there, biting his nails.

I reached for a fork in the center of the table, holding it up. "Bobby, where are you going?"

Then Finn stood up. "I have to get to the bar," he said.

Bobby moved toward the hallway. "I'm going to unpack," he said.

Then they both walked out, in opposite directions. Leaving the lasagna to me.

The Wedding Crashers

$\mathcal{S}$ ynchronization. To operate in union.

On a vineyard, synchronization meant watching and waiting until everything lined up.

You didn't step in too quickly.

You also didn't step out.

The night before Bobby's wedding, Finn got arrested. He would tell you that it wasn't his fault. He would be right and wrong.

We had been drinking that night at The Brothers' Tavern. Finn had been good friends with the previous owners and they'd agreed to let him throw an impromptu bachelor party for Bobby. My father had joined us and left. Bobby's friends had joined us and left. And eventually, Finn, Bobby, and I were the last people in the bar, a candle on our table, too much bourbon between us.

Bobby poured us each another round, and I rested my head on the table. Finn had his head in his hands. Bobby was the only one awake and he was wide-awake, wired. He slapped Finn on the wrist.

"Don't be a pansy," Bobby said. "We're just getting started."

Finn sat up, startled, and moved his glass closer to Bobby. "Hit me," he said.

Finn was anxious to give Bobby whatever he needed the night before his wedding. I, on the other hand, was ready to go home. Though that wasn't an option. When I said that my brothers each played a role in my life—one helping me to be better, one helping me to be better at being bad—I also should have said that I played a role in theirs. I fixed things for them, when they didn't even know yet that they were broken. For Bobby, that meant staying up all night to put jokes into his speech for school president, revising his first Valentine's Day plan with Margaret, which had involved a monster truck show with the football team. And on the night before his impending wedding, in a way he couldn't name, fixing things for Bobby involved alcohol and nonstop movement.

"I think Bobby wants us to go and do something, Finn," I said.

"I do!" Bobby said. "That's exactly what I want. Let's do something!"

There was nothing to do in Sebastopol at 12:50 A.M. But, Finn was up, ready to please Bobby. "Where should we go?" he said.

Bobby moved toward the door. "I have an idea," he said. "I know of a party."

"I love a party," Finn said.

We headed up into the hills to a private estate owned by Murray Grant Wines. The lush vineyards surrounded a Spanish mansion that could have held five of my parents' houses. All the lights were on, a party in action.

"What is this?" Finn said.

Bobby shrugged. "Some girl is getting married. One of the grooms-men was talking about it at the bar earlier this afternoon."

"Are you crazy?" I said.

"Maybe." Bobby smiled ear to ear. "I still want to go to a wedding."

Finn shrugged. "Fuck it, then. We're crashing a wedding if Bobby wants to," he said. "Besides, it's so late. Anyone who's still out at a party won't give a shit if there are a couple of new guests. They'll be glad to have new people to drink with."

Bobby nodded. "We are crashing a wedding," he said. "Genius."

Then Bobby put his arm around Finn.

This was the secret no one knew. For all of Bobby's accolades at the time (newly minted MBA from Stanford Business School, a primo first job lined up at a venture capital fund), he just wanted to be as comfortable in his own skin as Finn was. (Finn, who still had yet to be employed, except for an occasional bartending shift and the stipend he'd made selling one of his photos to the *Press Democrat*.) And tonight that meant Bobby doing something ridiculous to prove to himself that even though he was about to write his future in stone, he could still be anyone.

We went into the wedding reception, which was on its last legs. Finn was correct about that. The bride was in her slinky sheath dress, but everyone else was in bathing suits and jeans. They were all drunk, hanging out by the Olympic-size swimming pool. Which made it slightly less awkward that the three of us were walking in in shorts and T-shirts, Finn in his backward baseball cap.

Bobby made a beeline for the bar, saying hello to everyone he passed. The partygoers stared at him, confused, but they didn't really care too much. They were at a wedding in wine country, drinking Murray Grant's rosé blend, thinking it was good.

Bobby made a face as he downed his first glass, then ordered another.

Then Bobby pointed to the bride. "She looks beautiful . . ."

The bride had flaming-red hair and makeup running down her face. She might have been beautiful earlier, but now she was a wet mess, someone having thrown her in the pool. She was happy about that. She didn't care that she was a wet mess. That was how a bride was supposed to be. At least that was what Bobby said, toasting to the happy bride, before he walked right up to her.

Finn shook his head. "This isn't going to go well," he said.

But, the bride seemed to like Bobby, the two of them gabbing.

As we walked over to join them, the bride gave Finn a flirtatious smile, newly married and checking out Finn, striking a pose for him.

"Hello there," she said.

Finn nodded. "Hello."

Then she motioned toward Bobby. "He's getting married tomorrow," she said, her wild red hair flying.

"We know," Finn said.

Bobby leaned in to her, a little too close.

"The thing is," Bobby said, "I'm a little young to be getting married. You know? I love Margaret. I really love her. But maybe that's part of it. You look a little older. You probably are more sure."

The bride looked at Bobby, irritated. "Did you just call me old?"

"Older, not old."

The bride looked like she was going to cry, which was when the groom came over. He was also redheaded, and large. He smelled like a brewery. "What's wrong?" he said.

She pointed at Bobby and Finn. "They called me old."

Finn put up his hands in surrender. "No, we didn't."

"Are you calling Catherine a liar?" the groom said.

"Who's Catherine?" Bobby said.

Bobby put out his hand, which the groom slapped away. A group surrounded us, the happy couple and the Ford siblings, who had upset them.

"Easy," Finn said. "Let's take it easy here."

He put his arms out, trying to keep the group from closing in.

Bobby moved closer to Catherine as though she couldn't hear him, as though that were the problem. "I said you looked older, not old. Can we move on to whether I should get married tomorrow?"

This was when the groom threw a punch at Bobby's face.

Finn jumped in to protect Bobby, and pushed the groom onto the ground. He wasn't trying to fight him, just trying to get him away from Bobby.

"Get him out of here!" Finn yelled. He was thinking only of Bobby and his upcoming marriage. Protecting both.

As I ran with Bobby into the woods, the cops showed up, sirens blasting.

Bobby stopped where he was. "I have to go back for him," Bobby panted.

And he wanted to, he really did.

He started to race back toward the fight, toward the cops. But, even from the woods, we could see it was too late.

Finn was on top of a rich, redheaded groom—and the cop who was pulling him off was not there to save him.

～

I kept going over the night before Bobby's wedding—as if it held the secret to how I should feel, seven days before mine.

I was getting nowhere fast—lying on my childhood bed, staring at a photograph of Culture Club taped on the ceiling above. It had been there since I was a teenager, placed at my eye level, so Boy George would be the one to say good night.

It felt like he was taunting me with all the answers I didn't seem to have—when my phone rang.

I looked down at the caller ID, a happy Ben staring back. I wanted to pick up and tell Ben what Finn had just told me—I wanted Ben to be my person again, the one I told everything to. Ben always said the thing that revealed to me what I should do. Ben said that was giving him too much credit. It never seemed to me that it was giving him enough.

"Hey," he said when I picked up the phone. He paused, not sure what to do now that he had me there. "Thanks for picking up."

I kept my eyes on the ceiling, on George's face. I wasn't going to make this easier. Maybe I was done making it harder, but that was different.

"What are you doing?" he said.

"Staring at Boy George."

He laughed. "That bad of a day?"

"You have no idea."

He cleared his throat, asking me a question that encouraged me to answer him.

"You want to tell me?" he said.

"Yes."

"You going to?"

I shook my head as though he could see that. "How would you describe Bobby and Margaret? Would you describe them as happy?"

"Yes, I would." He paused.

"What?"

"I would describe him as happier than her," he said. "She seems a little lost."

That broke my heart for Bobby, for the reasons why Ben was correct, for the reasons it didn't matter.

"And my parents?"

"That is more even. That is blessed," he said. "I mean, next to you and Boy George, I'd say they are the happiest couple I know."

I laughed for the first time that day, some of my anger melting. Ben felt like Ben again, the two of us talking gently in a dark room, the world safer and more lovely for it.

"You still need to take that poster down. It's creepy. Milli Vanilli creepy."

"That's not a battle you're going to win, Ben."

Except that it was. I would have to remove everything from this room before this house was sold. The house. The vineyard. My childhood.

"So I oversaw the move today," Ben said. "Everything is on its way to London."

His accent crept up on me and warmed me to him.

"I guess you heard that . . ."

"I did," I said. "Thomas called looking for you."

"He mentioned something about that," he said.

"Considering what's going on between us, did you think that maybe you shouldn't have sent my stuff to London?"

"I did. I thought you might not want me to send your stuff anywhere without talking to you first. I thought that was the right thing to do. But I decided to move everything anyway."

"What would you call doing that?"

"Hopeful."

I covered my eyes with my elbow. "Ben, I should get some sleep."

"I had them leave the guest room mattress. I'm sleeping on that. Though I forgot to tell them to leave sheets. So it's a bit of a sad situation. Empty apartment. Old mattress. No pillow for my head."

"You could check into a hotel."

"That's sadder."

He paused. We both did. The silence between us was exhausting.

"I haven't shown up there. I've tried to give you space. But you do need to talk to me."

"I'm listening."

He got quiet. "I was ready for you to argue. Now I'm not sure where to start."

"How about with Michelle Carter?"

"I've told you about Michelle Carter."

What he'd told me was they had dated briefly the summer before we met—three months of briefly while she was filming a movie in New York. And that Michelle had crushed him. *Eviscerated* him. That was the word he used. Then she went back to London and got back together with her boyfriend. The famous actor—and often her romantic costar—Clay Michaels. The couple was tabloid fodder, glossy red carpet photos of them falling into the hands of girls at nail salons on a regular basis.

Ben had never even been photographed with Michelle at an event. He liked to joke: *If you weren't photographed with a movie star you were dating, was it like it never happened?*

And so Michelle became an anecdote for Ben to share about his dating life. The time he dated one of the most famous women in the world. How she completely and totally disappeared on him. *How else was that going to end?* Ben laughed. The way we laugh about the people who slayed us, when we're talking about them with the one person who never would.

"Does Clay know the truth?"

"Yes. He's always known that Maddie wasn't his."

"He isn't furious?"

"Apparently he has a kid that isn't Michelle's."

I was getting a headache. I pulled the covers up higher, contemplating Michelle's odd arrangement with her boyfriend, contemplating what else I knew about Michelle: her gorgeous house in London recently photographed for the cover of *Architectural Digest*, her gorgeous face chosen for *People* magazine's "50 Most Beautiful People."

Boy George stared down at me, laughing. He was laughing and not doing anything to save me. What could he do?

"When Michelle moved back to London, that was it," he said. "She got back together with Clay, and an old friend of mine, the guy that introduced us, said that they were having a baby at some point. But I never heard from her again." He paused. "Until I heard from her again."

"What did she say when she called you?"

"She said our summer fling resulted in a little girl who she was finally ready for me to meet," he said.

"When was that, Ben?"

He paused. "Five days after I proposed to you," he said. "Timing's a funny thing, isn't it?"

That was five months ago. Ben had proposed to me during a trip to Paris. He had known about Maddie for five months? That was longer than he had said yesterday. Had time collapsed for him? His engagement, the realization that he had a little girl. Everything melding into one long day. On one side there was our life, which we considered happy. On the other was this brand-new blessing, which could tear that life apart.

"I started to tell you that very night, but you were working late on the Porter case. And when you came in, you said, and I remember, get me a bottle of B-Minor and don't say a word until I've had half of it. You fell asleep after half of it."

"So it's my fault?"

"No, I was just trying to pick a time that it wouldn't hurt you."

"What happened?"

"You have this wide-open face. And we were having so much fun planning the wedding, getting ready for London." He paused. "And then I guess I couldn't find a time that seemed like it wouldn't hurt you."

I took a breath, softened to him. He probably should have stopped talking then. But he didn't. We never stopped talking, did we? It was what allowed us to say the thing that stuck. In the moment before we said the wrong thing.

"I know it's hard to understand why I kept Maddie from you. But it's hard for me too. It's hard to understand why Michelle kept Maddie from me for so long."

"Doesn't it make you mad, Ben?"

"It makes me fucking furious and it has been rather difficult for me to deal with."

Which was when I remembered seeing them on the street, Michelle's hand on Ben's back. He didn't look furious.

"I look at Maddie and I think, regardless of what Michelle did, I don't want to lose another second with her." He paused. "And I'm grateful to Michelle that she did tell me."

He cleared his throat.

"And now I'm telling you. I love you. And I'm going to do whatever I can to make things right for us."

I could hear how much he meant it—and I felt myself moving toward him, toward understanding. Which was when he started to talk again.

"Let's figure out how to get past this. I didn't do anything intentionally deceitful. It's not like I was unfaithful," Ben said.

Unfaithful. What a choice of word. As if there were one way to make someone lose faith. Adultery. That was Ben's measure of what was unforgiveable. It was what my mother was doing—with an impotent man. It was what my good brother was running away from so he didn't allow himself to do it to my other brother. Ben wasn't guilty of that. Except weren't there other unforgivable things you couldn't turn back from?

Last week I had known Ben. I had trusted him to tell me the truth, to ask me the questions that made me feel like I was moving closer to the truth. That was the trust between us.

"You still there?" he said.

I told him I wasn't.

Then we got off the phone.

~

I went downstairs and made a cup of hot water with lemon, then I went upstairs and into Finn's room, but it was dark. Maybe he was still at the bar. Either way, he wasn't there now—his bed made, his bag on top of it.

I moved down the hall. There was a soft light coming from Bobby's room. Margaret and Bobby in there together—reading, talking softly. They didn't look unhappy. They looked comfortable.

That left my parents' bedroom. The door was wide open. The door was never wide open when we were children—the bedroom was my parents' sacred space, none of us daring to enter.

My mother was already in bed, her curls swept back off her face. Her radio was playing softly—a twin on either side of her, both of them sleeping. She put her finger to her mouth. "Whisper," she said. "And tell me you have wine in that mug."

"No, hot water and lemon. Do you want a little?"

"Only if the hot water and lemon magically turns into wine."

I nodded and took a seat on the edge of the bed, motioning to the twins. "Are they sleeping with you?"

"They are sleeping with me," she said. Her voice low, like in demonstration.

I smiled. I couldn't help it. In a long, unruly day, this was the nicest thing she could do. My mother was acting exactly like my mother. Bossy, serious. It made me feel calm. So why did I decide to reward her by being mean?

"No Henry tonight?" I said.

She smiled, giving me a look that said it wasn't okay and, also, that she forgave me. "No. Not tonight. He's in rehearsals."

"Good for him."

"Good for San Francisco, actually," she said. "Henry is one of the most beloved conductors in the world. He ran the New York Philharmonic, and was chief conductor of the Royal Stockholm Philharmonic before that. He has changed the template for what an American orchestra can be."

"That sounds like an exaggeration."

"It's an understatement. He's mentored scores of prominent musicians. And he's brought contemporary American music back into vogue in this country. You should look up his bio on Wikipedia. Don't take my word for it."

I nodded in a way that said I'd get right on learning all I could about Henry. If *get right on it* meant never.

She paused, deciding how to shift gears. "Your fiancé called me," she said.

I nodded. "That seems to be what he's doing today," I said.

"He's very torn up." She shook her head. "I told him it was between the two of you. That I loved him, but I love you more and I support whatever you decide together."

"Thanks, Mom."

"I did tell him not to call your father, though." She shrugged. "I doubt your father will think it's between the two of you."

I knew she was right. My father would be furious at Ben, not for keeping the kid from me, but for getting himself into that situation in the first place, for not being responsible enough to stop it.

"Dad tells me you paid a little visit to Jacob McCarthy today," my mother said.

"He knows?"

"Of course he knows. Jacob called him as soon as you left there."

Jacob was a tattletale—why did that surprise me? Of course he was. The man lived on licorice.

"He wanted to make sure Dad wasn't having second thoughts," she said.

I perked up, hopeful that my father was going to see the error of what he was doing, just by being asked. Maybe Jacob's call would trigger a new conclusion. One where Jacob moved the hell away.

"He's not having second thoughts. This is what he wants. What we both want."

"Then why were you avoiding me today?"

"I had a feeling you weren't in the mood to be pleasant," she said.

"I don't like Jacob, Mom. I have a bad feeling about what's going to happen to our vineyard, to everything Dad worked so hard for, that you both have."

"Fine, but do you actually think you're going to change your father's mind?"

"No. I'm just hoping he'll at least wait until he's in a position to make a better decision, one that he's not making under duress."

She laughed. "He's not under duress."

"Does he know about Henry?"

She nodded. "Yes."

"Then he's under duress."

She sighed, but she didn't look hurt. She looked like she wanted to hear me. She looked like she wanted to be on the same side, as opposed to opposite ones, so we could get to the conversation she wanted to have, the one about Ben.

"Darling, we're supposed to sit down with the caterer . . ." she said.

"Should I cancel that? It's not about the deposit, though if we don't sit down with her, she is going to take that. She needs a final head count. She needs a final decision on the entrée."

"Mom, I can't really deal with that right now."

"I told her we're going with the fish," she said.

I looked at her, confused.

"I'm sorry, did you cancel the wedding and forget to tell me?" she asked.

"No."

"Well, I think that means part of you doesn't want to cancel."

"What about the other part?"

My mother looked me right in the eye. "If you want to fix things, you have to start somewhere," she said. "For you that somewhere is fish."

I interrupted her. "Do you remember when Finn snuck out of the house on his fifteenth birthday and hitchhiked to Los Angeles to go to a Phish concert?"

"It was his sixteenth birthday. And of course."

Her face went dark even remembering it. Finn ended up at a downtown Los Angeles police station, my parents driving five hundred miles in the middle of the night to pick him up. "Why are you bringing that up?"

"Because Bobby and I were the ones that you were mad at. Even though I was thirteen."

"Fourteen. And I seem to remember that you took it upon yourself to drive to the Queens' harvest party while we were gone."

"You were late, how else was I going to get there?"

"Very funny." She was less than amused, just remembering how I'd *borrowed* her car, driven up the road to the party. "I think we're getting a little off track."

"You grounded both of us, as long as you grounded Finn. Do you remember why you made that decision?"

"Apparently you do."

"You said Finn wanted to go so badly that he wasn't thinking clearly. But we knew how dangerous it was and we didn't stop him, or tell you and Dad so you could stop him. And you said that was unacceptable.

Because that's what we do for the people we love. We don't sit around watching while they make mistakes. We at least try to stop them from doing things we know they are going to regret."

"You realize I was talking about children as opposed to grown people?"

"Do the same principles not apply?"

She nodded. "I guess they do."

Then she took my hand and put it to her face. Josh and Peter squirmed beside her, curling in against her legs.

"So that's what you're trying to do?" my mother said. "Stop the people you love from doing what they'll regret?"

"Yes. Exactly."

She kissed the inside of my palm. "But which way is regret?"

Sebastopol, California. 1984

*T*he baby was crying.

All the children were crying. They wouldn't stop. He could hear them from the bedroom, Jen trying to soothe them. He wanted to get up and help her, but she had ordered him away. He had worked all night and was heading back to the vineyard soon. The clock read 10 A.M. He needed to sleep for at least an hour or two.

He was lying on the bed, staring at the ceiling. They had three children and they were going bankrupt trying to make this vineyard work. After that first vintage—when he thought he had the hang of it, that one lovely wine giving him a false sense of security—he realized he didn't have a handle on anything. The weather wasn't cooperating: two years of storms, one year of no storms at all. Three children.

Sebastopol was changing, diversifying, but it wasn't becoming a wine haven. And there was a man who wanted to buy the land back from him and turn it into a subdivision: McMansions on McMansions, ten of them, one acre of land each.

Dan didn't want to think about doing it, but he had to think about doing it. He had given himself five years, five vintages. If he sold the vineyard now, they could get out without losing everything. He would come out ahead. But even one more bad harvest, and he would be borrowing against what he had already borrowed.

He wasn't going to do that, not to his wife, not to his kids. The boys fighting, always fighting. If they moved back into the city, they would still fight, but he would be around less to hear it. And maybe they would cry less. That was possible too.

He looked up to find Jen in the doorway, the baby in her arms, sleeping. Jen smiled at the small victory. He smiled back at her. He loved her so much he thought it might break him.

"Hey there, baby," she said.

Jen came over and lay down next to him, putting their daughter between them. Jen had put her in a blue dress. Her legs stuck out beneath it, chunky and sweet. The baby was a mix of both of them. Bobby had been a spitting image of Jen, Finn of him. But this one, their daughter, on any given day, looked like both of them. And neither of them.

He put the baby on his chest, reaching for Jen's hand. "You okay?" he said.

She sighed. "I gave up," she said. "I gave the kids a bag of cookies."

"That was smart of you," he said.

"Each. Each their own bag."

He smiled, looked at her.

"Did you sleep at all?"

"Yes." He nodded, meeting her eyes, so she wouldn't worry.

"Liar."

She closed her eyes, about to fall asleep herself.

"We need to take the offer," he said.

She opened her eyes.

"I can get my job back at the university," he said. "I just got off the phone with Bill and he said they'd be glad to have me. And the real estate agent can get our money out of this. She knows a guy who's interested."

"That's what you've been doing instead of sleeping? Making that decision?"

"That's what I've been doing."

She paused, and he could see her relax. They would move to San Francisco. She could get a job as a studio musician. They could have salaries and buy the purple Victorian home they'd driven past in Pacific Heights. They could get help with the kids.

She looked at him and smiled. He loved that smile, and was willing to move mountains when it appeared. He had made it appear now by giving them both a break, by giving them a way to turn it around.

Then her smile disappeared on him. "Did you call anyone else?"

"What?"

"Did you call anyone besides Bill? To tell him the plan?"

"No." He shook his head. "Why do you ask?"

She moved closer to him for a second, one hand on him, one on her baby. Then she stood up, leaving the baby with him, sleeping quietly on his chest.

"I'm just trying to figure out who I need to call back."

He looked at her, confused.

"To tell that we're staying."

The View from 8 A.M., the Last Sunday of the Harvest

This was what I dreamed. I was getting married under the Eiffel Tower. The sun was coming up over Paris. Ben was by my side, wearing a green suit, smiling. It didn't feel like a dream because of that suit, which we'd bought together at a flea market in South Pasadena shortly after Ben moved to Los Angeles. The pea-green suit was intoxicating to him. He wore it every chance he had, so it added a verisimilitude to the dream to see him in it. It actually felt like we were getting married, the two of us reading our vows. But when it was time for Ben to put the ring on my finger, he threw it toward the tower's iron stairs, the ring landing somewhere high in the tower. "Go!" he said.

We ran toward the ring and the stairs. Ben started to climb, before I even reached the staircase. He was climbing the first of three hundred stairs, which would take him from the ground floor to the first level, the second three hundred stairs, which would take him from the first level to the second. He explained this mid-run so I'd understand where he wanted to go, even if he didn't want to explain why.

Just as I got to the base of the tower, I got drenched. I woke up to find my father and Finn standing over my bed. Finn was spraying me with water from my mother's self-created spray bottle, which she used to water her vegetables.

"What the hell?"

"I could ask you that," Finn said.

"You guys scared the crap out of me," I said.

My father smiled. "Mission accomplished. Let's go."

"Where to?"

"The Tasting Room," Finn said.

He pulled up the window shade and bright light streamed in. I tried to cover my eyes but it was no use.

My father motioned toward the back of my closet door, where my wedding dress was hanging, clean and hemmed. My mother must have done her handiwork while I was sleeping so it would be the first thing I'd see when I woke up.

He nodded. "Pretty," he said.

I ignored that, sitting up. "Why are we going to The Tasting Room at eight A.M.?"

"Why are you still sleeping at eight A.M.?" he said. "Is that what corporate lawyers do these days?"

My father had been up for five hours already. He had already had breakfast and lunch. It was time for a drink.

"Don't you know what today is?" Finn said.

It was Sunday, the last Sunday of the harvest. Five days until the weekend of my wedding.

I deserved more than water on my face to wake me up. Had I forgotten everything that mattered around here? There was an order to things during the last weekend of the harvest.

The official kick-off was the Sunday morning winemaker's tasting, when my father opened the previous year's vintage for the first time, sharing it with local winemakers. Tonight, we had family dinner in the wine cave. Then, on Tuesday night, we had the ultimate celebration: the harvest party.

Most years, the harvest party was the following Saturday night—the weekend after the harvest ended—but this year they had changed the plan. They had changed the plan because the next Saturday night they were supposed to be at my wedding.

"Let's go!" my father said. "Get out of bed."

"Can you guys just give me a few minutes?"

"No," my father said.

"You should pretend she didn't ask that, Pop," Finn said.

"I don't have time to pretend," my father said. "We're leaving in five minutes."

Finn reached into my suitcase and threw jeans onto my bed, a hooded sweatshirt.

"I don't want to wear this."

"Well, it's slim pickings," he said.

He headed for the door. "Unless you prefer your wedding dress?"

~

"So, little one," my father said.

We were in the back of Finn's pickup truck, heading to The Tasting Room, steadying the barrel of wine for the tasting between us. The truck was moving along at a steady pace, *The River* playing in the background. My father always played Bruce on the morning of the first tasting. Bruce Springsteen, my father's favorite, necessary for synchronization: the music the first grape was picked to, the music it should be tasted to during the official wine tasting. My father never changed it, certainly not today.

Finn took a left onto Main Street, taking the long way to The Tasting Room.

"Ben," my father said.

That was all. No question at the end of it.

Bruce played loudly.

My mother had told me that she hadn't told my father, which meant he didn't know about Ben. He didn't know anything beyond the fact that he knew me, and he knew I wouldn't be here like this if something wasn't up.

"You having doubts?" he said.

"You could say that."

"I just did," he said.

I smiled at him as Finn took a right off of Sebastopol Avenue, leading us into the sweet town of Sebastopol. It was dusty in its way but also full

of gems: the best ice cream in five hundred miles, a drive-in movie theater, a local saloon. Sebastopol's central drag had recently been usurped
by the new downtown industrial complex filled with artisanal foods and
fancy florists and a five-hundred-dollar-a-night boutique hotel, creating
a mini-Napa. But it was still quiet, lovely, at this time of day.

"You know, I almost married someone who wasn't your mother." He
shook his head. "A week before the wedding, I told her we should call it
off. I said it nicer than that, but I told her we should reconsider."

I looked at him, confused. "Is that true?"

He nodded. "My decision to become a winemaker didn't feel like a
choice. I had this great job at the university. Tenure track. But I spent
most of my free time thinking about wine. It felt like something I was
compelled to do. The woman, who was a poet, had this quote on her wall
about writing. I think it was Fitzgerald. Anyway, he talked about how he
had to write his books, how there was no choice in the matter. That was
how I felt about this."

He motioned to the land around him, small vineyards as far as the eye
could see.

"The truth was, that girlfriend . . ."

"The poet?"

"The poet. She hadn't made it that easy for me. She told me she wasn't
going to sit and watch me live my dreams in some small town when she
could be in London, Paris. She said if I insisted on making wine, spending
my life in a small California town, that was the last straw." He shrugged.
"That's how I named the vineyard."

My jaw must have dropped open to the floor. My father always said
that he'd come up with the name at The Brothers' Tavern, after midnight, five beers in. It was a detailed story that he'd recounted often.

"I don't understand," I said.

"Nothing to understand. I lied to you before. Don't tell."

I looked at him, floored.

He shrugged. "Your mother has always been a little sensitive about
it," he said. "She feels like she has been spending her life on a vineyard
that was dedicated to another woman. It doesn't matter that I chose the
vineyard over the woman."

I nodded, even though I wanted to say he was facing the same problem now. My father still put the vineyard first, my mother still felt like she was in second place. And so, what was my father trying to say about Ben? That the demons we were facing, we needed to face now? That we'd face the same demons on the other side of building a family together, building a lovely life, and trying to hold on to it?

"Thing is, whatever's going on with Ben, it's okay to walk away. It's also okay to get over it. The two of you have built a great life together, that matters too, it matters as much as whatever is going on that has made you doubt him."

"It doesn't feel that simple."

"Most of the time it is. Most of the time a person wants something more than anything else. You can tell because at the end of the day that's what they're willing to fight for."

My father looked away, sad and angry. Suddenly I wasn't sure if we were talking about me and Ben, or him and my mother. She had spent her life fighting for her family, for my father, and now she seemed to be fighting for someone else.

Finn pulled in front of The Tasting Room, waving at Bill and Sadie Nelson, who were walking toward the entrance. Bill and Sadie were winemakers from Healdsburg, and old friends of my parents', my father's first recruits to Sebastopol.

He pointed at me, and they smiled, waving big.

Finn got out of the truck. "Let's go, slowpokes."

"Give us just a second," my father said.

"I'll send out some of the guys to get that barrel," he said.

My father nodded. "Great," he said.

Finn disappeared inside, Bill and Sadie holding the door for him.

"So Ben has a kid?"

I was still watching Bill and Sadie walk inside and thought I heard him wrong. I turned toward him, shocked.

He reached into the back pocket of his jeans, pulled out a series of index cards.

"What a world," he said.

"You know?"

"Of course I know." He nodded. "Your mother tells me everything," he said.

"Why didn't you come out and say it?"

He looked up and met my eyes. "Because I didn't want you to miss my point, the way you're about to do, and jump to asking my opinion on what you should do about the fact that the person you trusted most in the world lied to you."

"Which is?"

"My opinion?"

He put his notes in his front pocket.

"If you want to get married, then you should. If you don't, you shouldn't."

"That solves it!"

"I do what I can." He laughed. "Thing is, either way we cut it, we shouldn't test the people we love," he said. "We do, but it's shitty and ultimately, regardless of what they did or didn't do, we're the ones who feel like we failed."

Then, as if that closed the case, he kissed me on the cheek and headed into The Tasting Room.

The Wine Thief

*T*wo times a year, my father did a tour of The Last Straw Vineyard for locals and wine club members, once at the start of the harvest and once the day of the harvest party. The rest of the year, the only place to taste my father's wines was at The Tasting Room.

My father wasn't unique in handing over the wine tasting responsibilities to Gary and Louise. Many people associated Napa Valley with going to a tasting room at a vineyard and drinking a bunch of wines for ten dollars or the price of a bottle of wine. But that type of stop-by tasting was usually only done by the big wineries—like Murray Grant—factory wineries, existing on the side of Highway 29, that were eager to take advantage of drunk tourists who didn't know better, who didn't care if they were drinking anything good, who only cared that they were drinking.

But most of the small vineyards in Sonoma County didn't have tasting rooms at their vineyards. They gave their wines to Gary and Louise to sell, Gary pouring the wine to folks who were serious about drinking it, pouring different wine for the folks who weren't and stumbled into his tasting room. If that sounded like snobbery, it wasn't. The measure wasn't people who could spend a lot of money on wine. Gary and Louise regularly lost money. The measure was appreciation.

Today, The Tasting Room was open only to winemakers. And the only wine on tap was ours.

There was no way to adequately describe The Tasting Room and make it sound as cool as it was. On the surface, it was a '50s-style diner. The soda counter had been converted to a wine bar. The fluorescent lights had been replaced with hanging lanterns and candles and wooden sconces. The tiled floors were washed and polished twice a week. Cork-filled vases lined the small tables.

When I walked in, I felt happy to be there, surrounded by this group of winemakers, who got together every year for the harvest. They had nicknamed themselves the Cork Dorks. The Cork Dorks: a play on the fact that so many of them were scientists. Some migrated to Sebastopol at my father's urging. Some came in the rush of the '90s, when Pinot Noir really hit the map.

There was Brian Queen, a former colleague of my father's from San Francisco State, who was one of the only Grenache producers in the region. Terry and his wife, Sarah, produced Sauvignon Blanc in upper Russian River. Lynn and Masters (her Robert Redford look-alike boyfriend) had recently gone over to the dark side, Napa Valley, where they were making a Cabernet Sauvignon that the *New York Times* had named as one of the best ten wines coming out of California.

And then there were Gary and Louise, The Tasting Room owners, who grew grapes in the backyard, grapes that led to arguably the most scrumptious sparkling wine you've ever tasted—inarguably, if you asked either of them. No one did. They just drank.

Everyone hugged everyone hello, no one, thankfully, asking about the wedding.

"Look who's here," Finn said.

He motioned toward the back door, and I followed his eyes to see my mother sneaking in. She had on a long white dress, Bobby by her side, looking dapper in his sports coat and tie. Jacob McCarthy walked in behind them, looking un-dapper in jeans and another of those zipper cashmere sweaters.

"I'm glad she showed up," Finn said.

I pointed in Jacob's direction. "Are you glad he did?"

My mother waved as she moved closer to us, Bobby walking up behind her.

My mother wrapped her arms around my shoulders, like it had been ten months since we had seen each other, not ten hours. "You snuck out," she said. "Why didn't you tell me that you were leaving?"

"We didn't think you were coming," I said. My eyes were on Jacob, who'd moved across the room toward my father and was saying a friendly hello.

My mother looked offended. "Of course I was coming. Margaret needed to talk to me. And then I was getting the twins off for the day. They had to eat, didn't they?"

"Someone else has to eat!" Louise said, running over, kissing my mother. Giving me a hearty squeeze, then a second one. "Do they not feed you in Los Angeles?"

Louise was a large woman, in every way: her stature, her kindness, her love of wine. I had never seen her completely sober, now being no exception. She held a mostly finished jelly jar of wine in her hand.

"I guess that's what you get for becoming a big-city girl," Louise said.

"Weight Watchers?" Finn said.

"Exactly." She laughed.

Bobby put his hand on my shoulder. "She's about to get even more big city. She is a very important real estate lawyer. And she's moving to London with her amazing fiancé."

He was trying to help. As usual, he was doing the opposite.

"Okay, folks, let's get this started!" Gary said.

He clapped his hands together, excitedly, and motioned to my father.

My father put the barrel by the table, pausing for dramatic effect. Then he took out his thief to a loud cheer.

My father's thief. A winemaker's tool that he used to extract wine. It looked like a swirly straw. And, in many ways, it was. My father put the thief into the top of the barrel, sucking from the free end of it to pull enough wine from the barrel to give everyone a taste. Everyone was quiet suddenly, like we were in a library. Then he gently pulled on the thief, filled glasses for everyone.

As he finished, the Dorks erupted in a cheer, Finn stepping forward to distribute the glasses.

My mother usually served the wine, which led me to look around the room for her. She was standing in the corner, hiding by the tall soda maker, like she wanted to disappear into it.

I was so busy staring at her that I didn't see Jacob move in front of me, holding glasses of wine, making it hard to escape.

Jacob held a glass in my direction. "Hey, there," he said.

"What are you doing here, Jacob?"

"Your father invited me."

I took the wine from him. "He was just trying to be nice," I said.

He smiled. "Then he succeeded," he said.

"Ladies and gentlemen!" Gary called out again. "If you'd please shut it!"

We all turned to the front of The Tasting Room. Gary stood next to my father, his arm on his shoulder. My father leaned into him, his old friend, waiting to hear what he had to say.

Gary held up his glass. "Jen, what are you doing standing in the back? Get up here!"

Everyone turned to see my mother, hiding by the soda maker. She smiled and smoothed her dress. Then she made her way to the front of the room to take her place by my father.

"I'm going to tell you all a little story," Gary said. "I was running a wine shop in The Haight, when this guy walks in and says I have the loveliest selection of wine he's ever seen. And he wants to show me a place where he thinks I'd like to move. I thought he was crazy. Then I got here. And I knew he was."

My father smiled.

"None of us would be here. Not without Dan Ford. Not without Jen Ford. And we are grateful." He held up his glass. "Even if you're cashing in your chips and getting the hell out. Though I can't quite believe you're selling out to the Murray Grant empire . . . How many chips did they give you, exactly?

Everyone started laughing, but there was an edge to it. No one in the room was a Murray Grant Wine fan. I turned to Jacob, who forced himself to smile, playing it off.

"What's the big plan, Dan?" Brian Queen called out. "Second honeymoon?"

Louise laughed. "You should be asking Jen that."

My mother stared anxiously at my father, asking him silently how to answer. No one knew that when they left here, they wouldn't be leaving together.

She pulled herself together and held her wineglass up, tipping it in my father's direction.

"Whatever Dan wants!" she said.

The Dorks cheered as my father awkwardly put his arm around my mother.

Bobby headed to the front of the room, Finn staying by the back door.

My father took my mother in, forcing a smile. I watched as he struggled. It was too much. I grabbed for another glass of wine, downing it as my father held up a bottle of unlabeled wine, faced his friends.

"I don't know if any of you all remember, but at one of the very first Cork Dork meetings, we sat around talking about it, doing the math on it, how much work a single grape requires. From vine to finish. A single grape the start of it, this unlabeled bottle right here in my hand the end of it, the eight hundred grapes inside."

He looked out at his group of colleagues and friends.

"We know the secret, right? It's not just eight hundred grapes in this bottle. It's everything else that makes it heavy. Patience and focus and sacrifice and . . . fucking boredom."

The Dorks laughed.

"Let's just call it time. This bottle holds the endless time that I was lucky to spend with all of you." My father nodded. "Thank you, guys," he said. "Thank you all, for today, and for everything. It has been a really good run."

Then, as was tradition, he uncorked the bottle and took a sip right from it. The Cork Dorks cheered.

My father didn't look sad. He looked happy, maybe for the first time since I'd been home. My father looked truly and seriously happy. He took a sip of his wine, nodding, appreciating what he had accomplished with this wine, with all of his wines. Lost in it. My mother looked up at him, their eyes meeting, sharing that moment, both of them having the same experience of the wine.

In spite of Henry.

In spite of what was happening between them.

Bobby was standing near my parents, smiling. Finn was by the back door, smiling.

I, on the other hand, chose this moment to drop my wine, the glass shattering on the ground.

Everyone turned toward me, just in time to see the tears streaming down my face. The winemakers froze, drinks midair. Bobby and Finn looked at me with mouths agape. My father's smile, disappearing. My mother's eyes going wide.

As I moved as fast as I could. Toward the exit.

The Ride Home

I ran out of The Tasting Room, needing air. I knew someone would head out after me, so I went directly to Finn's truck, opening the unlocked front door, searching for the spare key where he kept it under the driver's-side visor. I planned to drive myself out of there. I planned to keep driving until my father's last tasting was far behind me, until I could pretend it wasn't happening.

"I don't think it's there."

I looked up to see Jacob standing by the driver's-side door, holding a cup of water.

I wiped at my tears. "I don't want to talk to you," I said.

"I don't want to talk to you either," he said.

Then I took the cup out of his hands, drank it down.

"Uh . . . I brought that out here for myself."

I handed him the empty cup.

He looked down at it. Then he turned it over, no drops coming out.

"I was thirsty," he said.

I tried to focus on taking deep breaths. I couldn't calm down, though. Apparently when your parents split up, it didn't matter if you were a grown-up, it turned you into a five-year-old again: wanting them to promise you that everything was going to be okay. And wanting to make everything okay for them, the way you could when you were five, just by saying you loved them.

Jacob tossed the cup into a trash can. "You seem like you need to get out of here."

"I do, but I don't have a car."

"You want a ride?"

I laughed, shaking my head.

"The proper response is *thank you*. Or, *thank you anyway*. Only two options."

He wasn't wrong, even if I couldn't stand him.

I turned back toward The Tasting Room. My mother was walking outside to make sure I was okay. She caught my eye and started walking toward me.

Which was when I saw Henry. He was standing in the parking lot across the street, waiting for my mother, for wherever he was planning on taking her.

Had my mother told him to stay out of sight so my father wouldn't see him? Was she going to run to their meeting spot now that my father was distracted? Was I going to have to see them kiss hello?

Jacob tilted his head, following my eyes across the street. "Who's that guy?" he asked.

"Let's just go," I said.

Jacob looked surprised. "Okay." Then Jacob paused, remembering something, looking like he didn't know how to say what he'd remembered. "Thing is, my car's back at my place. In Graton. We could walk to it. And then I could drive you home."

"It's five miles!"

"More like seven," he said. "Remember your choices. *Thank you* or *thank you anyway*."

My mother was getting closer.

I glanced at Henry. He hadn't yet noticed my mother. He looked like he'd spotted me, though, like he just might decide to come over to introduce himself again. Fully clothed.

This was when I started walking.

Grown, Produced, and Bottled

*M*y father's favorite varietal of his wine, Concerto, was an ode to my mother's musical roots—and an ode to the word itself. *Concerto.* My parents loved what it meant. It originated from the conjunction of two Latin words: *conserere*, which means to tie, to join, to weave, and *certamen*, which means competition, fight. The idea was that the two parts in a concerto, the soloist and the orchestra, alternate episodes of opposition and cooperation in the creation of the musical flow. In the creation of synchronization.

Which was, precisely, what was required of wine.

Which was precisely what I had lost. Any cooperation. Leaving only opposition.

Jacob wanted to avoid downtown, so we wound up Sullivan Road into the hills—into the deep remoteness of the old apple orchards, stunning farmhouses, renovated barns. This route exemplified the very quiet I had run from as a teenager. It suddenly felt comforting to be back in it. It felt comforting and completely unchanged. Which maybe, at the moment, was the same thing.

I'd taken this walk with Ben one of the first times I had brought him to Sebastopol. Ben had immediately fallen in love with it—the hills, the crisp quality of the trees and the faltering terrain, farmhouses harboring stories.

Jacob and I walked quietly, neither of us anxious to talk, at least not to each other. Then, Jacob broke the silence.

"This is going to be a long walk if we don't call a temporary truce," he said.

I motioned toward the hills, the naked landscape around us. "It's going to be a long walk anyway."

Jacob nodded in agreement, which was about as close to a truce as we were getting. "It must have been weird growing up here," he said.

I turned toward him, startled to hear out loud the opposite of what Ben had said.

"Most people assume that it was idyllic."

"Because it's so pretty?"

"Something like that."

Jacob put his hands in his back pockets. "Growing up is never idyllic, is it? Or it'd be called something else."

I turned away, not wanting him to see how that made me smile. "My mother would say you had to use your imagination raising kids here because there wasn't much going on. It would force us to make our own fun. Turning the old apple orchards into mazes. Doing a weekly relay race that would end at the ice cream shop and with two scoops of their homemade ice cream. At ten in the morning."

"I grew up in New York City. Our relay races would involve a nanny. And end on the 4 or 5 subway heading downtown for a hot dog at Gray's Papaya."

"Sounds idyllic."

He smiled. "It wasn't bad."

Jacob bent down, picked up a handful of rocks. He started throwing them, one at a time.

"I remember coming to visit my grandparents when I was a kid. Of course, they lived in Napa, but they had this barn and I'd lie there staring at the stars," he said. "It's weird to live somewhere where you can't see the stars. I told myself when I was old enough, I'd get my own barn."

"Your own stars?"

He nodded. "Exactly," he said. "Kind of how you want your own skyscraper. You'll have plenty of those in London."

"Or if I stay in L.A."

It was the first time I had said it out loud. What I might do if Ben and I couldn't get past it, in a world that went on for me Ben-less.

Still, I felt my breath catch in my throat, thinking of London. My new office was in a small building near the Chelsea Arts Club, a short walk from our house, a short walk from Ben's architecture firm. Ben had done the walk when he had been in London the month before—in the morning and the evening—noting the places we'd most want to stop together. A coffee shop in a converted garden, a rooftop art gallery, every theater on the West End.

"Why would you stay in L.A.? I mean, if you didn't go to London. Would it be for your job? I only ask because I hated being a lawyer. I really hated it." He paused. "The five minutes I was one."

"I thought you said you didn't practice," I said.

"No, I practiced. After I left Cornell, I moved to New York and joined a law firm in the corporate restructuring division. But it was literally five minutes. I quit before lunch."

I nodded. I had friends from law school who felt like Jacob did, who absolutely hated the law. I didn't. That wasn't the same as saying I loved it. Suzannah loved it. She loved it because she loved confrontation and she loved being right—and law allowed her both of those things on a daily basis.

I didn't love it, but it had always felt like the right path. And when I doubted it, I thought of my law school graduation. My parents had driven to L.A., proudly treating my then boyfriend, Griffin Winfield, to dinner after. At dinner, my father made a toast saying that he was glad I was going to have an easy life. Griffin had given him a look, as if deciding how rude he wanted to be. Then he decided he wanted to be very rude. He told my father that climbing the legal ladder was hardly easy. Though he hadn't understood what my father meant. My father meant that law provided a path. If you worked hard, you'd be rewarded. You'd have a career you could count on.

Griffin didn't agree with that either. He thought it was talent that separated out the most successful lawyers. Though that was the main thing he didn't understand. My father never measured success the way he did—reaching the tip-top of something, as if there was an objective tip-top. My father measured it by how well you figured out what you wanted for your life—what you needed to be happy.

And this was where my mixed feelings came in. Recently, I had to admit I didn't feel happy. Maybe I was distracted by the wedding planning, or our move to Europe. All I knew was that I needed a change. And I was hoping London was going to provide it.

"So you want to stay in L.A.? For your work?" Jacob said.

"There may be a world in which I do that," I said.

"The world in which you tell me what made you walk out on your dress fitting?"

We reached the main strip of Graton, which wasn't really a strip at all, just two restaurants across the street from each other. But they were great restaurants, farm-fresh food from the gardens behind them. Spaghetti nights on Monday. With all the great food in Los Angeles, I still missed spaghetti on Monday.

"You tell me first," I said.

"About my botched wedding?" He shrugged. "My fiancé would say that she felt like I prioritized my work over her. We were getting married at City Hall, the week before we headed out here. Just a couple of friends and family at this restaurant in Tribeca afterward. Then, the morning of the wedding, she said that she didn't want to get married the way we were getting married. That she wanted a wedding that counted more, with a fancy dress and a ten-piece band and an expensive cake."

"You don't buy it?"

"She hates cake."

We passed through the entire town and were heading up the hill in the direction of my parents' house.

He paused. "We weren't in a good place," he said. "And it's hard to get married when you're not in a good place. It feels fake."

That I could relate to. It was what made me sad about finding out about Maddie the way I had. It would be locked in with the wedding, what I knew about Ben, what Ben had left out about himself.

"Do you guys still talk?" I said.

He pointed back in the direction of town, pointing out a house over on State Street, a barn to the side. "We live there," he said.

"You guys are still together?"

He nodded. "Yep. We are still together. Very much so."

I started doing the math in my head. He had a girlfriend he'd referred to at the bar: a free-spirited, vegan type.

"She's the one who loves chia?"

"She's the one who loves chia."

It was blocking me up, reconciling the two things about her that Jacob had shared. "The one who wants a big, fancy wedding?"

He nodded. "We are all complicated people," he said.

There was that word again, used as an excuse, used to justify something that felt like love.

He smiled. "As are you, I'm guessing."

"What do you mean?"

"I don't know Ms. L.A. Law, but you seem pretty connected to Sonoma County. Unless that's your thing, storming into people's offices and demanding they not steal your home?"

"Very funny."

"Just saying . . . building a life so far away from a place you love so much? That's complicated."

I smiled, a bit surprised at the insight.

"Lee, that's my girlfriend, doesn't like it here so much," he said. "I was hoping you could help with that? Show her what makes it so great."

"My father says people either love Sonoma or they feel trapped here."

"They should put that on the brochure," he said.

Jacob looked back in the direction of his house, then kept moving.

"So why did you leave? Sonoma, I mean?"

"You wouldn't understand."

"Too complicated?" he said.

I tried not to laugh. "No, it's just, our family saw a bunch of really tough harvests. I wanted a life that felt more stable."

He nodded, considering. "It's kind of ironic though, don't you think?"

"What?"

"Well, you still ended up in a bar, in your wedding dress."

89

I looked at him, disconcerted. Why did Jacob think he knew me well enough to say that? Why did it bug me if he wasn't right?

I sped up, Jacob hurrying to keep up.

"What happened with Ben?" Jacob said. "Tell me. I have a gift for it."

"For what?"

"For telling people the reasons they shouldn't be as mad as they are."

"You talk too much. Has anyone ever told you that?"

"Has anyone ever told you that you have trouble answering questions?"

"Just yours, and that's probably because they go on and on!"

He smiled, but he stood there waiting for an answer. "So . . . what happened?"

I tilted my head, considering what to say. Which was when I realized why I was so hurt that Ben hadn't told me about Maddie. It wasn't just that he'd kept his daughter from me—it was the explanation as to why. "I think Ben doubted me."

He was quiet. "We all doubt each other," he said.

"My parents didn't. My father saw my mom in a car and that was the end of the story."

"Was it the end of the story?" Jacob said.

"No. What does that say?"

Jacob paused, and I could see him deciding to tell me that he knew there was something going on with my father and my mother.

"That there is no one way," he said.

We headed down the long driveway, quietly, Jacob looking up at the sky, the clear blue of it.

"It's been dry," he said. "All harvest. Not sure your father told you that."

My father rarely gave me details about the harvest when I wasn't home, or maybe I shouldn't be letting myself off the hook like that. I rarely asked him the specifics about his work and he had stopped offering them. Which was starting to feel like a fitting punishment for the fact that soon I wouldn't be able to ask him anymore.

"It makes me nervous," he said. "I think we're going to get soaked, and your father's most valuable grapes are still on the vines."

I followed his eyes up to the sky, which was cloudless and calm. "It doesn't seem that way," I said.

Jacob started walking again, slowly moving toward the house. "It never does."

He paused.

"I feel like we're going to get all the way to your parents' house without me saying the thing I think would be the most helpful in regards to Ben," Jacob said.

"You have a thing?"

"I have a thing," he said.

"Go for it."

"If you're not careful, you run out of time."

I tried to figure out what he meant.

He pointed straight ahead, down the driveway. And I realized what he meant was he had run out of time to tell his thing because we were no longer alone.

On the doorstep was the cutest girl in the world. Wearing heart leggings. The girl who looked exactly like her famously beautiful mother.

And Ben. Her father.

Part 2

The Crush

Ben and Maddie and Georgia and Jacob

The day I met Ben, he was wearing glasses. Tortoise-rimmed. Glasses he never wore, but he had forgotten his contact lenses. If I had seen him without those glasses, it would have been too much. He was take-your-breath-away good-looking. Suzannah said he looked like Superman: the same strong jaw and cheekbones, the same ridiculous shoulders. But he had one up on Clark Kent as far as I was concerned because he had these great eyes, green and deep and honest. And when he focused them on you, he seemed like he was going to do it. Make everything okay.

Ben had come out to Los Angeles for a profile *Architectural Digest* was running. He and a handful of other architects had been included in their "New Talent" issue—a title Ben thought was hilarious, considering he had been a working architect for a decade by then. But he was glad to take the work that came with it. He had an hour after the photo shoot before he had to head back to New York. We were sitting in a hotel bar near the airport, drinking watered-down martinis. Ben wanted to go over contracts—that was what he'd said. But he also said, out loud, that he was doing something else. Ben said that was finding out if the girl on the phone matched the idea of her in his head.

"It's a lot of pressure," he said.

"For me?"

"For me," he said.

Ben looked like he never felt pressure. He sipped his martini, looking sexy in a button-down shirt and jeans, a sports jacket.

"Why pressure?"

"Why pressure?" He smiled. "You know why."

He paused.

"That woman, on the phone, is the best part of my day. She makes me laugh and she makes me feel happy. She makes me feel like everything is going to work out as soon as she says hello to me."

My heart skipped a beat. I nodded, my way of saying I felt the same way.

"If she is the best part of my day, in person, I'm going to have to do it."

"What's that?"

He smiled. "You know, change everything for her."

Then he reached for my hand. He reached for my hand—his palm cupping my fingers, his fingers running through mine—like we were touching for the thousandth time—and he still had no intention of ever letting go.

How could I not be his after that? This was how he said hello.

~

It would be too simple to say that I never felt good about myself until Ben. And it wouldn't be true. But everything I was trying to reconcile— who I'd been growing up in Sonoma County, who I was trying to be as a woman building a life in Los Angeles—he was my partner in it. Maybe it was that he grew up similarly to the way I did: in a small town outside London—his father a carpenter who worked around the clock, Ben help- ing his mother raise his little sisters. He'd received a scholarship to study architecture at the University of London, had built a career for himself there, and then in America.

I understood the thousand steps between where he'd started and where he'd ended up. And, more than that, I understood the versions of him he contended with along the way: the version of him that was proud of what he'd built and the version buried far beneath that still felt like an outsider. Which might have been why all the versions of me I'd ever been—all the versions of me that I hoped to be—made sense when I was with him.

Deep in my soul I felt we understood each other, we loved each other. So—despite all the reasons I maybe should have—I didn't feel threatened by Michelle. I didn't feel threatened by any of Ben's previous girlfriends. The thing was, I was in. The first drink together establishing it for me, every day proving it. Ben was my yellow buggy.

~

Ben opened the refrigerator to get Maddie some milk. He handed me the bottle, trying to get me to talk to him. I couldn't seem to meet his eyes.

Maddie was sitting at the kitchen table having an enormous piece of chocolate cake, her arm protectively blocking the plate as if she were afraid someone was going to take it away from her before she could finish.

Jacob sat across from her, his eyes focused on those bites. He didn't look toward Ben and me, standing by the refrigerator, getting the milk. But I knew he was trying to listen.

"What happened to you not showing up here?" I said.

Ben poured the milk into three of the glasses. "We needed to talk," he said.

"So you bring Maddie?"

"I also brought you a suitcase full of clothes including a dress for the harvest party, the purple one that looks so pretty. What about a thank-you for that?"

"I'm serious."

"Yes, we needed to talk and we needed you not to kick me out." He held up the empty glass. "I still can't tell if you want the milk or not. The cake is going to be much better with it."

He flashed those eyes at me, and I wanted more than anything to let it all go—to just decide that everything was okay.

And maybe I would have, but he headed back toward the kitchen table and took the seat next to Maddie, leaving me the one between him and Jacob.

"She's serious about that cake," Jacob said as we sat back down.

He wasn't wrong. Maddie was precise in her bites, not like the twins, who would tear through that cake in the time it took Maddie to eat one bite. She moved slowly, savoring it.

Maddie felt my eyes on her and looked up. "Would you like some?" she said.

Her tiny, British accent could make you melt it was so cute. And there was this: She held out the fork to share, which looked like it pained her to do, to share anything with me—the cake or her father.

Who could blame her? She had just found him for herself. And now she was being forced to meet the woman he was going to marry? Who might want to take her father away from her. And her cake.

I smiled at her, anxious to relieve her anxiety. "That's all for you, Maddie," I said. "But thank you."

She nodded, relieved. "You're welcome."

Then she turned back to her chocolate cake.

Ben looked between us. I kept my eyes on Maddie, avoiding looking at him or at Jacob, who watched me, amused.

Ben gave Jacob a look. "So catch me up. How do you know Jen and Dan?"

"I'm a local winemaker," he said.

"Kind of," I said.

Jacob gave me a smile. "I own Murray Grant Wines," he said. "We're based in Napa Valley."

"I know Murray Grant Wines." Ben smiled condescendingly. "Everyone near a grocery store knows it."

Jacob ignored Ben's insulting tone. "I guess that's true," he said.

"You're Murray's son?"

"Grandson."

Ben took a bite of Maddie's cake, winked at her. He didn't turn back to Jacob when he spoke next.

"I didn't know Murray had much to do with Dan," Ben said.

"He didn't, but I do."

"Why's that?"

"We're purchasing The Last Straw Vineyard," Jacob said.

Ben turned toward me, shocked, compassion filling his eyes.

"We're planning to keep the vineyard in the tradition of Dan's work, to offer a biodynamic option to our customers. The vineyard will be run exactly the same."

Ben smiled, tightly. "If Dan's not here, it can't be run exactly the same."

"Dan isn't worried about it," he said.

Ben leaned in. "How much money did you have to pay him so he wouldn't be?"

The tension between them was thick. I should have enjoyed it, neither of them in my good graces. But I didn't want to watch it either, which maybe Jacob sensed.

"I should probably get going . . ." Jacob said. It was less a statement, more a question. Did I want him to go or did I want protection from the talk Ben would demand we have as soon as we were alone?

I didn't meet his eyes. I didn't want protection from Ben, at least not from Jacob.

"You need us to call you a cab?" Ben said.

His eyes were still on me. "No," Jacob said. "I'm going to walk."

"Who's walking where?"

Margaret walked into the kitchen, more like breezed into it, smiling, animated. She wore workout clothes, a sun visor, her long hair swept beneath it. She looked around the table and noticed Ben.

"Ben!" she said. "When did you get here? Did you come up for the family dinner tonight?"

Ben stood up to hug Margaret, wrapped his arms around her. "Of course."

He smiled, happy to see Margaret, happy to be going to the family dinner. He hadn't missed it since we'd started dating. The intimate family celebration before the big harvest party celebration. Ben loved it so much that he flew from a meeting in New York one year to be there for it. Another year, he cancelled a trip to London. He loved it as much as any of the Fords did.

Margaret smiled. "We were hoping you'd show up," she said. "And who is this cutie pie?"

Ben looked at his daughter, smiling. "This is Maddie," he said.

"Maddie?" Margaret said.

"Ben's daughter," Jacob said.

"What was that?" Margaret said.

Ben drilled Jacob with a dirty look, but I stifled a laugh, enjoying the confused look on Margaret's face.

"Maddie, this is Margaret," Ben said. "Margaret is going to be your aunt."

Maddie nodded, uninterested.

Margaret looked like she'd swallowed paste. Then quickly recovered.

She bent down so she and Maddie were eye to eye. "It's nice to meet you, sweetie."

She forced a smile, looked at Ben and me.

Then she motioned to Jacob.

"Do we know each other?" she said. "You look familiar."

"I'm Jacob McCarthy. I think we met once at a pickup party for Angus."

"Right," she said. "Great."

She looked back and forth between Ben and Jacob, noting the tension.

Then she forced a smile, motioning to Jacob. "You're coming with me," she said.

Sebastopol, California. 1989

*M*urray had been the one who told him that you have to give farming—winemaking included—ten years. Ten years to figure out how the land beneath you was going to work. How you were going to work it.

This would mark year ten—the beginning of it, the end. Today was the harvest party, a small party. Dan had taken the extra money this year and built a winemaker's cottage, where he could do his work. It had been Jen's idea. She'd thought that they needed a separation between church and state.

He'd thought it was a bad idea, but he hadn't argued with her, and he was glad he hadn't. He was glad to be sitting on the porch of his cottage now, watching the festivities happen—tons of good pizza and free beer for the workers.

It wasn't much of a party, but it was something. He was glad to do something for them. They had earned it. And they were happy sitting in chairs that Jen had set up, umbrellas shielding them from the sun, Bob Dylan playing in the background.

It had been a good harvest despite the cold temperatures. The grapes had held on, and he had no complaints. Or, he had one complaint. His five-year-old daughter had taken this opportunity to announce that she knew what she wanted to do for a living. She wanted to be a winemaker like him. It broke his heart. It broke his heart and made him happy all at once. He didn't like to think about her out here, without having him to protect her. Now the vineyard was a joy for her, a pure and unadulter-ated joy. What if it became something else? But you don't get to choose for your kids, not once they were grown-ups: not once they were five, going on fifty.

She was sitting on the porch with him, reading a book, when Murray walked up.

"Dan," he said. He was smiling, holding a bottle of his wine in one hand, holding his grandson in his other, his grandson, Jacob, who was visiting from New York City.

Dan's daughter dropped her book and ran away. She ran toward her brothers, who were playing catch. Finn picked up another glove as soon as she got there, wanting to play, Bobby biting his nails. This was a two-person catch and he didn't want to include his sister. But Finn put his arm around Georgia protectively until Bobby relented and threw her the ball. This was the interesting part. Jen had pointed it out, and now Dan would notice it too. Bobby always threw the ball so Georgia could catch it. Bobby threw the ball softer than Finn would throw it to his sister. He threw softer and he waited longer. He moved to her level as opposed to asking her to climb to his. This was why they didn't intervene too much, letting the kids work it out. Because Finn seemed like he was the one tak-ing care of his sister, but, in the ways it counted, Bobby was too.

"How are you doing, Murray?" Dan said.

"Good. Good. No complaints."

Dan motioned toward the pizza, smiling. "Help yourself," he said.

Murray nodded, picking up a piece of the greasy pizza, handing it to his grandson, Jacob taking a big bite.

"You want to go play?" Murray said to him.

Jacob nodded and ran out into the yard, toward Dan's children—the kids dancing, Jen dancing. Then he ran past them to a tree in the shade, guarding his pizza, and pulled out a comic book.

"He's a city kid. Not much for the outdoors." Murray shrugged. "I'm working on it."

Murray took a seat beside Dan on the steps, Dan pouring him a glass of wine.

"I was just thinking of you when you walked up."

"Were you?"

Dan nodded. "I was thinking how you were the first to tell me that it takes ten years for a vineyard to become itself. That I should be patient and I would get there."

Murray took the wine, tilting it in Dan's direction. "I was right, wasn't I? This has become something lovely. Don't you think?"

Dan smiled. He knew Murray meant that. But he also knew Murray profited ten million dollars last year, which meant more to him.

Murray smiled back. "I want to make you an offer," Murray said.

Dan shook his head, impressed by the old guy's perseverance. "You've made it. I've gratefully declined."

"Remind me why?"

"I can't do what I do for a hundred thousand cases of wine."

"Five hundred thousand." He shrugged.

"Five hundred thousand."

"You thought Sebastopol was going to turn into a bastion of wine-making, didn't you? It hasn't happened."

"Yet." Dan smiled. "There's time."

Murray took a long sip of the wine. "That's true."

"More people are coming out. There are two new vineyards up the road."

Murray nodded. "Also true. I think I passed one on my way in. What is that? Five acres?"

Dan ignored his tone.

"If you're so sure Sebastopol isn't going to become anything, why do you want my little vineyard so badly?"

"I don't. I don't want it at all, really. I want your winemaking. I want you to come and work for me. You can keep control over your vineyard, which I'll fund as a thank-you."

Dan took a sip of his own wine, hoping that Murray couldn't see in his eyes what that kind of money would mean to him. He would have financial security. And he could still do what he wanted. He could still make wine. He could stay in this house, with his kids, without worrying about it. But that was the thing about how Dan made wine. It wasn't just about the wine for him. It was about the land and how he was changing it, ten years in or not. He was still getting there, and wherever he was going, he knew that Murray and his offer were going to send him in the wrong direction.

"I'm not going to do that," he said.

"Well." Murray tipped the wine in Dan's direction. "There's time for that too."

The *Terroir* Has a Story

My mother loved to tell a story about the day she fell in love with my father. They were having dinner at a small Chinese restaurant before her performance that night, before he was scheduled to fly back to Northern California. Over stuffed cabbage and pork dumplings, she asked him what a winemaker did. What he actually did: *If you do your job,* he said, *then you make good soil.* She liked how he said it, even if she didn't understand what he was saying. It took her a while to understand what he did mean.

My father believed that the most important aspect of winemaking was the soil. That his wine got better, from year to year, because his soil did. He would monitor his soil carefully, treating it with the nine biodynamic preparations. Preparations made of teas and organic compost, seven of them buried in the soil, two of them sprayed and spread over the vines. Cow horns buried deep into the soil during the winter. No chemicals, nothing added from outside the farm. This created a lot more work, but it also created a more stable ecosystem. This was what he was the proudest of, that he had made the land stronger.

My father said that this was what most people missed. If you took something out of the soil without putting it back in, the wine would suffer. The soil would suffer. You had to figure out how to get it to a better place than where it had started. My father was of the belief that, if you did that, winemaking took care of itself.

Many of the factory winemakers would disagree. After their grapes were off the vine, that was when they started intervening, making their wines do what they wanted them to do, adding chemicals and eggs and sulfites to aid the fermenting process, to refine their wines. My father didn't add anything to the grapes. His winemaking facility was stark: a sorting table; a destemming machine; open-top fermenters. He would wait for the grapes to ferment on their own. Spontaneous fermentation. Where for fifteen to thirty days, the grapes begin the process of turning into alcohol. No help from chemicals or additives. No help from cultured yeast to make fermentation predictable. The patience it took was extraordinary. The faith it took too.

My father said this was the best part of winemaking. When the grapes you had taken such good care of did their thing, not because you were forcing them, the wine beginning to ferment because it was ready. The wine fermented because after the care you had taken with the grapes, they knew what to do. They used their own juices to move toward the wine they were meant to be.

If that sounds hokey, you should watch it happen. It was inspiring every time. The grapes sat in their tanks. My father punched them down—until, like that, the grapes revealed themselves as something new. My father able to give them the foundation they needed and step back.

Here's why my mother fell in love with him, she said. She was sitting at the Chinese restaurant, hearing him talk of soil, about the importance of foundation. And she heard the rest. His belief, at the center of his winemaking, that with work, you can give something the strength at the beginning that it needs later on. Before it even knows how it's going to need it.

∼

Ben and I walked through the vineyard, Maddie a few paces ahead of us. She was quiet, focused, staring at the grapes—at certain shoots—as if she was trying to figure out which were the good shoots, which ones should get to stay.

Ben touched my wrist. "So I have a plan if you're ready to hear it," he said.

"For what?"

He slowed to a stop, smiled. "Us, of course," he said. "Making this okay for us."

"What's that?"

"We're not going to talk about what happened," he said.

"That's your plan?"

"That's my plan," he said, proud of himself.

Then he started walking again, keeping Maddie in his view. I tried to understand what he was doing.

He shrugged. "Talking about Michelle. Maddie. It's just going to make it worse. We're better off talking about the weather."

"Are you serious right now?"

He nodded. "Bobby says it's been an ideal harvest. And it looks like it's going to finish out that way, don't you think?"

I looked up at the sky. It looked blue and bright. I didn't know what I thought, but I didn't want to talk about it, not with him. He held my cheek in the palm of his hand, forced me to look at him.

"Please try it this way," he said.

"Until when?"

"Until you remember that this isn't what defines us."

He looked at me, challenging: Did I want to try and make this okay? I took a deep breath. I did want this to be okay—and maybe he was right. Maybe this only had to be as big as I let it be. So why was I letting it be everything?

"I know you'll fall in love with Maddie. You're already falling in love with her."

"This isn't about Maddie."

"It is, a little. If for no other reason, you'll forgive me for keeping her from you even if you don't accept why I did it. You'll forgive me because of her."

Then he leaned in and kissed me on the cheek, the softness of his lips jarring me, reminding me of something I had almost forgotten.

He smiled and motioned toward Maddie, who was bending down in the gardens. The tea gardens. Her chubby fingers were touching the top of the leaves tentatively. Aside from the stinging nettles, which were far in the back, she was safe. So I didn't make a move to stop her, letting her explore the leaves for herself.

"Is it just me or do I have a future farmer on my hands?" Ben said.

"She does seem to love it here."

"She does, doesn't she?" he said.

Then he looked at me out of the corner of his eyes, taking in how Maddie was having an impact on me. How could she not? This adorable little girl studying the gardens, thrilled at the idea of what she was going to find next. And yet, if I was falling for Maddie, the reverse was certainly not true. She was avoiding any kind of contact. She was pretending it was just her and Ben.

She looked up when we got close, smiling up at her father. Ben bent down beside her, cupping his hands over the flower next to hers. "Hi," she said. "What are these, Dad?"

Dad.

Ben smiled at her, pointed toward the sign behind them. "It says they're dandelion leaves," he said.

"For what?" she said.

"I think they help to feed the land. What's the fancy word for that, Georgia? For the land?"

Maddie met my eyes and looked like she didn't want any information from me, even about this. Ben ignored this. He motioned for me to bend down between them, explain it to her.

"What's it called, Georgia?" Ben said.

I wanted to throttle him. "The *terroir*."

Maddie nodded. Serious. "The *terroir*," she repeated.

I started to explain that *terroir* wasn't just about the land. It was also about the winemaker, how he interacted with that land, bringing out different things in the geography and climate than someone else might. But Maddie looked up at me and smiled—her smile just like Ben's. It stopped me from saying anything. It stopped me from doing anything except smiling at her too.

Then she stared at the plants, considering, the same way Ben would do. This stopped me even more.

I bent down so I was by Maddie's side, Ben moving out of the way.

"The teas are put into the soil to help take care of it. They all do different things for the soil in the vineyard and for the compost."

"What's compost?"

I smiled. "You don't want to know."

Maddie smiled back, moving closer so I could be tucked in among the flowers, beside her.

She pointed toward the yarrow. "What does this one do?" she said.

"The yarrow tea helps the soil make the grapes. It fills the soil with potassium and sulfur."

I picked off a piece of yarrow and held it closer to her nose so she could smell it.

"Should I smell?" she asked Ben.

Ben smiled, nodded.

She moved in close, making a face. "Yuck," she said.

I laughed, not blaming her. I should have reached for some lavender instead.

Maddie picked up a chamomile flower, gingerly putting that to her nose.

"What's this one do?"

"You just picked out one of the most important teas," I said.

Her eyes got wide, pleased with herself. "I did?"

"Yes. That's the final tea that goes on the vineyard, and once all the grapes are picked, my father spreads this out over the whole vineyard to help the vines know it's time to sleep for the winter."

"Like milk and cookies."

I laughed, Ben joining in, touching Maddie's back. "Exactly like that," he said.

Ben looked at me and smiled, as if to say, see? We can figure this out. The California sun shining down.

I smiled back, agreeing in spite of myself. And there was something deeper happening as I explained to Maddie how the vineyard worked. I remembered my father explaining the same thing to me when I was a little girl: how when he'd opened up the vineyard to me, garden by garden, it had felt like he was opening up an entire world, the most important piece of the world, the most magical. Everything he taught me about the vineyard became etched in my mind, like a prize.

Maddie held up the tea. "What's it called?" Maddie said.

"Chamomile," I said.

"Chamomile," she repeated. "I think my mum likes chamomile tea, right, Dad?"

I was still lost in the moment, feeling connected to Maddie. And to Ben again. Then I saw his face.

He looked nervous. "I'm not sure, Maddie," he said.

Maddie ran up ahead, toward the hillside, toward the barrel room and the cave. Leaving Ben and me alone. Ben forced himself to smile.

"I'm sorry she said that," he said.

"Why?" I said.

He paused, starting to say something, then stopping. "I don't know."

"What aren't you saying, Ben?" I said.

He shook his head. "Nothing," he said, but he looked down, shielding his eyes—the way he did when he was keeping something from me. It was usually something insignificant that he was withholding: like when he'd forgotten to take out the garbage or drop off our rent check. Though, apparently, it could also be something less insignificant: like what he felt he needed to keep to himself now.

The Last Family Dinner (Part 1)

*B*en put Maddie down for a nap and I went to the kitchen to find my mother. She was standing by the farmer's sink, washing the vegetables she had picked from her garden for dinner: tomatoes and cucumbers and onions and garlic and broccoli filling her small woven basket. She was still wearing her gardening hat. And she had the music on high.

She was dancing to it. She was dancing this awkward little two-step in front of the sink. It wasn't surprising that she was dancing or that she was doing it oddly. She and my father both danced terribly and they both loved dancing, especially together. Growing up, I'd often walk into a scene just like this one: the two of them awkwardly two-stepping, arms happily flailing, in front of the tomatoes.

My mother was dancing, alone now, looking at her vegetables, not turning toward me. "How does pot roast sound for the family dinner?" she said.

I came up behind her, resting my head on her shoulder. I wanted to bury into her shoulder. I wanted her to make it all okay. As opposed to the reality. That she was part of the problem.

"I'm only asking to be polite," she said. "About the pot roast. Not because I'm planning to do anything differently. Finn and Bobby already requested it separately. And I'm glad there's something on which they agree."

"Sounds great, then."

She smiled, pleased with that answer. Then she moved to the right of the sink, motioning for me to help her clean the tomatoes.

"I wish everyone would stop calling this the last family dinner, though," she said. "It seems dramatic."

"Isn't it also the truth?"

She looked down, ignoring the question, handing over several tomatoes.

"The tomatoes are on their last legs," she said. "Do what you can. It's that time of year. The end of the harvest, which means rest. Which means your father can focus on other things. But also the end of the tomatoes."

"A mixed bag," I said.

"Indeed." She started chopping a cucumber. "I saw that we have two more joining tonight?"

I looked at her. "You met Maddie?"

She nodded. "Where do you think the cake came from?" she said.

I started washing a tomato, ignoring her gaze.

"What happened?" she said.

"He thinks we need to be together in the same place to get through this."

"No. I understand what he's doing here, but what happened, that you're letting him stay? At least for the family dinner? And don't tell me that he loves it. Though he does love it. Maybe more than your father."

I shrugged. "I'm so mad at him and then I think I shouldn't be. Which makes me mad in a new way, if that makes sense?"

"Not really . . ."

"It feels like he's still withholding part of the story. That I'm going to have to pull it out of him. It feels really hard to talk to him."

She looked at me, waiting. "Did you consider that if you keep trying to talk to him, it will get easier again?"

"I don't think I should have to work that hard."

She laughed, tossing her cucumber into a bowl. "That is love, baby girl. Working hard when we don't feel like it."

I put the vegetables down. "Is that what you're doing, Mom?"

She looked up at me. It seemed like she was going to argue but then she wiped her hand across her head, water smearing on her cheek. "I guess that's fair. I guess I'm not working so hard right now, but it didn't happen because of one misunderstanding."

"That's what you think this is?"

"Ben was put in a bad situation. He got a call finding out that he has a kid. He had to try to handle that however he could." She shrugged. "No one is saying he's handled it well, though."

I felt like she was finally listening, understanding the two ways I felt. On the one hand, I felt terrible for Ben that he'd been dealing with this, but I also was angry he hadn't trusted I would deal with it with him.

"Of course, it doesn't matter how well he handled it," she said. "What is going to save you two is how well you do."

Her phone buzzed and she looked down. It was Henry, Henry smiling. It made her blush, looking like a schoolgirl, which made me roll my eyes.

I peeked over at the phone, at the text message.

La Gare. 10 PM?

La Gare. That was the French restaurant in town. The only restaurant in Sonoma County that served that late. The only restaurant in Sonoma County my mother could get to after family dinner. The last family dinner, celebrating the last harvest.

My mother met my eyes, knowing what I'd seen on the phone. But as she started to say something, she closed her mouth. "I'll call him back later, but not because you're being mature about it," she said.

"What would you like me to say, Mom? Have fun on your date?"

"Would that be so hard?" She paused, shutting off the water. "Or maybe just don't look at me with such anger. I'm not looking at you with anger."

"Why would you look at me with anger?"

My mother looked at me. "I'm just going to ask you this once but I want you to think about it. Have you considered that your desire for us to keep the vineyard has less to do with us and more to do with you?"

She motioned toward the vineyard. I followed her eyes, and looked out the window at the vineyard below: foggy and swirling in the late afternoon wind.

The grapes were getting heat, but getting something else too in that wind, getting a certain amount of peace.

"Well?" she said.

"No," I said.

My mother looked at me, anger in her eyes. "No, you haven't considered it? Or no, it isn't true?"

"Have you considered why you're willing to give this place away?"

"I have considered it. And I have my answer, darling. It's just not one you like."

I heard a beep, Henry texting again. "He should really play harder to get," I said.

My mother pursed her lips. "Go away," she said.

"Does he know you hate French food?"

"Go away, please."

I wanted to explain it to her so she'd hear it. As much as my mother said I was making this about me, it seemed like she was doing the opposite. She wasn't making this enough about her.

"It just feels tragic to me that everything you and Dad worked for, you're just handing off to someone who is going to blow it. Who's not going to honor your legacy."

"Even if you're right, and I'm not saying you are, that's our tragedy."

"That can't be your opinion."

She took off her kitchen gloves. "You want my opinion? I'll give you my opinion. Worry less."

"What are you talking about?"

"I'm talking about the fact that you're a smart, accomplished woman who has worked very hard to build a great life for herself. And you still think your main job is to make things okay for everyone else. For your father and me, for Bobby and Finn. It's why I felt relief the day you moved away from here!"

"You cried. And sent me a map of Sebastopol, so I'd remember where I came from."

She rolled her eyes. "The point is, I thought, now she is going to take care of herself too. But you're just falling back into your old ways. Focusing on our problems instead of your own."

"That isn't true."

"Are you sure about that?" she said, her eyes angry. "If you ask me, Sweetie, then you're going to have to get over that Ben did something wrong and listen to your heart."

"It's related, Mom. It matters."

"My goodness. You sound like you're arguing a case. What matters is what you want to do."

Then she pointed at the tent, the sailcloth tent, on the edge of the patio.

"We never would have paid for a sailcloth tent just for the harvest party. We could have run around on the lawn for all I care. Someone needs to get married under that sailcloth tent, it is too beautiful to waste."

"You think that's a good reason?"

She turned the water back on, looking away. "Well. It's not a bad one," she said.

Spontaneous Fermentation (and Other Ways to Lose the Love of Your Life)

*W*hen we were kids, Bobby and Finn used to ride their bikes down to the candy store in the center of Sebastopol. I loved the ride—and my mother wouldn't let me take it alone. But, man, was it fun when Finn and Bobby let me join them: the easy climb down the hills into the center of town, the hard ride back, candy melting in our pockets speeding us along. One time, on the ride back toward home, a car pushed us off the road. It was going so fast around the final turn, giving us no choice but to ride ourselves into a ditch to avoid getting hit head-on.

The car pulled over. It was a group of tourists, who had just been up at The Last Straw Vineyard. My father, at that time, was doing food and wine tours for elite tourists willing to pay fifty dollars a pop for a private tour with him.

They were apologetic, drunk, and apologetic, Finn telling them that it was okay. They felt like they needed to do something to make it right, though. One of the women checked out our skinned knees, covering us with ointment. Her husband offered to drive us back to our parents, Bobby refusing the offer after we stole a peek in their trunk. The trunk was filled with cases of wine from every vineyard on the road and many from Napa Valley—including Murray Grant Wines. They weren't discriminating. They weren't taking a special trip to visit my father. They weren't even drunk on good wine. They were drunk on anything they could get their hands on.

They took off, heading back to their fancy Healdsburg hotel—the three of us walking our bikes in the direction of home, agreeing to keep the incident from our parents, otherwise that would be the end of the bike-riding to the candy store. They got confused on the dirt road. And no one was hurt. So there was no reason to make a big deal. Except that I remember all three of us being angry with them in a way we couldn't explain, in a way I could only explain when I thought of my mother's question about the vineyard: Was I sure that I wanted to hold on to the vineyard for my father as opposed to for myself? Was I sure that I was thinking of my mother and my father only?

We didn't want them anywhere near our vineyard. We didn't want anyone near it who wasn't going to appreciate it.

So maybe the answer to my mother's question about the vineyard was no.

~

I got into a bubble bath. I wanted some peace and quiet. Ben hadn't reappeared from my bedroom, which let me know that in addition to nap time, Ben was checking in with Michelle, letting her know that Maddie was doing well, telling the story about how she loved the vineyard, how she was a future winemaker. Why did that feel like its own injury?

A second injury. There was a magazine by the bathtub. And Michelle was on the front page, staring back at me, all legs and glowing hair, a dress that cost more than the entirety of my closet.

I closed my eyes, sinking into the water, when my phone rang, Suzannah on the caller ID.

"I don't know whether to kill you or come up there to save you," she said when I picked up. "I had to sit in on your deposition in Santa Monica. I think I peed eight times. No one was pleased."

I felt myself take a deep breath in, relieved to hear her Southern drawl, mad and loving and true.

"Saloom is pissed that you aren't here, by the way."

Saloom was the managing partner of the firm. His defining characteristic was that he was pissed.

"And don't tell me that it's Sunday or that you're taking this week off for the wedding anyway," Suzannah said.

"What should I tell you?"

"Did Ben show up?" she said.

"He did."

"Okay. Am I still a maid of honor?"

"Do you think you should be?"

She paused, considering the question. "Well, on the one hand, I can't fit into my dress. On the other hand, I bet that you look stunning in yours."

I laughed.

"In all seriousness, I just keep thinking about the turtles," she said.

"What are you talking about?"

"The turtles. Ella's turtles."

She offered no further explanation, leaving me to figure out what she was saying. I'd bought her daughter turtles for her birthday, mostly because she wanted a dog, and Suzannah had said no way. But she was happy with the turtles. She named them Lily and Jake. And she absolutely loved them. What that had to do with my current situation, I had no idea.

Suzannah got tired of waiting for me to figure it out. "Remember how Ella left the door open and the male turtle ran away? And the girl turtle was so sad, she never left her shell again?"

I took a deep breath in, sinking deeper into the bubbles. "You're saying if I let Ben go, I'm going to be sorry?"

"No, I would never say anything that dumb."

"So what are you saying?"

She sighed, loudly. "I'm saying we make up all sorts of stories when really we should just keep the door closed."

There was a knock on the door, and Margaret walked inside, without even waiting for an invitation. She sat herself down on the edge of the tub, her hair wet from her own shower, her hands full with towels and the baby monitor and hair clips and a spoon and an open container of yogurt. She rearranged, leaning over the tub, putting one leg inside.

"Holy shit, are you okay? I passed out when I saw her there. Maddie's her name?"

That was the thing about your brother marrying his high school sweetheart. You'd known her since you were a tiny person. She'd sat before you in many more inappropriate positions than this. She thought nothing of walking in on you in the tub and going about the business of prying. She was your sister too.

She was dripping all over with that hair, her voice low, confirming Maddie wasn't the only child taking a nap. The twins were down as well, which was probably the reason Margaret had taken a minute to shower herself.

She pulled her hair into two tight buns, the spoon in her mouth. "What a shit," she said. Then she motioned toward the phone, talking loudly. "Tell Suzannah to call back later."

Suzannah screamed through the phone. "Tell Margaret I'm already hanging up and going back to doing your work. So Saloom doesn't fire your ass!"

Margaret took the phone away, leaning in with a demanding look.

"Well, what's the story, already? I have so many questions."

"What are you talking about?"

"Do you know who the mother is?" she said. "Some ex-girlfriend?"

I pointed at the soaking magazine, a wet Michelle staring up, still too pretty.

She picked up the magazine. Confused. "She works at *People*?"

I closed my eyes tightly, ignoring her.

"What was Ben thinking, showing up with her here? You know what? Back up. Bobby didn't say a word about this, so I assume you haven't known for long. When did you find out?" Her eyes got wide. "Did you just find out?"

"Margaret, I just need a minute alone."

"No way." She shook her head. "The twins are taking their nap. We're talking."

I pulled myself up, pissed. "You want to talk, let's talk. But you go first, Margaret."

I was silent, watching Margaret's face, Margaret letting it sink in that I knew about her and Finn. At least I knew there was something I shouldn't know.

Her voice got incredibly quiet. "Finn told you?"

She shook her head. Like that was the betrayal here.

"It's not what you think," Margaret said. "Between me and your brother."

"Which one?" I said.

She drilled me with a look. "You trying to be cute?"

"I'm trying to take a bath, but apparently that isn't happening." I pointed at the sink. "Can you hand me a towel?"

She shook her head. Then she reached over, grabbing the towel, putting it on the bathtub's edge, but too deep in, the towel falling into the soapy water. "Finn. Between me and Finn."

"Do you realize how wrong that is? That you even have to specify that?"

"I could do without the judgment, okay?" She paused. "I didn't do anything wrong. I didn't."

"So who did?"

She looked at me. "Bobby."

I closed my eyes. "Margaret, if you're about to tell me that my brother cheated on you, don't. I don't want to hear it."

"No, but there are a lot of ways to disappear on somebody."

"What was his?"

"I don't know . . ." Margaret shrugged, not wanting to say it. I was angry, but then I could see why. I could see why she was hesitating. As soon as she started talking, she began to cry.

I put my hand on top of hers. "What happened?"

"Our marriage. Getting married young. The miscarriage young. And then we decide to wait to have a child. Bobby wants to wait and we wait too long."

I squeezed her hand, remembering it all too well: Margaret losing the baby five months into the pregnancy. She was devastated, only pulling out after the wedding, only pulling out when they were entrenched in their life together.

"We spent years trying to have the twins. All those fertility treatments. And I was the one who wanted that, but he wanted them too. Then they arrive. And what does he do?"

"He's not helpful?"

She wiped at her tears, but they kept coming, the towel I'd left on the sink now her handkerchief. "He is helpful. He was absolutely amazing with the twins. Matching me feeding for feeding. Diaper change for diaper change."

"I'm not sure how that means he disappeared," I said.

She smiled. "It means I disappeared. At least as far as he was concerned."

"You're mad at him for being a devoted father?"

"No, I love that he is a devoted father. But it just made it obvious that there was not a whole lot there when the kids weren't. Do you know when the last time we had sex was?"

I shook my head fiercely. "I don't want to."

"You don't want to? *I* don't want to."

"So you've started sleeping with Finn?"

"No, I'm not sleeping with Finn," she said. "It was stupid, what happened. Finn came over on July Fourth. For drinks. Burgers. Bobby was running late, of course, and we'd both had too much to drink. And he had his camera there, you know? He had come from doing this terrible shoot of a couple's dogs. I asked to see his photographs and so he showed me. He showed me the photographs of the dogs. And we laughed about how ridiculous they were. We were really laughing. And it was stupid. But I kissed him."

I looked at her, speechless.

"But he pulled away. I could tell he didn't want to, but he did. He put his beer down and walked out. Got in his car. Drove away. Actually, he sat in his car for a solid five minutes. Not getting back out. Then he drove away."

I felt myself audibly exhale, relieved. Finn had stopped it, whatever Margaret had started. There was no unfaithful act. Except then I looked into Margaret's face, my relief turning to something else. The longing I saw there stopped me in my tracks. It mirrored perfectly the longing I had seen when I looked at Finn.

She shook her head. "The thing is, Finn . . . he was my friend. He was my friend when I was fifteen years old and I knew he liked me even then.

He liked me for the reasons I liked me. But I chose Bobby." She shrugged. "I chose Bobby for all the reasons that everyone chooses Bobby. I just didn't take it into account."

"Which part?"

"The part where someone looks at you, really looks at you, when you walk into a room. You either have that with someone or you don't. And if you don't, you're fucked." She paused. "That's what I wished I had known going into this marriage, that we didn't have the one thing you need most."

I thought of Ben and how he made me feel when I walked into a room, like I was the only one there. I derived meaning from that, Margaret deriving meaning from its absence. Though wasn't that just a story we were telling ourselves? Synchronization: You look up just when someone is looking at you. Your eyes meet and you feel like he recognizes your beauty. You look up and he is looking the other way and you tell yourself he never wanted you in the first place.

Margaret shook her head, trying to fight her tears. "Finn looks at me like that. I'm not turning us into *Dynasty*. I'm not sleeping with my husband's brother, as much as I may want to."

"Margaret, this isn't about Finn. You need to talk to Bobby."

Margaret shook her head, wiping away her tears, composing herself. "I fucked everything up," she said. "And if you want to judge me for that, then judge me."

Which was when Bobby stormed into the bathroom. Holding it with his bitten-down fingers. The other side of the two-way baby monitor.

"I think I'll judge you, Margaret," he said.

Sebastopol, California. 1994

They were spending the season in Burgundy. Or Dan was.

He was in the south of France and the countryside looked a lot like Sebastopol: rolling hills, sky. He didn't love it here the way he loved it in Sonoma County, though. He didn't love anywhere like Sonoma.

He hadn't been here since he was twenty-three years old, interning for the best Burgundy producer in the region. He hadn't wanted to be here now, but he had no choice. Two devastating harvests in a row, no wine he was proud to distribute. They needed the money. It had seemed like a good opportunity to come back. This was a renowned vineyard: They had finished high at the Judgment of Paris, they had finished the highest in many competitions since. And he understood why. This land, this soil, was agreeable. It was made to do exactly what he needed it to do.

But Dan missed his vineyard. He missed his kids, their voices far away on the weekly calls, Jen even farther. And the days he didn't miss them were worse than the days he did because they brought something else. Guilt.

Dan felt guilty for being apart from his family, and guilty for being away from his vineyard. He'd left Terry to harvest for the season, knowing of course that Terry wasn't going to do it the way he would. He would do fine though, and the money Dan was making here would allow them to make up the difference they lost—not just for the bad harvests, but for a bad harvest to come.

That was all a million miles away from the south of France, from the quiet life he was living on the vineyard with Marie, the winemaker here. They would read books at night, have long dinners, talk occasionally of their other lives, of Jen, of Marie's boyfriend in Spain. He was a chef, who opened a restaurant in San Sebastian, who wanted Marie to come and join him there. Marie had no intention of leaving her vineyard to join him there.

Marie didn't want to follow the chef. Not anymore. She wanted Dan. He wanted her too, though not in the same way. He wasn't harboring the illusions she was, that he could leave everything and stay here with her. People did such things for love, or what they named as love so they could justify doing what they wanted regardless of the people who needed them.

But their closeness was weighing on him, like a drum in his ear, in his heart. It was starting to feel like an answer to a question he didn't know he had been asking. He hoped she didn't notice. He brought up Jen twice to avoid her noticing. She nodded and smiled. Because it didn't matter to her. This wife that lived on the other side of an ocean was as irrelevant as the chef. Marie was young. What mattered to her was what she wanted.

They were eating dinner, the way they did many nights together, no one else within twenty miles of this place, a fire in the fireplace, music, her bad French music, on the stereo.

Marie couldn't cook like Jen could. Marie was an amazing winemaker, but in the kitchen she made two things well. She made a green garlic soup and toasted bread. They had that most nights. Tonight was no different.

Except for this. When Marie disappeared from the table, he cleaned the dishes. He cleaned the dishes and got ready to retire for the evening. Turning down the music, wiping off the table. Then she walked back in. Naked.

"Come here," she said.

He smiled. "What are you doing?"

"Nothing. What are you doing?"

They had spent days walking in the vineyard together. They had taken bike rides down the coast and slept on the beach. They had drunk too much wine one night and fallen asleep on the couch head to feet. When he woke up, he hadn't moved. He had gone back to sleep.

He shouldn't have done those things, but they were on one side of a line that kept him with his wife. She was starting to feel imaginary so far away. But he knew she wasn't. Just like he knew that wasn't what Marie was asking for now.

He had drunk an extra glass of wine. She had encouraged it. It was making it hard to walk out the door. It was making him think that he shouldn't walk out the door. Maybe he should walk toward her instead. No one would know. He would barely even know. When he went back to Northern California, wouldn't Marie feel as far away as his family felt from him now? She would.

She was beautiful. She was naked.

And she wanted him.

What he did next would determine everything.

The Last Family Dinner (Part 2)

*W*hen my parents decided to build the barrel room, Finn nicknamed it the Great Barrel Room, mostly because it ended up costing them more than my parents had spent on their actual house, red door included. The Great Barrel Room, slightly off the wine cave. It was an inviting room, with its wooden rafters and a stone fireplace, white lights wrapped around the oak beams.

My father had built the room for Bobby and Margaret's wedding so they would have a place in which to get married.

It housed some of my father's most valued wine barrels and was home to the few tastings my father did on the property. It was also where, in recent years, we'd started having our family dinner during the last weekend of the harvest.

Family dinner. The most intimate celebration with the people for whom the harvest meant the most.

But first, it had been for their wedding. Their gorgeous, intimate wedding, the happiest bride and groom. Bobby was truly joyous his entire wedding day, not leaving Margaret once the entire evening.

Which made it ironic to be sitting in there tonight: the room where we got to witness that kind of love, while Margaret and Bobby were standing outside of it, fighting.

My mother had set a gorgeous table, covered with daisies and baskets of fresh raisin bread, homemade herb butter. She refused to bring out the meal, though, until everyone was there. But everyone wasn't there. Ben sat between Maddie and the twins, all three kids stuffing their faces with the homemade bread (the twins picking out the raisins). My parents were at either end of the table. Then there was only me, surrounded by empty seats, where Finn should have been seated, where Bobby and Margaret should have been seated.

Finn was nowhere to be seen. He hadn't even arrived home yet. And Bobby and Margaret stood out in the cave, arguing loudly, in the way you did when you were yelling, but keeping your voices down at the same time. The rest of us pretended we didn't hear them—my mother focused entirely on the twins, on giving them more buttered bread, on ignoring my father's gaze.

My father, meanwhile, was the one closest to the doorway. He gripped the edge of the table, trying to decide whether to go outside and interrupt them.

"You can't seriously be saying that!" Margaret yelled.

My father caught my eyes and shook his head, looking down at the bread baskets in the middle of the table, the drooping daisies. He wanted to do something to turn this meal around—this meal that he looked forward to all year. His kids back in one place, the new family members along with them. All celebrating another harvest, another job well done.

My father banged on the table. "You know? Let's just eat."

This was directed at my mother, but I jumped up ready to do it, so there was activity. "Good idea," I said.

I headed for the serving bench, past my mother, before she could argue that she was going to do it, past Ben, before he could get up and help. I kept moving toward the pot roast, like it was going to save the evening. Maybe it would. My mother's pot roast, with its plump tomatoes and roasted onions, too much brandy.

I put on her oven mitts and gingerly picked up the pan, the roast rich and robust, not suffering from its extra time waiting for us.

I put the roast down in the middle of the table.

"That looks wonderful!"

We looked up to see Margaret entering the barrel room, Bobby behind her. They had smiles painted on their faces, Margaret's aimed at the pot roast, Bobby's aimed at the twins.

Bobby took the seat next to mine, Margaret sitting on his other side, looking like she'd rather take the seat on my other side, the one between me and my mother. Finn's seat. But she sat where she always did between Bobby and my father.

Margaret scooted the chair over so she was near my father, as near as she could get, like he was going to protect her if Bobby threw the succulent roast at her. She was smart. Beneath his smile, he looked like he wanted to do that.

I reached over, tentatively tapping Bobby on the back, trying to be comforting to him. It was a mistake. Bobby looked like he was about to explode, and my touch only tightened him up.

Bobby looked across the table, nodding in Ben's direction, their first and only hello. Ben gave him a nod back, giving me a supportive smile.

Then Bobby reached immediately, and deliberately, for the wine.

At another moment, Bobby would have wondered what had changed with Ben and me that had Ben sitting at this table. But Bobby wasn't thinking about that. He wasn't thinking about anything except what he'd overheard in the bathroom.

Luckily, Josh called out to Bobby, distracting him. "Daddy . . ."

He looked across the table at his son. He gave him a genuine smile. "Yes, what?"

"Where's Uncle Finn?"

Bobby bit his thumb, Margaret answering for him.

"I'm sure he'll be here soon," she said.

Bobby looked away from the twins, toward Ben, just in time to see Ben put his arm lovingly around his daughter, Bobby noticing for the first time the child that wasn't his.

"Who's the kid?" he whispered.

Margaret hadn't told him. I wasn't going to break that news. Not when the rest of his world was unraveling before him.

Bobby didn't want an answer, though. He was already reaching over and pouring himself some wine, not pouring any for his wife.

My father clocked that he ignored Margaret's glass and took the bottle from Bobby, pouring some for Margaret himself. Margaret smiled at him gratefully.

"Thanks, Dan," Margaret said, taking a long sip. "This wine is really delicious. What are we drinking?"

"Concerto," my father said.

"Soon to be *Wine Spectator* magazine's 'Pinot Noir of the Year,'" my mother said.

"One of *Wine Spectator* magazine's 'Pinot Noirs of the Year,'" my father corrected. "And I had very little to do with it. Lots of strong, warm weather. The fruit just presented itself."

"To you," my mother said proudly, my mother, who was pre-gaming with us, her real meal a few hours away. *La Gare. 10 PM.*

I must have been giving her a look, because she turned toward me. "What?"

Ben tapped on his wineglass with a spoon, all eyes turning toward him.

"Would it be okay if I said a few words?" he said, holding up his glass and directing the question to my father. "We are just so happy to be here."

"Who's *we*?" Bobby whispered.

Then the door swung open, a woman's loud laugh making its way into the barrel room before she did.

"Is Finn bringing someone?" my mother said.

Which was when they entered, the loud-laughing woman and Finn.

The woman wore an outfit that matched her laugh. She had on a wildly short dress, her ample boobs falling out, the dress emphasizing her long blond hair, her longer legs. A real-life Barbie.

The twins and Maddie stared at her, mesmerized.

Finn held her hand, unsteady on his feet, slurring a little.

"Hey! I'm sorry I'm late. Bill didn't show up for his shift." Finn put his arm tightly around his guest's waist, brushed those boobs. "I've brought my friend Alexis to make it up to you. Alexis, this is my family. Family, this is Alexis."

She waved, leaning in closer to Finn. "Hi there," she said.

My mother smiled, jumping out of her seat. "Hi, Alexis," my mother said. "I'll set a place for you next to Finn."

My mother grabbed a woven placemat, plates for pot roast and pie, as Finn introduced Alexis around the room, finishing his introductions with the people he wanted to meet Alexis most.

"Alexis," Finn said. "That is my brother, Bobby, and his wife, Margaret."

He was rubbing her ass the entire time.

Bobby kept his eyes ahead of him, Margaret too.

Ben met my eyes, questioning what was happening. "You okay?" he mouthed.

I shrugged, at a loss as to what to do, watching Finn snuggling into his friend.

"Why don't you two help yourself to the roast?" my mother said.

Alexis shrugged. "I don't eat anything with a face. Except for shellfish."

I stared at Alexis, ready to slap her, not for her statement but for being here at all. As though it were her fault.

"Alexis is actually a vegetarian," Finn said.

Bobby laughed, but it was a mean laugh. Angry.

"Thanks for translating," he said.

Finn looked at him, confused, uncertain why Bobby would be upset with him. He was oblivious that Bobby had found out about him and Margaret, too focused on his own asinine agenda: to move on from Margaret. Alexis was here for Margaret's benefit. Bobby wasn't supposed to know.

"Ben," my father said. "You were saying?"

"What?" Ben said.

Ben's eyes were still on Alexis and Finn, confused.

My mother touched his arm. "You were giving a toast, Ben," she said.

"Right . . ." Ben raised his glass, trying to remember. "I was just going to say, I'm happy to be here. And I want to raise a glass to Dan and Jen for always making me feel like a part of your family, even when I haven't deserved it."

Finn laughed. "When was that?"

I pressed hard into his thigh.

"Ow," Finn said. Then he raised his hand in mock surrender. "Just checking where we were on the honesty meter."

Bobby shook his head. "Is that what you were checking?" he said.

"Eat," my father said loudly, everyone looking at him. "Let's eat."

We all began eating, Finn keeping his hand over Alexis's shoulder, groping her. Then he did the worst thing. He started to turn toward Margaret; Margaret, who was focused on her roast, shaking. Shaking in the face of Finn's cruelty, of Bobby's anger.

"Son of a bitch," Bobby said.

Bobby dove for Finn, knocking him off his chair, the two of them landing on the floor, legs hitting chairs. Finn's elbow knocking into the wall, crushing it.

Everyone was up from the table at once. My father moved toward Finn and Bobby, Ben moving to help my father. My mother and Margaret ushering the twins and Maddie away.

My father pulled Finn off of Bobby just long enough for Bobby to punch Finn in the face. Hard. The force of it pushed Finn back, leveling him, blood dripping down his face, through his cracked skin.

Finn held his jaw, shocked. His shock turned to anger, fueling him forward.

"Are you crazy?" Finn said.

"Screw you, Finn."

The two of them were on top of each other again. Finn was on the offense now as much as the defense. He pushed Bobby through the front door, tumbling toward the lawn.

Finn tackled Bobby on the grass, the vineyard steps away, Bobby rolling over on top of him, ready to take another swing.

But Ben grabbed on to Bobby's shoulders before he could, holding Bobby back and away, my father reaching down and pulling Finn up to standing. All of them stuck together.

Finn pulled away, straightening his shirt.

"What the fuck, Bobby?" Finn said.

Bobby, almost breaking loose of Ben, lunged at Finn again. But Ben grabbed him back. "What the fuck? You're asking me what the fuck?" he said. "What about Margaret?"

"What are you talking about?"

"What about Margaret?" Bobby said.

With that question, Finn got quiet, aware that Bobby knew. He knew about him and Margaret. His eyes locked with mine, where I stood with my mother, two feet away.

"Don't look at her," Bobby said. "She has nothing to do with this. Look at me."

Finn turned back to Bobby as Margaret ran outside, the twins and Maddie safely ensconced elsewhere. My mother put an arm around her protectively, not sure what else to do.

Bobby gave Finn a look, disgusted.

"You're my brother," Bobby said.

"Nothing happened, man," Finn said.

"Oh, nothing happened? Okay," Bobby said. "You've always fucking wanted her."

Finn shook his head, laughing angrily. "Whatever, Bobby . . ."

"This isn't even about her," Bobby said. "It's about me, you wanting my life."

My father and Ben stood between them, holding them back. But they weren't watching carefully. They were too mad, and I could picture it. One of them swinging, hitting Ben or my father in the head. Or both.

I moved toward both of them. "Why don't you guys calm down and take this up tomorrow?"

"Why don't you worry about yourself, there?" Bobby said, his voice harsh.

Ben immediately got protective, defensive. "Leave her out of it, Bobby," he said. "She has nothing to do with this."

Finn laughed and turned away from Bobby for the first time. "You've got to be fucking kidding. Now you're in the business of protecting our sister, Ben? That's impressive."

Bobby turned toward Ben, confused. "What is he talking about?"

The vein was throbbing in Ben's forehead. "Finn, now is not the time."

Finn shook his head. "Exactly. What are you doing bringing your kid here?"

"Your kid?" Bobby said. "That little girl is your kid?"

Bobby was connecting the dots, and for a minute it seemed like he might turn all his Finn-anger at Ben. Bobby moved to tackle Ben, Finn joining in. The three of them locked together.

"Hey!" my father said.

He jumped in between his sons and his future son-in-law, separating everyone out. He pushed Finn first, his eyes holding tight on Bobby, warning him, warning them both.

"That is enough," he said.

His voice was serious and steady, enough to stop them in their tracks. Finally.

Everyone stared at him, no one used to seeing him that angry. The anger, alone, stopped everyone in place.

"Bobby, you're going to go talk to your wife." He pointed toward the house. "And Finn, you're going anywhere else."

They both stared at him.

"And I really don't care what you both have to do to act like grown men until then, but at five A.M. tomorrow morning, I expect you both in the vineyard, for my final day."

Then my father walked back into the barrel room, everyone separating. My mother followed my father inside. Bobby moved toward the twins, Ben toward Maddie, Finn walking the other way. Finn walked out into the vineyard. Past the gardens and the winemaker's cottage. Getting lost among the high vines, the evening wind swallowing him.

Until I was left alone, or mostly alone.

Alexis appeared in the doorway. "I think I'm going to go," she said.

Exile on Main Street

*M*y father had a theory that what was of equal importance to the wine you presented in your vintage was the wine you left out of the vintage. In winemaking, this was known as declassification. Declassification: a fancy word for what wines you were willing to throw out. The decision was made as early as when the grapes were picked. It was made as late as after investing months fermenting the wine.

I always thought that was what made my father such a great winemaker. There were some winemakers who wouldn't declassify anything that came from their vineyard—the factory winemakers, the big producers. They didn't care about quality control to begin with and they didn't care about it at the end. They wanted high yields, regardless of weather, regardless of rot. Give it a shiny name and sell it for five dollars. Someone would be glad to drink it.

My father believed in low yields, working from the best grapes, balanced pruning. The year of the second awful harvest, after sweeping fires, my father declassified more wine than he bottled, even though it meant he risked going broke in the process. Even though it meant that he risked everything.

~

"I shouldn't have brought her to the house," Finn said.

We drove toward The Brothers' Tavern, Finn slipping around in the passenger seat even though he swore he was fine to drive: a full-on fistfight with his brother over his sister-in-law apparently sobering him up.

"I'll apologize tomorrow," Finn said. "First, to Ben. Then I'll apologize to Dad."

"Great, sounds like a start."

He looked over at me, trying to read my tone. His lip was bleeding, his eye starting to swell—the package of frozen peas my mother had grabbed for him useless on the dashboard. "Thank you for giving me a ride," he said.

"I didn't have a choice. Dad made me."

He looked out the window. "He shouldn't have. I'm a better driver drunk than you are sober."

He reached for his peas, holding them to his face.

I checked the clock. I promised Ben that we'd talk after I took Finn to work. Ben didn't quite understand why I had to go into town with Finn, even though he wasn't mad at Finn.

Ben was mad at me that I hadn't kept my family out of our relationship. Ben had been the one who screwed things up—and, arguably, it had been a mistake to bring Maddie with him. But I hadn't protected him from my family. Wasn't that the job? It was about the two of you. And you told the rest of the world that you had it figured out or that you would. That was love, after all. Loyalty in the face of despair.

Finn ran his tongue over his busted lip. "I've been trying to keep my space. To do the right thing."

"I know that you have."

He tossed the peas back on the dashboard. "She kissed me. I was the one that walked out."

"You just need to explain what happened to Bobby. I can explain it to him. You can talk to Margaret and just tell her it was a mistake."

"A mistake?" He shook his head, laughing. His bloody lip was splitting open against the pressure. "Bobby isn't going to see this as a mistake."

"Finn, if I explain to . . ."

"No."

"Why?"

He shook his head. "'Cause you can't fix this. I know you try to fix everything, but you can't fix this."

"I just want to help."

"Start by helping yourself."

His tone was dismissive, and it stopped me. "What's that supposed to mean?"

"Nothing. You're just acting like you know the right thing for everyone when you don't even know the right thing for yourself."

"That isn't true."

"Really? Then why are you still thinking about marrying someone you don't love?"

I gripped the steering wheel, my heart starting to race. "I love Ben."

"Georgia, he has a kid you didn't even know about."

"So? You're saying if I loved him I should have known?"

He shook his head. "I'm saying if you love him, why'd you run?"

I gripped the steering wheel tighter, hurt and angry. No one had said that to me, and his words—in a way I didn't want to admit—penetrated.

So I didn't focus when I turned onto Main Street. I forgot about the curb. I forgot about how, when you turned onto Main Street, the curb jutted out five feet, making room for the fire hydrant.

The fire hydrant that I hit. Muffler first. Jolting us, me into the steering wheel, Finn into the dashboard.

The water shot upward, spraying the front of Finn's pickup, soaking the empty street, Finn's bag of peas exploding all around him.

Finn held on to the dashboard, bracing himself. "Are you okay?" Finn said.

I reached up, touching my forehead, feeling for blood and nodding that I was fine.

Finn nodded, relieved that no one was hurt. Then, once he knew that, he wanted nothing more than to kill me himself.

He gripped the dashboard, the water coating the windshield, like a rainstorm.

A tornado.

"You really shouldn't be behind the wheel!"

I shut the ignition and jumped out of the truck, stepping into the soaking spray of the fire hydrant, surveying the damage. Finn's headlight was dented, his muffler tipped. I tried kicking it back into place, water in my eyes.

Finn screamed at me. "What are you doing? And where are the keys?" he said.

Then he slid into the driver's seat, motioning for me to take the passenger side.

"Get back in the car," he said.

I kept kicking but it was no use. The muffler wouldn't go back into place, nothing would go back into place.

The Brothers' Tavern was still several blocks away, but its lights were visible in the distance. Finn could make it by himself. He was going to have to try. I started walking in the opposite direction.

Finn called out the car window. "What are you doing?" he said.

I turned around, still under the spray, getting drenched. "I'm leaving you."

"Why?"

"You're an asshole, Finn. You weren't talking about me and Ben. You were talking about Bobby and Margaret, at least the version of them you want to be true."

He laughed. "Really, then why are you running away from me?"

"I'm walking."

"Semantics. You're running. You're just not very fast about it."

Finn called out after me as I walked fast down Main Street, soaking wet. My wallet was still in Finn's truck, my phone too.

"Come back!" Finn said.

But I turned left onto Green Street.

And I saw him standing there in front of the small French restaurant that my parents used to go to when I was growing up, the only restaurant in town that served after 10 P.M.

Henry.

He stood under the awning, backlit by the open sign, the streetlights. His hands were in his big pockets, his cashmere sweater hanging over his stomach. He was looking at the menu longingly, though he must have felt my gaze, because he turned toward me.

I walked over to him, pulling my hair behind my ears, tugging on my drenched shirt.

He smiled. "Hi there, Georgia."

He took his hands out of his pocket, like he was going to reach out to shake mine, or dry some wet streaks from my face, or both. Thankfully, he thought better of it.

"You're . . . wet," he said.

"I had a fight with a fire hydrant," I said.

He looked at me like that was the weirdest thing he'd ever heard. For that, at least, I didn't blame him.

"Are you looking for your mother?"

"I'm actually looking for you."

This surprised him. He stepped back, looking uncomfortable. "Why's that?"

I tried to think of how to answer him. What was a good answer? Why had this little confrontation seemed like a good idea? Maybe because there was no one else that I was able to talk to. Not Ben, or my brothers, or my parents. I had no idea what I wanted to say to any of them, but I knew what I wanted to say to Henry. I wanted to tell him to stay away.

"I thought we should talk."

"Okay . . ." he said.

I wasn't sure where to start. I looked at Henry, as if that would provide a clue as to why my mother loved him. He was so different from my father: city intellectual to my father's outdoorsman, large to my father's lean and lanky. Of course, that wasn't the right question. The right question was why my mother was giving so much up for him— her family, her home, the farm around it that she had nurtured with her own hands.

"Your mother just texted me that she may not be coming."

He reached in his pocket, showed me his phone like proof.

"I'm meeting my son instead, actually. He's never been to La Gare."

"You have a son?"

"I do, yes."

"You're divorced?"

"No, I'm not technically."

I looked at him, confused. Henry was married? He had a wife somewhere, wondering where he was, two homes breaking up so he and my mother could run off?

"I have a son, but I was never married to his mother. We were close friends. We still are." He pointed at the menu. "Would you like to join us for a bite to eat? My son is a winemaker. He's relatively new to the area. I think you'll enjoy each other."

"No, Henry, I think that may be the last thing I'd like to do. No offense."

"None taken." He paused. "It's nice to see you again," he said.

He looked like he wanted to see me as much as I wanted to see him. Which did the strangest thing. It warmed me to him.

Then he leaned forward, looking me in the eyes, and a weird thing happened—suddenly, I was the one standing at attention.

"It's easy to think you understand what's going on between your mother and me," he said. "It's always easy from the outside looking in."

I gave him a look, warning him to avoid suggesting I was on the outside of anything involving my mother.

"What I'm saying is that I do love your mother very much," he said.

"And you think that makes it okay to break up a family?"

He shook his head. And I saw it, his edge. The kind that meant he wasn't going to play nice. "That's her choice, not mine."

He paused, softening, but pressing on.

"Your mother has taught me a little about winemaking. It's fascinating to me. Perhaps because it isn't unlike music. Timing is everything."

I was unsure what he wanted me to take from that.

"When your mother walked into rehearsal for the first time, she had on this green jumpsuit which she thought looked sophisticated but she looked ridiculous. She was the most ridiculous and beautiful woman I'd ever seen."

He shook his head fondly.

"I'd just had my son, though. And by the time I left his mother, she had already met your father." He paused. "So if you want to understand why your mother's with me, you have to ask someone else. But for me, I've been waiting thirty-five years for the two of us to fall into rhythm."

I was floored, hearing him talk about my mother that way, and seeing what happened in his eyes. There was an intensity there. It was intoxicating to witness that kind of intensity—that kind of passion, really— honest and raw and irresistible at the same time. Irresistible in how sure of itself it was. And my mother was on the receiving end of that intensity. How could she turn away from it?

"What makes you think I want to hear any of this?"

He smiled. "Because you came to find me tonight," he said.

"To tell you to go away."

He shook his head. "That's not going to happen."

Again, that edge—and worse, a certainty. He was certain that my mother and he were a done deal. He was certain that they belonged together—the way my father was certain of the same thing.

It made me want to ask him a question. Not if he understood what my parents' love was like—what it had been like to grow up in the glow of it—because how could he? And he didn't care as much about that as he cared about being with my mother.

But that wasn't my question. I was wet and freezing and exhausted. I wanted to ask him if he could lend me twenty dollars so I could get home.

Then the restaurant door opened. And he was standing there.

In his sweater vest glory.

Jacob. I started putting pieces together. Jacob grew up in New York. I only knew Jacob's mother, not his father. Was Henry his father? I didn't know Henry's last name, but he had moved here from New York. I knew that. I knew Jacob was a winemaker. Maybe this was the story. These two men, father and son: Henry destroying my parents' marriage, Jacob destroying their livelihood.

Jacob held out his hand, offering Henry his half-smile. If he had a piece of licorice he'd have offered that too.

"I'm Jacob McCarthy," he said.

"Henry," Henry said. "Henry Morgan."

"Good to meet you, Henry," Jacob said.

I breathed a sigh of relief as Henry walked inside and away.

Jacob did a double take, looking through the window, after him. "That wasn't *the* Henry Morgan, was it?"

"You know about classical music now?"

"I know enough to know about Henry Morgan," he said.

He gave me a smile, not commenting that I was dripping like a wet dog.

"What have I missed?" he said.

I pointed at the closed door. "Henry is my mother's non-lover, and according to him, her soul mate," I said. "And my brothers tried to kill each other over pot roast. And there was an incident with a fire hydrant."

Jacob took a breath, as if overwhelmed himself. "That's it?"

"There is a theory that I don't love my fiancé. And I need money for a cab."

Jacob reached into his coat pocket, held out his wallet. "I can help with that part," he said.

He peeled off a fifty-dollar bill, handed it over.

"Thanks," I said. "Are you meeting Lee here?"

He nodded as if remembering her. "Lee. Yes," he said. "We keep meaning to go other places, but this is the only place open by the time we can eat. She's at Foo Camp and running late."

"Foo Camp?"

"Foo Camp." He nodded. "That's what they call this computer camp Lee is attending. This guy Tim O'Reilly runs it up here. He basically is at the forefront of everything technological. Lee idolizes him. It's like hacker nerd dreamland."

"Lee likes chia and computers and Vera Wang. She's interesting."

"To both of us." He smiled, considering that. Then he pointed to the restaurant with his wallet. "You want to come in and have a drink?" he said.

I looked down at my outfit—wet jeans, a white T-shirt. "I shouldn't," I said.

Jacob reached out and held his hand over the back of my neck, like he was going to touch my skin, hold me there, warm me there. I felt a chill. I felt a chill where his hand almost was.

"Come in," he said. "That way there can be two of us looking stupid when Lee explains the algorithm that is going to change the way we log in to secure websites."

That sounded better than heading back to the house, but I shook my head. "Henry's in there."

"The non-lover."

I nodded.

He shrugged. "Another night, then."

I smiled, putting the money in my pocket. "I'm not paying you back, though."

"Why's that?"

"You're taking my family's vineyard. I figure you can give me fifty bucks."

He nodded. "Fifty bucks seems fair."

I turned to go, walking in the direction of the main drag, the only place to catch a cab.

But I looked back at Jacob. He was standing there, watching me go.

He nodded, his way of offering encouragement for the rest of the night apart. Like he wished he was joining me for it. If I didn't know better, a little like that.

"What's that look for?" he said.

I shrugged, considering how to say it. "You just keep showing up. Exactly when I need you."

He smiled. "Some people would say that's a good thing," he said.

Then Jacob walked inside.

The Vintner Drinks Alone

*W*hen I got back to the house, Ben was sleeping on the couch, trying to wait up so we could talk, the TV on, his shoes still on. But he was sound asleep. I put a blanket over him and headed upstairs. Maddie and the twins were in bed with my mother. Maddie fit right in, just one more, squeezed under my mother's arm.

The light was off in Bobby's bedroom, the door was closed tight. And I imagined that Margaret was in there with him, that they were starting the process of working things out. But when I opened my bedroom door, Margaret was there, a box of tissues beside her, sleeping with her feet up by the pillows.

I threw on a dry sweatshirt and closed the door behind myself, heading down the back stairs to the winemaker's cottage, to the only free place to sleep.

My father was up, drinking a glass of wine on the porch, looking over his incredible spreadsheet. His spreadsheet was the difference between him being a good winemaker and a great winemaker. It listed every grape, every clone, on the entire vineyard. It listed where they were fermenting in the cellar, how long he was going to let each ferment, the combinations that were going into the final product. The spreadsheet was his ultimate work in progress. He would make changes throughout the entire winter, based on the wine's taste and its color. That was the part that made him a good winemaker, he would say. Not that he was willing to make the changes, but that, in the end, he was also willing to change it back.

He kept his eyes on his spreadsheet, marking it. "Avoiding every-one?" he said.

"Not you."

He looked up and smiled. "Aren't I lucky, then?"

He patted the bench beside him, and I sat down, tossing off my shoes, pulling my knees up. I took a first breath, lavender and chamomile and honey filling the vineyard air. It took me back, remembering how it used to calm me, a night just like this one. I'd stay up past bedtime, sitting beside my father while he worked on his spreadsheet, my father stopping occasionally to show me what he was doing.

He put the spreadsheet down and poured me a glass of wine. "Finn doing okay?"

I nodded, relaxing into the safety of this porch, the vineyard like a beautiful barricade, keeping everything wrong and unwanted away.

"Thank you for dropping him off," he said.

It didn't feel like a good time to tell him that I hadn't.

He handed over the wine. "That's the 2005."

I took the unlabeled bottle, the glass shiny and blue. My father could have meant several wines from that vintage, but referring to it in that way, it was clear he meant the 2005 Block 14: the one wine on his spreadsheet that he never messed with. The first wine he'd ever made, an expression of a single site. Every year, those were the grapes he picked after the har-vest party—everything else off the vine except for them. These were his most valuable grapes, juicy and rich from the extra time on the vine. He saved those grapes for last and fermented them as they were.

Some years Block 14 turned out well, some years not well. Biody-namics at its most pure. And, 2005, it turned out gorgeous. The fruit was present in every sip of the wine, a rich, dark berry explosion. It won my father two national awards, his distributor insisting he charge ninety dol-lars a bottle. He liked to joke that 2005 was the wine that paid for all the wines. Tonight, it was like drinking comfort. Ripe and simple.

"Not bad, huh?" he said.

I breathed into the wine, thick with chocolate and jamminess, the way only the best Pinot Noir was. "Beautiful."

"Beautiful. I'll take it."

I motioned toward his spreadsheet. "How's it looking?"

He smiled. "These last grapes came off lovely," he said. "The whole southwest corner came off lovely. I'll feel better when Block 14 is off the vines, but I'd like to give them a little longer to ripen fully."

"Forecast clear?"

"Forecast clear, but they've been wrong before."

He pointed to the last page of his spreadsheet, the weather services lining the top. He updated each of them daily, all five of them showing sunny skies.

"Jacob is getting into my head," he said. "He thinks they should come down."

"Why would you listen to him?"

He picked up his wine, considering the question. "He's paying me plenty to."

"Well, not enough, in my opinion."

"Good thing it's my opinion that matters."

Then he tipped the glass in my direction, looking at me, and smiling a little sadly.

"Not that you asked, but it might help to separate out what's going on with the vineyard and with our family from what's going on for you and Ben. They are all separate things."

It all felt like the same thing: the loss of the vineyard, the coming apart of our family. Finn and Bobby and Margaret. My parents. Ben and Maddie. Michelle. It all felt tied up, like the same thread was running through them. Where there had been trust—to keep each other safe, to make each other feel loved—there was none. Maybe it *was* tied up. Synchronized to come apart the moment my father turned his back on the vineyard and we were all too busy to stop him.

"Not that you asked, but it might help you to stop thinking of them as separate things. Everything is falling apart."

"Not everything is falling apart," my father said.

"Did you see your sons trying to kill each other tonight?"

He nodded, considering that. Then dismissing it.

"Finn and Bobby are fighting over the wrong thing. But at least they're fighting."

"And how is that good?"

"Because that's the only way to get somewhere better." He shrugged. "If you fight, you work it out. If you don't fight, you move into your own corners, and nothing gets decided there."

I looked up toward the house. All the lights were off. Everyone sleeping where they shouldn't: my mother in my parents' bedroom without my father, my father apparently resigned to that. The man who had built a vineyard from nothing, who had kept my family together in spite of everything. He was just giving up. That was suddenly the scariest part.

"It's not like you," I said.

He looked at me. "Not to fight?"

My father had fought hard for the vineyard his entire life—he fought for everyone in our family. "Yes."

He poured more wine, pointing at my empty ring finger.

"You either," he said.

Pancakes at The Violet Café

*T*he last harvest that Finn and Bobby were still living at home, Finn and Bobby and I moved into the winemaker's cottage. My father stayed in the house with my mother. My father allowed us to do this as long as we worked the entire harvest start to finish. It was my father's last chance to show us fully what running the vineyard would be like. He wanted us each to have that knowledge. Of course, we took it as an opportunity to stay up late and smoke cigarettes and avoid homework. The three of us spending time together and talking, really talking. The way you often avoid doing with your siblings while growing up— everyone too busy doing other things.

It was only recently that I realized the knowledge my father wanted us to have. It wasn't about the vineyard. It was about each other.

~

Five days before my wedding, I woke up in the winemaker's cottage, in the extra bedroom, in another world. Finn and his angry words snaked through my head most of the night. Was he right that if I truly loved Ben I'd have reacted differently? It felt simplistic to think so, but in my own way I was being simplistic too. As if Ben's wrong freed me to stop behaving right.

I slid out of the cottage, past the cold toast and jelly my father had left on the table. My father was already gone. No such thing as a day off during the final days of the harvest.

I headed up toward the main house, toward the one person that could make me feel better about what Finn had said, about what my father had said, toward the one person that I needed to try with most. Toward Maddie.

She was already up, dressed in her heart leggings, watching *Beauty and the Beast* in my mother's bed, lying with my mother, and the twins—in their fireman uniforms.

It startled me for a second, seeing the three of them there, watching morning movies, like the three of us had done, growing up. The twins like Finn and Bobby. Maddie, a little like me.

My mother looked sad lying there and I bent down, kissed her on the forehead.

"What's that for?" she said.

"It's a new day."

My mother studied me in my faded jeans and a tank top, my hair piled into a messy bun on top of my head. "Then don't you think you could use a shower?" she said.

I gave her a smile and turned toward Maddie. "You sleep well?"

Maddie nodded, her eyes on the movie. "We watched *Beauty and the Beast.*"

"Last night also?"

Maddie smiled, eyes on the television. "Twice," Maddie said.

My mother shrugged. "Don't judge," she said. "I learned a long time ago to pick my battles, and it's not like they aren't learning something," she said.

"What's that, Mom?"

She pointed at their happy faces, intent on the princess. "Commitment," she said.

I looked at Maddie, trying to get her attention. "Maddie, what's your favorite breakfast in the world?"

"Pancakes," she said.

"With chocolate chips?"

She looked at me like I had just solved a code. "How did you know that?"

"Would you let me take you for some, if your dad says it's okay? There's a place near here that has the world's gooiest chocolate chips."

"Just you and me?" She looked skeptical about that. I held her gaze, letting her know she could trust me about the chocolate chips. And everything else.

She turned toward Josh. "Can I borrow your fireman hat?"

He nodded, handing it over, too entranced by the movie to care.

Then Maddie looked at me.

"Can we put the movie back on as soon as we get back?"

My mother gave me a look. "Pick your battles," she said.

And like that, I agreed.

~

The Violet Café did have the world's best chocolate chip pancakes. They were made with five different kinds of chocolate chips. Dark, milk, white, bittersweet, espresso. And they came in a stack of five large pancakes that were impossible to finish.

Maddie, in a feat that I hadn't seen since my own brothers would attack their plates, managed to do just that. She moved slowly through them, eating a pancake at a time, dipping each piece in maple syrup, in a dollop of powdered sugar. The waitress came over to ask if she was done, and she waved her away. She was a professional.

"I love pancakes," she said.

"Are these up to your standards?"

She nodded enthusiastically. "Yes," she said. "They are."

She looked like she might throw up, the effort of eating and making conversation too much, but then she rallied, and reached for her milk-shake.

"Mum takes me every Sunday for pancakes to a café near our flat. The pancakes there have lemon in them. Lemon and lots of chocolate chips. If that sounds bad, they aren't."

I smiled. "If you tell me they're good, I believe you."

She smiled back. "These are better though. Daddy would love these pancakes . . ."

Maddie looked down, realizing something. Probably something as simple as this: I'd know that too. I'd know many of the things that she knew about her father.

"We could bring him some if you like?" I said.

She smiled. "And more for me?" she said.

"Sure," I said.

Maddie went back to the business at hand, scraping her fork along the plate. "Mum told me that you were a nice person," she said.

I looked at Maddie, surprised. "She did?"

She nodded. "She said you're Daddy's friend, like Mum's friend Clay."

She took another bite while I considered that. Michelle stepped outside of herself to help. Didn't that mean she had good intentions?

"Clay took me out for my birthday. We were visiting California for Mum's movies, and he took me to a restaurant where they have spicy lettuce. And lots of burger. Korean food. If that sounds bad, it was."

I couldn't help but laugh. It was all I could do not to reach over, touch her little face. "We won't go there, then."

She looked up. "Clay lives in California now, in Los Angeles. Near Daddy."

"Well, then you have to introduce us to him."

Her eyes got wide. "Clay and Mum aren't good friends since he moved to California. But we still are good friends. So maybe he'll come here. For my next birthday."

Then something occurred to me, something I didn't want occurring to me. I understood why Ben hadn't wanted me to know the circumstances around how Michelle reached out to him.

Maddie shook her head. For a second I thought she had made the connection that I had. That her young mind was astute enough to know where Clay had gone and why he had.

"No," she said, tears springing to her eyes.

I moved closer to her. "Maddie, it's okay."

She shook her head from side to side, the tears falling. "No, it's not."

Then she pointed down and I realized the depth of her sadness. Her plate was empty.

~

On the way out of the restaurant, Maddie ran into a pretty woman with thick, dark hair, wire-rim glasses. Fireman hat first. The woman was sitting at the counter, eating a bowl of oatmeal. A small container of chia seeds by her purse.

Lee. Why should I be surprised? Jacob had said they came here most mornings, but it was different to see her in person, spooning up her oatmeal.

Maddie raced for the door, sideswiping her, Lee swaying to hold on to her stool.

"Whoa there!" she said.

"Sorry!" Maddie said.

Then she reached for my hand, needing my protection from this strange lady who could yell at her, who could do anything. I took Maddie's hand and gave Lee a smile.

"We are post-pancakes," I said.

Lee laughed, throwing her head back. "Don't worry about it for even a second." Then she pointed at her healthy breakfast, picking up her spoon. "I wish I was post-pancakes too."

Maddie jumped up, the fireman hat falling over her eyes. "If you get some, I'll share with you."

Lee gave Maddie a sweet smile. And I took her in. Up close, behind those glasses, her skin was porcelain—like a doll. Which maybe was why Maddie couldn't take her eyes off of her either.

Lee looked back up at me. "She's adorable," she said.

"I can't take any credit. She's my fiancé's daughter."

Lee nodded. "A good thing to come with the deal," she said.

Maddie smiled at Lee, her new fan. She was used to being told how cute she was and milking it after. She was, after all, the daughter of a movie star.

Maddie picked up Lee's package of seeds. "What are these?" Maddie said.

"Those are chia seeds," Lee said.

Maddie looked at them, confused, putting them down. "Yuck," Maddie said.

She laughed. "Yes, that seems to be the consensus. She sounds like my fiancé."

I must have cringed, hearing those words. Lee tilted her head, as if noting it, considering something.

"Is that why you look so familiar? Did I meet you through him? He's a local winemaker. Jacob McCarthy?"

I shrugged. It wasn't a lie, but it wasn't an answer either.

She adjusted her glasses, looking confused. "Maybe you look like someone else I know," she said. "I'm Lee. For the next time I confuse you with someone that you're not."

I laughed, feeling guilty about withholding from her. I pointed at the chia seeds. "I've heard a lot about those recently," I said, wanting to tell her something true.

"You need to try them, then . . ."

She licked her spoon to clean it—and then dipped it into the oatmeal, making me a seedy bite. I didn't want to take it, though there didn't seem to be much choice. It was such a familiar gesture—as gross as it was—so openhearted.

I took the spoon, swallowing it all at once—her oatmeal and her seeds and her licked spoon—the slimy, gooey mix.

"What do you think of the chia seeds? Friend or foe?"

Maddie started tugging on my shirt, done being hospitable. Done with any more adult conversation. "Come on!"

That saved me from answering. I smiled and handed her back her spoon.

And Lee waved good-bye as Maddie took my hand and ran out of there.

Perfect Red

*W*hen we got back to the house, there was a large SUV parked out front. It seemed odd, but not for long—as soon as we walked into the house and Maddie ran upstairs, back to her movie, I went into the kitchen. And found Ben standing by the coffee machine, holding a mug and laughing.

With Michelle.

Michelle Carter. In my kitchen.

She was gorgeous, and effortlessly stunning, wearing a long silk dress and cowboy boots, her red hair pulled up into a loose bun. She held a mug herself. My mug. Like it belonged to her, like she belonged standing in my family's kitchen, leaning comfortably against the countertop, leaning comfortably, hips open, into Ben.

Ben looked up, noticing I was there. "Hey," he said.

Then he motioned toward Michelle.

"Michelle came to pick up Maddie a little early," he said.

My heart was beating so hard, I actually thought they could hear it. I forced a friendly smile. "Is that right?"

"I apologize for just arriving!" she said. "My phone is useless in wine country."

Ben smiled at me, his eyes apologizing. "They have to get back to London, but she wanted to come by the house so you two could meet."

"Or meet again," Michelle said.

She spoke in this powder-soft voice, which forced you to lean forward just to hear her. I drilled her with a look, disliking her powder-soft voice, disliking that she was trying to add levity to the awkwardness of that meeting on the street. At another moment that would have been what was called for, but after my conversation with her daughter, it was the last thing that was called for.

Michelle gave me a smile, which lit up her face, making her seem younger and older than she was, almost like a different species. As pretty as she was when she wasn't smiling, when she did—smile at you—it was trancelike. Making it hard to avoid being mesmerized by her. Michelle knew it. Of course she knew it. Every man in the world told her.

And if I wasn't intimidated enough by the idea of her, the perfect woman standing territorially close to my fiancé—and staring at me post-pancake, un-showered—certainly sealed the deal.

"Benjamin has told me wonderful things about you."

She put her hand on his arm, as though she had ownership over Benjamin, whoever he was. As though I was someone they were meeting.

"Did he?" I said.

"He did," she said.

Michelle smiled, and it wasn't lost on me. She didn't want it to be lost on me—her eyes piercing me, like a challenge.

Michelle held my gaze, until I turned back to my fiancé. "Ben, can I talk to you alone for a second?"

Ben glanced at Michelle, embarrassed. "Of course."

"It's nice to see you," Michelle called out as I stormed out of the kitchen, the softness of her voice rising just enough that it was impossible to miss it.

I walked out the back door, toward our patio, as Ben followed behind. I didn't know where I was leading us, which might explain why the two of us ended up in our wedding tent.

We ended up where we were supposed to be married in five days, the sun shining down on it, burning through.

"I'm so sorry, Georgia," he said. "She showed up early."

I tried to catch my breath, the chill from the vineyard rising up behind me, making little sense with that sun.

Ben shook his head. "She insisted on coming over and saying hello."

"You didn't want to give me a heads-up?"

"I tried to call, you didn't pick up your phone."

My phone was upstairs. I hadn't brought it to breakfast and I didn't have it now. Another thing I didn't know about having a child. You always had your phone. Ben had assumed I had mine.

"I thought that it would make it less weird for the two of you to meet, but obviously that was a mistake. I'll tell her to go."

He shook his head, looking a little bit angry.

"Michelle wants you back. That's what you left out."

He tilted his head, confused. "What did you say?"

I started to tell him how I'd done the math based on when Maddie had said she'd last seen Clay. Michelle and Clay had ended their relationship, Michelle had reached out to Ben. She'd made a decision to make herself available to him, she'd made a decision that she wanted that.

"That's what you haven't told me. And then you just let her come here?"

"No . . ." he said.

"Why aren't you looking at me, then?"

Ben shook his head. "She's . . . Michelle is complicated. She's confusing wanting to take a shot with me and wanting to take a shot with Maddie's father. It's not the same thing."

"It is, actually. That's who you are, Ben."

Ben's eyes got cold. "Why do you care what Michelle wants from me?"

"She is the mother of your child. That has weight."

"Not to me, just you," Ben said.

It didn't feel appropriate to say the obvious, which was that it mattered to Michelle too. Apparently, it mattered to her more than anything, including her own relationship and whatever hurdles she had to overcome to tell Ben the truth.

"This is a woman that eviscerated you. And now she wants you."

He shook his head, frustrated. "I never said she eviscerated me," he said.

I looked at him in disbelief, that word locked in my brain from the time he'd volunteered it. Even if he was choosing to forget, it had power that she had disappeared on Ben. And that she wanted the opposite now. This was hard enough when I imagined that Michelle was still with Clay, like the magazines said she was, like Ben had let me believe she was.

"Look, let's focus on what matters, okay? Michelle knows that the best thing we can do together is be good parents to Maddie. She knows that. She knows that I love you. She knows that I'm marrying you."

"Why?"

"Why am I marrying you?" he said.

It didn't feel like a great time to ask that question. But I wondered: If what I'd thought was connecting us—honesty, friendship, a deep understanding—was gone suddenly, then what was between us?

"Why are you looking at me like that?" Ben said.

"Why are we moving to London, Ben? Is it for the job? Or did you find the job so you'd have a reason to be near them?"

"I wanted that job long before I knew about Maddie. You can't really be suggesting I'd be that duplicitous. You can't suggest you don't know how long I wanted that job."

Ben wasn't wrong. It was a low blow. He had wanted that job and I knew that. We had talked about it late at night, many times. This was his dream job—working for the London firm, designing homes all over Europe. We had talked about whether my career would allow the move. The firm's new London office made it easy. My desire to live abroad, to live in one of the greatest cities in the world, made it preferable.

But when he reminded me of that now, it just felt like another thing he was trying to prove.

Ben moved closer to me. I moved away.

"It's hard for me to turn my back on Maddie," he said. "When she needs me."

"Who's asking you to?" I said.

"Well, being there for Maddie, that means not turning my back on Michelle, either."

"Meaning what?"

He shrugged. "I'm still trying to figure that out."

That stopped me, especially when Michelle's version of his being there probably meant I wouldn't be.

Ben shook his head. "Let's relax for a second," he said. "Let's take a walk."

I heard a knock and looked in the direction of the house. We both did.

My mother stood by the sink, waving at us through the window to come inside. Michelle and Maddie were visible behind her, Michelle kneeling down so she and Maddie were eye level with each other.

My mother waved again as though the reason we were stuck in place was that we hadn't seen her. Her words ran through my head. *Be careful what you give up.*

Still, I met his eyes, taking in his smell, his sweetness. "I think you should leave."

"You can't be serious," he said.

He reached forward and held my face, trying to make me look at him. Except I couldn't look at him and not see all the stories he had kept private about his life this last year. There were breakfasts with Maddie, secret cards and phone calls, a million stories that he hadn't shared— including the story about how much Michelle still loved him.

Wasn't the ultimate form of fidelity whom you told your stories to? Ben had stopped telling me his.

Ben leaned forward. "If the situations were reversed, I would look to understand as opposed to the opposite. You know that I would. What does that say about what you want from me?"

I had no answer for him. All I knew was that my heart had moved in my chest, right into a place where it felt heavy and stuck.

"We're getting married in five days, Georgia. Five days. Don't you still want that?"

Ben met my eyes, asking me to say yes.

I didn't say anything.

Then he walked out of the beautiful and empty wedding tent.

Sebastopol, California. 1999

When she reached for his arm, Dan followed her into the dining room, irritated and tired.

"I just need to talk to you for a minute," Jen said.

It was the night of the harvest party and he didn't have time for this conversation. In a couple of days, Dan would have endless time. He was closing down for the season. The grapes had come in early. He was already putting chamomile on the vines. He would take her, his lovely wife, down the coast. He would take her to Los Angeles, a night at the symphony. He was ready to give her what she needed, just not tonight. Except tonight was when she wanted his attention.

"I got an offer," she said. "To go to New York for five months. And substitute."

"What are you talking about?"

"I'm talking about the symphony. It's not in the city. It's outside, but it's a good symphony. And they need a cellist. I'd be working with Henry Morgan again. Do you remember Henry?"

Dan did remember Henry and he didn't like him. Jen had dragged him to Portland when Henry was in town, a guest conductor at the prestigious symphony there. They had drinks afterward at their hotel, Henry and Jen talking about music into the early morning hours. Dan would have excused himself and gone up to sleep, but he felt like he couldn't leave them alone together. He didn't like the way that Henry looked at his wife. He didn't like the way Jen seemed to enjoy it.

"He's a fantastic conductor."

He bit his tongue, staying quiet. This was a trope of Jen's—Henry's brilliance. A trope that presented itself every so often. Not regularly enough to cause alarm, but enough to cause irritation. Jen noting any new symphony he moved to, Jen sharing a photograph of his son with a gorgeous model. As if that proved Henry's brilliance.

"You want to take it? We could let someone take over the vineyard for a year."

"We'd be back before then. I'd go next week. And we'd be back before the grapes finished coming in. You'd only miss part of it."

"The quiet winter."

She nodded. "The quiet winter."

Though of course nothing was quiet these days. It was an exciting time to be in Sebastopol. It was the boom. Everyone was coming to Sebastopol. Winemakers were buying land, making Pinot Noir, people moving up from San Francisco to open restaurants, to open music stores. Sebastopol was getting a hotel. It was the community he'd always wanted. He didn't want to leave it.

"You don't want me to take it," she said.

"I didn't say that," he said. Then he used the only ammunition he could think of. "But it will disrupt things for the kids."

"They're not kids anymore. They're in high school. It won't be the worst thing for them to experience school in New York. Your daughter will love it. She'll never want to come back."

He relented. "They'll be fine. What are we really talking about?"

She shook her head. "You won't like living in New York. You didn't even like living in Burgundy. It made you queasy living away from here."

What made him queasy was Jen bringing up the south of France, Marie standing in front of him. What he'd almost thrown away just to touch her. He had walked out of the room, though. Didn't that count for something?

"Jen," he said. "Why don't we talk about this tomorrow? We can sit down and see how we can work it out. Because if you want to do this, we need you to do this. That's important."

"I have to tell them tonight."

"Okay. So you do want this?"

She shook her head. "It is flattering that they want me still."

"Of course they do."

"There is a version in which I go alone. And you come and visit. We could do that too."

He wasn't going to separate again, not after what had happened last time. He didn't think he was strong enough. Marie, standing before him.

"I'd rather go with you."

She smiled, but it wasn't loving.

"What?"

"That's not the same thing as you saying you want to come, Dan."

"I said I'll go. I'll go. What do you want from me, Jen?"

"What do you want from me?" she said.

She waited. It was clear that she wanted everything. She wanted the devotion that she gave to him. She wanted him to stop standing there, pretending he didn't know these things.

He watched as she walked away from him. He should have stopped her. He should have insisted that they go because he knew how much she wanted it, even if she wasn't saying it. She wanted to go back to New York if for no other reason than to remember how much she didn't need to be in New York anymore. Having a taste of that life again would show her she had picked the one that mattered more to her.

What was there to debate? There was one thing for him to say. *The details don't matter, we'll figure it out.*

He was ready to say it, what she most needed to hear.

"Jen," he said.

But when she didn't hear him, he didn't say her name louder. He said it softer, like that was the very same thing.

Home

I didn't want to go back into the house—not until Michelle was gone—so I headed toward the vineyard, toward the winery, calling Suzannah on the way.

"What's going on?" she said.

"I ended it."

"What?" She sounded shocked. "What do you mean, you ended it? You're getting married in five days!"

"Maddie's mother showed up here and she's still in love with Ben."

"So I take it that you didn't listen to my turtle analogy?"

"How does that apply?"

"Someone opened the door for her!"

I moved deeper into the vines, wanting to feel something besides what I was feeling. "How could he not tell me she wanted to be with him again?"

"How can you let her win?"

"I didn't know it was a contest."

"Of course it is!"

I thought of Michelle, stunning and sure of herself. She wasn't particularly fond of me, though she was great with Maddie. And I could see how, given the chance, she'd be great to Ben.

"Then I'm going to lose."

"No you're not. So she's a little famous. A little gorgeous."

"Can someone be a little gorgeous?"

"So she's more than a little gorgeous," she said. "She's incredibly gorgeous. You're not so bad either."

I laughed.

"Seriously, you're smart and successful and the most loving person I know. Not to mention gorgeous in your own right. Michelle Carter has nothing on you."

"Says my best friend."

"And the man you're supposed to be with," Suzannah said.

She was quiet.

"It's not too late to work this out with him."

"Why are you pushing me to forgive him?"

"Because you did the wrong thing."

My heart dropped. "Why are you saying that?"

"Because I have to." She paused, as if considering how to convince me of that. "Charles cheated on me in high school. Have I told you that? I'm sure I've told you that."

She had told me a hundred times. It was the first story Suzannah had shared, my first day at work, or, after work, when she'd taken me for a welcome-to-law-firm-hell drink. Law firms like to make enemies out of their female lawyers, she said. Let's be best friends instead. Then she proceeded to prove her friendship by telling me that her husband had been unfaithful. Only halfway through the story did it become clear that Charles had cheated on her in high school. That she remembered it like yesterday, walking in and seeing him with the head of the drama club and clocking him in the head.

"If I hadn't forgiven him, I would have given up an entire life with him. Our family. All the good things. I was rewarded for forgiving him. That is what I'm trying to say. Forgive Ben. You will be rewarded."

"There is a difference here. Charles was fifteen when he lied to you."

She paused. "Details. The point is, you guys are supposed to be together. You have the kind of relationship that is hard to find and even harder to keep. Just like ours, me and Charles."

I shook my head, feeling like the opposite was true. Otherwise, how had we ended up here?

She was quiet. "Why don't you come home?"

I thought of Los Angeles and my empty house there. I thought of London, which felt impossibly far away. I looked around at the beautiful vineyard, which was about to belong to someone else.

Suddenly, I had no idea where that was.

The History of Wine

*M*y father liked to say that to understand how to make wine, you had to understand the history of wine. And wine's history was long and deep, moving from its quiet beginnings in the fifth century BC in Southern France to the rest of the world. A history that archeologists had constructed from the scrapings of 2,500-year-old pottery containers holding the world's oldest wine, flavored with thyme, rosemary, basil—the Roman invasion, hundreds of years later, introducing wine across France.

It was a long time before winemaking touched down in America. Early vineyards failed in Ohio and Kentucky. California had only gotten into the game two hundred years ago, with Sonoma County housing the first commercial winery, Buena Vista Winery. John Patchett followed suit and planted the first commercial vineyard in Napa Valley. Prohibition had nearly knocked out those early efforts. The wine revolution brought it back in a broader, more organized manner, leading to the modern era of winemaking—the pioneers of the 1960s and '70s putting California wine on the map, readying it for the blind tastings in Paris, California wines the winners, prying open the hold that French wine had on the world.

My father said the history mattered, mostly because it explained the first thing you had to understand about wine: Wine came from itself. Even wine that was supposedly indigenous to its land still utilized grape clones from Europe, mined everything that had come before to try to get somewhere better.

I found my father standing by the sorting table, a worker beside him, the two of them going through the grapes. They were picking out the whole clusters that he was going to use. When you used whole clusters, stems and all, it added something to the wine—a richness, but a tartness too. The tartness was something that my father strove for, so he wasn't throwing much away. This wasn't a harvest for throwing away.

"You look frantic," he said.

"I need a job to do."

"Let's hurry up and give you one, then," he said.

My father pointed at the open-top fermenters, the destemmed grapes resting inside.

"The grapes may need to be pumped."

I got up on the ladder and looked down into the tank. The red grapes were spitting, almost bubbling, like a stew.

"They look good, don't they?"

I nodded, not trusting myself to speak, afraid everything with Ben would come pouring out.

My father motioned up at me. "I have more jobs, if you come down."

I sat down on top of the ladder, several feet above my father, looking down at the winery below, moving along, beautifully, as if to music. It calmed me, helping me to take a much-needed breath.

"Or you can just sit there, lazy."

"Dad, why aren't you angry at her?"

My father's eyes narrowed. "Careful, kid . . . I'm not going to start into this with you."

"I'm just trying to understand."

"Which part?"

"What are you going to do when you leave here?"

He paused, deciding whether he wanted to say it, whether he was going to tell me the truth about what he was doing or push it off. "You remember the harvest I spent in Burgundy?"

I nodded, the difficult time moving to the front of my mind: the harvest of my father's absence, the two awful harvests that forced my father's absence. My mother was so sad that winter without him, distracted and lonely. I was so desperate to make her happy that I initiated dance parties on Friday afternoon—the two of us jumping around the kitchen to Madonna. Though her heart wasn't in it. She was almost dancing well, which gave her away.

My father nodded. "I'm heading back there to visit a friend."

I was shocked to hear him say that. I wanted to ask him what friend he was talking about, but—remembering my mother's sadness—I didn't really want the answer.

"I'm going to travel the world. I'm starting there. I'm renting a yacht from someone who my friend knows."

"You hate boats."

"Who doesn't?"

Mom. That was the answer. She loved boats. And she loved the ocean. But she wasn't going with him. So why would he go without her? He was planning the dream trip, her dream trip. Like the sky and the rain and the soil, was this something else he thought was going to line up—that it would be enough to make her want to come back to him? If not, would he just take this other person instead?

Synchronization. You get into the wrong yellow buggy and build a life with someone. You do everything in your power to build a new one when that life falls apart.

My father climbed the opposite ladder, moving toward the top of the second fermenter, from the opposite end.

Then he motioned toward the compost piles, Bobby and Finn standing by them, ignoring each other, working on the feed. He was happy, looking at his sons. "They've been working all day, not saying a word."

"Why are you smiling, then?"

"People get more work done when they don't talk."

He bent over the grapes, kneading them softly. Which was when I saw it, sneaking out from beneath his white shirt. A scar, white and winding, in the center of his chest.

I moved closer to him. "Dad, what is that?"

"Nothing." He pulled up his T-shirt, blocking my view. "It's nothing . . ." he repeated.

He kept studying the grapes, not taking his eyes off his task.

"What happened? Did you hurt yourself working?"

He was getting more and more irritated. "Georgia, can you drop this?"

"You want me to drop everything these days."

"Not everything. Just this."

"And Henry," I said.

He drilled me with a look, angry that I had the nerve to bring up Henry when he so clearly didn't want to discuss it. Except that I was angry too. I was angry at all the secrets around here, at all the things that we weren't talking about: my mother's relationship, the fact that the most beautiful woman on the planet was in love with my fiancé.

"Henry isn't even about Henry. It's about a car going off the road."

"What are you talking about, Dad?"

He looked up at me. "Do you remember when your mother and I were driving into town a few years ago and the pickup went off the road? Do you remember? Neither of us was badly hurt, but we had to go to the hospital."

"Of course. Mom called me hysterical."

He motioned toward the scar on his chest. "When this happened, when we got in that car accident, it changed things. When I lost control of the car that night, it changed things around here . . . and really it changed things for your mother."

"Why?"

He shook his head. "It scared her when I got hurt like that. And I think your mother had to consider that one day she was going to be without me, and what was her life going to look like then."

"Her answer was Henry."

He nodded. "Yes."

"So you're letting her do that. Even if it costs you the vineyard?"

"Even if it costs me the vineyard," he said.

My father stepped down the ladder, moving back toward the destemming machine. Then he looked out at the vineyard, at everything he was giving up. Which was when I understood: My father didn't want to be here without my mother. If he was going to be anywhere without her, it was going to be somewhere far from here. It was going to be far from everything he was proud that they had built.

"Dad, we can figure out another way."

He shook his head, angry. Angrier than I had seen him about all of this—angry that my mother was putting them in this position, angry that he was competing with someone for her affection, and just angry. It both relieved and scared me.

He headed toward the door.

"This is the other way," he said.

Then, he was gone.

Note by Note

$\mathcal{M}$y mother was in a towel in the corner of the bedroom, standing in front of her cello. Dancing. She was dancing around the cello, swaying, happily, or trying to stop from tripping over her feet, or both.

This was her first minute free from her grandchildren, from Maddie. She was getting ready to go to Henry, and I watched her for a moment, thinking of my father's words. He thought that he understood what was happening in a way she didn't: She was scared. She was scared that if she didn't get out of this version of her life now, she never would. My father would leave her, one way or another, and all she would be left with was the fear she already had. That she had chosen the wrong life.

You become your mother in the oddest ways, at the oddest time. Today, I had become her because I was afraid of the same thing.

She pulled her towel up. "We have to stop meeting like this."

Instead of yelling, she sashayed toward me, trying to get me to dance with her.

Though instead of dancing, I reached for her, and held her to me as I started to cry. The two of us fell to the floor.

"What is it?" my mother said.

"You still love Dad."

She nodded. Then she paused, before answering. "With all my heart."

"So what are you doing? Covering your bases?"

"That's not the reason," she said.

"Then what?"

My mother shrugged, trying to decide whether she was going to keep me as her daughter in this moment, or if she was going to trust me with something she wasn't going to be able to take back.

"When I met your father, I fell madly in love. Head-over-heels, turn-my-whole-life-around in love. When I look at him, when he touches me, I still feel that way." She shrugged. "I don't know how to explain how Henry makes me feel."

She shook her head, like it was the last thing she wanted to do. She motioned toward her cello.

"Henry loves it when I play the cello."

I wanted to tell her that Henry already said that, in a way that I wished I could get out of my head, how much he loved that. But I could see in her face that if I said a word, she was going to bolt, so I stayed quiet.

She shrugged. "Henry loves it when I play the cello in a way that is hard to explain. He stands there watching like I'm the only person in the world, listening, note by note, like each note matters to him. Because it does. And it's not just that he loves music, or that he loves me. It's this third thing, where those two things meet. It makes me feel . . . understood."

She paused.

"I understand everything about your father, but your father doesn't understand me the way Henry does. And I don't fault him for that. But it is an amazing thing to be with someone who really sees you."

She paused, and my heart started racing, trying to reconcile what she was saying with what my father said.

My mother sighed, looking down. "I see your father and I love who I see."

"But Henry sees you?"

She nodded, looking back up, meeting my eyes. "But Henry sees me."

She stood up and started getting dressed. Without further explanation. And I understood what my father didn't get about my mother. It wasn't about her fear of losing him. It was about her fear that she had lost herself. It was about what she had given up for him. Henry didn't just see my mother as she was. He saw the girl who was sitting in the yellow car, her cello the most important thing in the world to her. He saw who my mother would have been if she had told my father to get out of her car—the imagined life she would have led then.

Who could blame her for wanting a second chance at that? Suddenly, not me.

I stood up and walked up behind her, wrapping my arms around her.

"Mom, I just want you to be happy."

She nodded. "I am happy."

Though she was crying when she said it.

Falling Out of Sync

*D*esynchronization. Your fiancé lands his dream job on the other side of the world only to find out he has a daughter down the block, her mother still in love with him. Your mother is tired of doing too much work in her marriage at the exact moment someone returns to her life promising to do all the work instead.

Everything seemed to be lining up so the wrong people were together. So the right ones were apart.

In all my years growing up in Sonoma County, the drive over CA-116 had never felt so fast. In fifty minutes, I was in the Murray Grant waiting room, staring up at the pear. I'd planned on waiting for Jacob to walk out of his meeting, but Jacob wasn't going to walk out of any meeting. There was a note taped to his office door. AT THE FACTORY.

I got back into the car and hit the gas, moving fast toward the large Murray Grant Wines facility, where they bottled and shipped all their wines.

There was a security guard outside too busy watching ESPN to notice or stop me.

I stormed past him, opening the wooden door and entering the factory. It was angry and cold. A large conveyor belt was bottling the wine bottles. Cranes were pulling crates of wine toward the shipping area. I thought of my father bottling his wines by hand, waxing each shut.

On the second floor was a hallway with several large glass offices. Through the glass, I could see Jacob standing in one of them. No cozy white couches there.

He stood before a group of four men in expensive suits sitting around a conference table. Were they having a meeting about how they were turning Sebastopol into the new Napa Valley? Selling factory wine. Making them a lot of money to buy more small vineyards, turn them into something other than what they had been. Someone's home.

I ran up the stairs toward him and stormed into the office.

Jacob looked at me in the doorway, the men in the business suits staring.

I knew I was being crazy. I knew it even before Jacob's look of confusion and outright irritation confirmed it.

"Hey, Georgia. Could you give me a minute?"

"No."

He looked at me, then back at his meeting in progress.

"I need you to give me a minute, okay?" he said.

The security guard had made his way up the staircase. "Everything okay?"

Jacob tried to wave him off, trying to stay in control, to make it less of a scene. "We're fine, Caleb," he said.

Jacob turned toward the businessmen. "Would you guys excuse me?" he said. "I'll be back in one second."

Jacob quickly steered us out of the office, past Caleb, the security guard.

"You want me to escort your friend outside?" Caleb said.

"I'm doing that myself, Caleb," Jacob said, moving us down the stairs, keeping his voice low, now trying to control his temper, in addition to everything else.

Jacob slammed through the front door of the factory, leading us back out to the parking lot, toward his Honda.

"I can't believe you," he said.

He was moving so fast I was basically running to keep up with him.

"What makes you think you can just walk in here like that?" he said. "That was my board up there. Do you have any idea how embarrassing it was to have that meeting interrupted?"

"You need to sell me the vineyard, Jacob."

He stopped walking. "What?"

"I want to run it."

Jacob stared at me, dumbfounded. But as soon as the words were out of my mouth, I felt the weight of their truth. It was what I had been feeling from the minute I returned to Sebastopol. This was my family's home, and I didn't want to give it up. I didn't want to give up how I felt being back at the vineyard, despite everything that was going on with my parents and my brothers and Ben. I felt like myself here.

He shook his head, and started moving again, faster than before.

"You have no idea how to run a vineyard."

"My father will stay on and teach me. That's not your problem."

"Except you keep making it my problem when you show up demanding I do something I'm not going to do. My grandfather ran this company for fifty years. Do you have any idea how hard it is to get the board to take his grandson seriously? Even without crazy women interrupting my meetings?"

We got to his car and Jacob opened the trunk. It held several boxes of files. Jacob began searching through, reaching for a file.

"Look, I understand you're having an emotional reaction to the vineyard's sale, but . . ."

"Is that what I'm having? An *emotional* reaction?"

"What would you call it?"

Jacob grabbed the file out of the trunk. Then he grabbed another file. But Jacob seemed to still be searching—and it seemed like maybe he wasn't actually looking for anything, busying himself as an excuse, so he could get himself together.

"Thing you don't get is that you can't save your family like this. I know you think you can. It doesn't work that way."

"That isn't what's going on."

"It is or you would have waited downstairs like a normal human being."

His eyes cut in a way that surprised me. It felt both intimate and mean.

I felt my anger rise up. "Just let me buy the vineyard back. I'll give you interest for your trouble, higher than anything you'd have made in the bank."

He shook his head. "I made a deal with your father in good faith, and he wants to honor that deal. That doesn't make me a jerk. That makes me someone who isn't going to change plans because his daughter is panicking."

"Stop pretending this is about my father. It's about your business model telling you to take on his type of vineyard for reasons that have more to do with money than anything you're admitting out loud."

He shook his head, irritated. "Whatever."

"And we both know the worst part of that transaction. You're going to change his vineyard into a lesser version of itself. You're going to destroy it."

"We're not going to destroy . . ." Jacob paused, his face red. "Your father knows what he signed on for by selling to us."

"I'm just asking you to let me hold on to the vineyard until I can find someone to run it who will do it like he did." I got quiet. "You know, for when he realizes how much it still matters to him."

He stared at me, like he'd heard me on that. This was about my father and it was about me. It was about me feeling like I was the one person who understood what my father actually needed. And maybe also what the vineyard did. The vineyard needed to stay in our family. It was as much a member of it as the rest of us. It was the shining member that brought us together again, and reminded us it was the most important place to be.

Jacob met my eyes and paused. It seemed like he had heard me, like he saw me. And it seemed like he was going to do the right thing.

But then slowly, evenly, he shook his head. "Your father is welcome to stay on and help run the vineyard. He knows that we would love to have him. He knows that was our preference."

I stared at him in disbelief. "Wow, just when I thought you might understand. You're just a corporate asshole."

He laughed. "Name-calling. That's a good tactic."

"You have the cute office in Yountville, it's a good front, but this is where the dirty work gets done. The factory. The factory with your asshole board and your punch-the-clock workers. And everyone else who could care less about making good wine, who could care less about what my father has spent his entire life doing."

He put his hands up. "You know what? I'm done. I don't need to explain myself. I'm trying to do a good thing for this company. I'm using vineyards like your father's as models for more sustainable winemaking, for us to generate a better product. That's a rough road with these guys. It's an expensive road. Not that you give a shit, but you're making it a hell of a lot harder."

He turned back to his trunk, really angry now.

"You need to stay away from here. And me."

"Believe me, that's all I want."

"Really? So why do you keep showing up here, then?"

He started to close the trunk, which was when I noticed a duffel to the side of the files. His toothpaste and toothbrush on top. He followed my eyes and closed the trunk the rest of the way, slamming it shut.

"Is everything okay?" I asked.

He laughed. "Now you care?"

"Did you have a fight with Lee or something?"

"No, I just thought it would be a fun change of pace to sleep on an old mattress at the Yountville Inn."

He started walking toward the factory, picking up the pace, trying to get away from me. I struggled to keep up, Jacob looking up at the sky as he walked, as if that was the only way he could think of to avoid making eye contact.

"Look, I'm doing the best I can to take over this company. That's my priority and that's what I need to focus on now. As far as I can see, you and I have nothing to talk about anymore."

"So what? I should call your lawyer with any additional questions?"

"Just don't call me, okay?"

Then he looked up at the sky again.

"It's definitely going to rain," he said. "Your father needs to take those grapes off the vines now."

"That's what you have to say?"

He headed for the factory door, not turning back. "What do you want me to say? That's what matters."

No Secrets

I drove back to the house, the sun fading out as I wound down the driveway. The SUV was gone, taking the Wicked Witch of the West Coast with it. And taking her lovely daughter. I expected Ben to be gone too, but he wasn't. Ben was lying in my childhood bed, surrounded by papers and notecards. It took a second to realize they were the seating charts for our wedding.

"I didn't leave," he said.

I lay down next to him. "I noticed that. Why not?"

He touched the seating charts. "These charts needed completing."

He held out the charts for me to see—the big, beautiful charts that were hanging over us, one of the reasons that coming back for harvest had felt unreasonable. We had no idea where everyone was sitting, what they were eating when they got there.

I looked down in grateful disbelief. They were done. The charts were done. Everyone was in a seat. Everyone was next to someone that would make them happy.

"I've been working on them since you kicked me out. You can look through and see that they are pretty much perfect. I even put my uncle Merle downwind. You know, because of his halitosis."

"Ben, that's sweet of you . . ."

"I also called the caterer. And she can come up here tomorrow. Though I figured with the harvest party we should wait until the day after tomorrow. But we can get it done then. One day and the rest of the planning is done. And I'll take care of it. I hope you won't think this is unmanly, but I seem to have a knack for this wedding stuff."

I couldn't believe it. It was a small thing and yet it was the kindest thing he could have done—taking care of the charts, taking care of the caterer. So all that was left for me to consider was what it would feel like to walk down the aisle. Toward him. So that was something I could enjoy thinking about again, being in my dress again, moving toward our future.

"Here's the thing. We are good together. We belong together. And it's easy to look at Michelle and decide she means more than she does, but it's also easy to look away from Michelle. For me, it is. That's what I'm trying to say. I love you. And that is my choice."

He was looking at me, his eyes unshielded, his heart open.

"And I know you think it's out of some loyalty, but it has nothing to do with loyalty. It's about love." He smiled. "From the second we met, I knew that nothing could pull us apart."

I tried fighting what popped into my head—except, perhaps, the mother of your child.

He held up the seating charts, his form of truth. "And what I want more than anything is to walk down the aisle in your favorite place in the world and get through this together. That is what I'm going to do for you if you let me do it. I'm going to keep us strong."

Ben always got there a minute before I did. This time was no exception. I could forgive him or not. We could move forward or not. But if I stayed with him, he would make me happy I stayed. He would spend his life making me happy.

And then he proved it.

"What if we stayed here after the wedding?" he said.

"What are you talking about?"

"What if we stayed in Sebastopol? We could stay and figure out the vineyard together. We could figure out a solution so that your family wasn't just giving everything away that they've worked so hard for."

"What about London?"

"We don't have to be there immediately. London can wait."

"You'll help me fight? To get the vineyard back?"

He nodded, serious. "I'll help you fight to get the vineyard back," he said. "We'll find a winemaker to take it over, one who does things your father's way. We won't let him give this place to Jacob, just because your father is struggling. Just because he stopped believing in this place."

Ben moved toward me slowly, pulling my hair back from my face, smiling. "I don't deserve a second chance, but sometimes when someone doesn't, that's exactly when you need to give them one."

I thought of all the second chances around here that weren't being handed out. Between my brothers. Between my mother and father. I thought about how much happier they would be if they could hand them to each other. To themselves.

"No more secrets?" I said.

"No more secrets," he said.

Like that, I forgave him.

Part 3

The Union

An Invitation

My father once said watching wine age was like listening to music. He said it was the strangest mix of music and chemistry, in which you listened to every note to know what the grapes needed: when they should come off the vines, how long they should be given to ferment into the wine they wanted to be, how the wine should be racked, transferred, blended.

Racking and blending were the primary ways my father interacted with the grapes once they were off the vine. Racking involved transferring wine from one container to another, to get rid of the sediment that might have settled, to allow the wine to aerate better. Then, after the wine was racked, came the blending. My father blended different clones, one or several, depending on what the wine needed. The initial barrel wines were more like spices in a stew. The final product was the joining of the different clones, the making of the stew. That was the job. Like you were a chef. You had to see what belonged together.

As I got older, my father would take me with him to taste the newly blended wines—to help put the final touches on what he'd created. He'd share that first taste with me, trusting me to tell him that it was ready. It felt impossible that he was never going to do that again—that we, together, were never going to do that again. It felt impossible that someone else was going to finish the wine that he'd taken so much pride in starting.

~

The morning of the harvest party, the sky was clear and stunning. The type of California sunshine that made you believe again was shining down. We had a tradition in our house of spending that morning out in the vineyard. The vineyard was mostly stripped at that point, except for Block 14.

My father tried to time the harvest party to when Block 14 needed to come off the vines. We picked them as a family, staying up all night after the harvest party, picking the grapes before the sun came up.

And, every year, the morning of the harvest party, we would check on the grapes together. Even when we were little, my father would bring us to check on those grapes and make a group decision as to whether they needed longer. All of us peeking at my father's spreadsheet, the weather conditions, the grapes themselves. Do they leave the vines today? Do they stay on longer?

But when I looked out the window, no one was in Block 14. The grapes swayed quietly, so rich and ripe on the vines.

Ben wrapped his arms tighter around me. I could feel his newfound appreciation that we were on the other side of it, his mistake, my reaction.

"Good morning," he said.

He looked so happy. And I remembered the joy I felt at making him that way.

He smiled and looked out the window, to see what I saw. Block 14, empty. Then he turned back to me, trying to make it better.

"What do you say that we go into town? Get me some of those pancakes Maddie can't stop talking about?"

I smiled in agreement as Ben leaned in closer, kissing me. As he did, his phone rang. He ignored it, but I could feel his body tense.

I pulled away from him. "Michelle?" I said.

Ben turned to his phone, checking the ID and quickly silencing it. "Yeah . . ." he said.

"Are they back in London?"

"Not exactly. They stayed in San Francisco last night," he said.

He paused as that registered.

"Maddie wants to come to the harvest party tonight."

I looked at him, confused. "She does?"

"I can tell her it's not a good idea."

I jumped right in. "I don't want you to. If Maddie wants to be there, I want her there."

Ben nodded, appreciative. "That's very sweet. But I'm just not sure how we would handle Michelle."

"What do you mean?"

"I think she wants to be there too."

I wasn't sure how to respond to that. "What? Why?"

"Michelle is a very good mom, despite her other faults. And I think she wants Maddie to know we all get along. I can tell her no, but I just . . . I don't want to alienate Maddie by alienating her mother. If that makes sense?"

It did. I nodded, getting that, and trying to process what to do. "So let's invite her too," I said.

"What?"

"You should invite Michelle."

"To the harvest party?"

Ben looked like that was the last thing he wanted to do, the scene in the kitchen flashing before his eyes. Why would he set himself up for another terrible encounter?

I moved closer, trying to figure out how to explain how important it felt to rectify our awkward first meetings, to begin to all move forward. Michelle was going to have as much power as I handed her, and I was done handing her any.

Ben shook his head. "I don't think that's a good idea."

"If we're going to make this work, we need to make things right. We need to all be on the same page."

"Michelle is on her own page." Ben took a breath in, as if he didn't know how to explain it, as if he didn't want to explain it. "Isn't tonight going to be hard enough? I don't want spending time with Michelle to be another hard thing."

"Maybe this is one thing that doesn't have to be," I said. "Let's just decide that."

He looked skeptical, but he nodded. "Okay, then. Whatever you want is okay."

I smiled. "Good."

He smiled. "Good. I'll call her now."

Then he moved closer, kissing my neck, wrapping his arms around my waist.

"Well, not right now."

People Who Screw Up

*B*obby stood by the kitchen table. He was drinking the green drink he had most mornings, the green color that made it hard for me to look at, let alone ingest.

Bobby was in his suit already, the newspaper open in front of him—the only indications of the fight the cut by his lip, his bruised hand.

Even though he heard me walk in, he didn't look up. He sat down, turning the page of the newspaper.

"Beautiful day for a harvest party," he said.

I took a seat beside him. "It is."

He turned to the back of the first section, reading the sports rundown. "Dad was just here," he said. "He wants to wait on Block 14. Have the family pick them together after the harvest party, like usual."

He motioned toward his green drink. "You want some?" he said.

It was an offer on the other side of what he wasn't giving away: any information on how he was feeling. It was the last thing I wanted, but I took a sip of the thick mess of it so he would feel like I was on his side.

He smiled. "Pretty good, right?"

I motioned toward his suit. "Where are you going?"

He took the drink back, gulped down the green. "I've got to go into the city for a work thing," he said. "I have a lunch, but I'll be back in time for the harvest party. Don't worry."

Bobby started gathering his things.

"I'm already running late," he said, standing up. "I should go."

"Can I at least drive you there?"

"Didn't I just say I was late? If you drive, who knows when we'll get there."

I started to argue, then I remembered the last time I had attempted to drive one of my brothers somewhere.

He reached for his briefcase. "Just say it already."

"Say what?"

"Say whatever you think you need to say to convince me that Finn didn't mean any of this. That neither of them did."

I looked up at him, feeling the weight of his stare. He didn't want me to try to make things okay between them. He didn't want things to be okay between them.

"Where is she?"

He reached for his thermos, poured the rest of his juice inside. "She's taking the twins to see a friend of ours in Healdsburg."

"She's missing the harvest party?"

"No, they're coming back tonight, but I can't handle her being in the house today more than she has to be. I thought it was a good idea for us to have a little space."

"What does Margaret think?" I said.

"What does it matter what she thinks?"

"You need to talk to her, Bobby. Shutting her out isn't going to do what you think it's going to do. Margaret would never do anything to hurt you."

"Do you think that makes this better or worse?" He shook his head. "I knew that things weren't great between us. I'm not an idiot. But knowing things aren't great and finding out your wife is in love with your brother? Those are two different things."

"That isn't what this is about, Bobby," I said.

"You sure about that?"

He paused, biting his thumbnail. Bruised hand meeting bruised mouth.

"Do you know she's been talking about having another kid? Why would she talk about having another kid if she was feeling as badly as this? Maybe she thought that would fill it, what she was missing with me . . ."

"I think that you and Margaret need to sit down and deal with this."

He drilled me with a look. "I think you should have told me. That's what I think."

"Bobby, I didn't know."

"I'm not talking about Margaret. I'm talking about Ben. He has a kid?"

I nodded, unsure how to read my brother's expression. "Does that make you hate him?"

He shook his head, surprising me. "No, not at all. It makes me sad for him."

He started walking toward the door. Then he turned back.

"People screw up, you know. You shouldn't hold it against them. You shouldn't expect everyone to know everything you're thinking about or not getting from them. It doesn't mean they don't love you. They screw up."

I nodded, even though Bobby wasn't talking about Ben—the kindest thing I could do for him was pretend that he was. I realized that was what was so hard for him. Bobby wanted to be the one who never screwed up, who we all looked up to, Margaret especially. He confused that with love. He confused how she saw him with how she needed him to see her.

Bobby sat back down. "I don't want your sympathy," he said.

"You don't have it," I said.

Then I took his hand.

High Yields

After Bobby left for San Francisco—for work, for a Margaret-and Finn-free day—I headed into Santa Rosa. I drove to the courthouse in the center of Santa Rosa—a small courthouse where the biggest business was traffic tickets. I had two enormous files in my hand, files I had found online that backed up my case. The case I was about to make to someone behind the small courthouse desk.

As it turned out, I knew the person I was making the case to. Kirby, from high school, was standing behind the desk.

Kirby Queen—Brian Queen's daughter. We hadn't known each other that well in high school despite our fathers' desire for us to be friends. She had been the captain of the volleyball team. She looked ready to go to the gym now, standing there in a pantsuit that looked more like a jumpsuit, looking bored.

She perked up slightly when she saw me standing before her, but only slightly. Whatever she remembered about me from high school, it wasn't really about me but about Bobby. The one meaningful interaction we'd ever had was when she'd confessed that she had a crush on him.

"Look what fell off the vine!" she said. "What brings you to Sonoma County?"

"Hi, Kirby."

"I heard you were getting married, or maybe *heard* is the wrong word. I read you walked into town in your wedding dress. If it had been your wedding day that would have been news, but when everyone found out there was no wedding, it hit the Twitter feed."

I felt my skin getting hot. "That's embarrassing."

"Sure is."

I opened the files on Kirby's desk. A legal case from the 1800s stared back at Kirby, *Philbert v. Philbert*, a small family case in which the grown children weren't informed of a property's sale. In that case, it had been a horse farm. Since their trust was linked with the land, the grown children had contested the horse farm's sale, contending that they were losing out on future earnings.

My law firm had used this case once while representing a greedy billionaire whose father had built shopping malls all over Los Angeles. He was planning on selling one for one hundred million and the son was trying to stop him. Now I was using the case for something else.

"What can I do you for?" she said. "Because I'm not reading any of this."

"I'm filing an injunction to stop the sale of my father's vineyard."

"Your father is selling his vineyard?" She looked shocked. "My father didn't mention it."

"Yep, to Murray Grant Wines."

"Whoa. No way! Those corporate scumbags?"

I nodded, happy that Kirby was stuck on that, my desire to go up against a major corporation, and not the illegitimacy of what I wanted to do.

"Their grandson, the one who is taking over Murray Grant Wines, he sucks. He's a major asshole."

"You've met him?"

"No, I read about him. On Twitter. Give me your filing."

She grabbed the appropriate paperwork, smiling, happy to be in the know about this. That was fine as long as she was willing to do her job here and get the lawsuit going. The reason corporations often won lawsuits was that they out-lawyered the small guy. Maybe I didn't have a leg to stand on, but I had the manpower to see this thing through. And I was going to use it.

Kirby shrugged, apologetically. "You're not going to be able to see the judge until next week. And it's probably going to be Judge Riley, once he comes back from his fishing trip. He's gonna be in a bad mood too, irritated he's at work again."

I nodded, knowing I'd lose in front of pretty much any judge. But that didn't matter. What mattered was getting him to hear my argument for why my father couldn't sell the vineyard without approval, to create work for Jacob's lawyer, to create trepidation for Jacob's board about getting involved. Why would they want to get involved with a small vineyard that was making waves? They could find another small winery with a good reputation. The upside wasn't worth it.

I looked at Kirby, hoping she'd help with the second part of the plan, knowing it was critical that she did.

She smiled, thrilled to be on the inside of this secret. "I, of course, won't tell anyone in the meantime," she said.

"Thank you."

She nodded seriously. "Of course. I would never."

Which proved that the second she was on her own again, she would.

~

I felt pretty pleased with myself as I walked out of the courthouse.

Then the phone rang.

It was someone else I'd gone to high school with. Ethan Tropper. Ethan Tropper, who had once convinced Finn it was a good idea for them to break into my father's liquor cabinet, while Bobby stood guard in the hallway, replacing all the bourbon with Dr Pepper. Ethan Tropper: former juvenile delinquent, current deputy sheriff of Sebastopol.

"This is Deputy Sheriff Ethan Tropper. I've got someone here who wants you to come and get him," he said.

This was what he said instead of *hello*.

"Finn?" I said.

"Finn," he said.

"I'm five minutes away."

"Congratulations," he said.

Then he hung up.

The Starkville City Jail

I didn't have much choice here," Ethan said, leading me down the hall toward the small jail cell where Finn had spent the night drying out, Ethan not officially booking him, but not letting him roam the streets either.

"These last couple of months, it's been a lot. Disorderly conduct, drunk driving, sleeping in his car."

"Seriously? That isn't a crime."

Ethan nodded. "It is here," he said.

I didn't like thinking of what it had been like for Finn since Margaret had told him how she felt about him, Margaret both closer to him than ever, and further away, Bobby unavailable for consolation. It just about broke my heart to picture him sitting in jail, Ethan Tropper the only one who was available to talk to him.

"Last night was the last straw, especially after the fire hydrant incident."

"What did you just say?"

"The fire hydrant incident. Finn rammed his truck into a fire hydrant. Finn destroyed public property."

"What makes you think it was him?"

"I don't think. I know. I was able to decipher the marks left on the fire hydrant and match them to the chipped paint on Finn's truck."

Tropper looked amazingly proud of himself for this great detective work, or for rehashing what he had seen on *CSI: Miami*.

I raised my hand, unwilling to let my brother take the hit, at least for that. "That's on me, Ethan. I was driving the truck."

Tropper cocked his head. "That was you? You hit and ran?"

Then Ethan reached in his pocket, and for a second, I thought he was going to take out his handcuffs. He took out a key instead.

Ethan opened the jail cell door, a tiny room with a toilet and a mattress and a pine tree air freshener.

Finn rose up from the twin mattress, Ethan jokingly knocking on the jailhouse bars.

"You decent?" Ethan said.

"Decent enough," Finn said, smiling. He was slightly disheveled, but I'd never have guessed that he'd spent the night in jail if that hadn't been where he was standing. Smelling of trees.

Ethan walked out of the cell, locking the door behind himself, the click deafening. "Give me a few minutes to sneak you past Sheriff Elliot. And summon your sister here for her hit-and-run altercation from the other night."

I drilled Ethan with a look. "It was a fire hydrant, Ethan, not a person."

Ethan got in my face. "What it is, my lady, is unacceptable."

Then Finn stepped forward, putting his hand on Ethan's shoulder. "Let's just calm down here, okay? You need to ignore her. She wasn't even in the truck. She's just trying to help me out."

"Is that true?"

Finn gave me a threatening look. "Tell him, Georgia," he said.

"I guess," I said, convincing no one.

"Come on, Ethan. Think about it. You think I'd let her drive my truck?"

Ethan looked back and forth between us, trying to decide if that was something he was willing to accept, which was when his walkie-talkie went off, Ethan picking it up.

"We're not done here," he said, pointing to me. Then he turned to Finn. "But I will deal with Elliot for you, Finn."

Finn smiled. "Thanks, Ethan. I appreciate it."

Ethan smiled back, no one immune to Finn's charms, female or male. "No problem, pal," he said, heading out, giving me a look as he went.

Finn looked at me. "Way to narc on yourself."

"I didn't want to leave you in the cold."

"I've got Ethan covered."

I looked around the jail. "Obviously."

Finn shrugged. "Yeah . . ."

We hadn't spoken since our blowout and he looked uncomfortable. He was embarrassed about our fight, this stint in the city jail, apparently one of many stints. But what was there for him to say? The Ford children didn't apologize to one another. We did what my mother had told us to do as children. We held out a hand and the other sibling had to take it. Everyone willing to move on.

This was what he did. He reached out his hand and took mine as he sat back down.

"My hands are a little clammy," he said. "I haven't washed them for twelve hours."

"You really do suck at apologizing," I said.

He smiled. "Thanks for coming to get me," he said.

"You okay?"

"Yep. It's no big deal. Just needed to dry out."

"Ethan says you guys have a standing date, like a weekly poker game. Without the poker."

He shrugged. "Ethan likes my company."

I shook my head. "Finn . . ."

"You want to start, Miss Hit-and-Run?"

He shook his head, getting serious all of a sudden. And looking older than he was.

"I know. It's going to stop. I'm stopping it."

"How?"

"However I can," he said.

Then he nodded, like he was resolved. Resolved and exhausted—done with his own nonsense, done with how he was feeling.

He looked down at his fingers, shaking his head. "Maybe it was sleeping here last night, but I keep thinking about the night before they got married. That wedding we crashed together. Do you remember?"

"Your first arrest?"

"Very funny." He looked up and sighed. "Do you know what I was thinking the whole time? Maybe they won't be able to get me out of here in time for the wedding. That I would miss Margaret and Bobby getting married."

"And that made you happy?"

"It made me sad, actually. What do you think that means?"

"That you love your brother."

He smiled. ". . . And don't say that you love your brother."

I paused, trying to think of what to tell him, sitting in this depressing jail cell. Finn needed to figure out how to be somewhere else, both of us needed to be somewhere other than where we'd been.

"I was out of line," he said. "What I said about Ben. Sometimes it takes people a minute to figure it out."

I smiled, grateful and relieved to hear him say that.

"But, the thing is, you just used to be so fearless when we were growing up. Fearless and fucking happy. I don't know. I want you to be happy like that."

I smiled. "I was happy, wasn't I? What happened?"

"Adulthood. Ambition. Compromise."

I laughed. "All things you have managed to avoid."

He shrugged as a smile crept up. "I hear there is a famous movie star in town. Someone by the name of Michelle Carter?"

"How did you hear that?"

"I've been in jail, not . . . in jail."

I smiled.

"Ethan's been giving me hourly reports. Michelle spotted at the ice cream shop. Michelle spotted at The Tasting Room. Michelle spotted on Main Street and Fifth Street and at the Sebastopol Inn." He paused. "What is she doing here?"

"We invited her to the harvest party."

"Why?"

"I'm making an effort with Ben. And that means making one with Michelle."

"Can I be the one to make an effort with Michelle?"

"Come on, she's not that pretty."

"Yes. She's that pretty. She's prettier." He paused. "Since she's com-ing, maybe you can set me up with her," he said. "With Michelle. That would fix everything in terms of Margaret."

"You think?"

"No," he said, but he smiled while he said it.

Then he paused, looked at me seriously.

"I need you to tell me I'm not completely fucked," he said.

"You're not even close."

Finn stood up, motioning around the jail cell. "Let's be honest. I'm close."

The Wine Cave

We got back to the house and Finn went inside to take a shower. I went down toward the vineyard and found my parents in the wine cave, walking along the aged barrels. They were working through the wines that they were going to serve that night, choosing from among the wines that had just finished fermenting. They were standing there together, working side by side, like they had been standing there eighteen months ago when those wines had begun the work they were getting ready to finish. My mother never gave herself credit for everything she did for the wine. It was the reason that she didn't seem to see it now—how much she loved it.

I watched them for a minute before moving closer. My mother leaned into my father. They looked happy together.

My mother looked up. "Hey," she said. "Where have you been all morning?"

I didn't know if the better answer was stealing their vineyard back for them or bailing their son out of jail.

I looked back and forth between them, bracing myself for their wrath. "I was actually down at the courthouse."

"The courthouse?" My mother perked up. "Getting your marriage license?"

"I filed an injunction," I said.

My mother tilted her head and gave me a look. "For what?"

"The vineyard. To stop the sale of the vineyard."

My father laughed. "That's not going to work."

I plowed onward. "Ben and I can't match what Murray Grant is paying you for the vineyard, but we can come close if you take a share of the money in percentage of future earnings. And either way, we will figure out a way to make you whole."

They shared a look with each other, my father crossing his arms over his chest. "So what's the plan?" he said. "You're just going to give up your job?"

"No. My firm has a San Francisco office."

My mother laughed. "Oh, so you're going to be a lawyer and run the vineyard?"

My father shook his head. "You and Ben don't want this place. You think I want this place."

"I love it here, Dad."

"Enough to give up everything you've worked for? Your marriage and the firm . . ."

"The vineyard isn't getting in the way of any of that."

He looked at me seriously. "Then you have no idea what the vineyard is," he said.

My father turned back to his barrels, done talking. My mother looked away.

I left the wine cave and headed up the hill, toward the house, quickly. I knew they were angry, but I was angry too. It left me thinking of my mother's words. *Be careful what you give up. You get it back however you can.* I was floored and scared by everything my father seemed to be giving up here. And maybe it wasn't my job to convince him that he was making a mistake—maybe I shouldn't have even been trying—though I wasn't just scared for him. I was scared how untethered I felt, thinking about losing the vineyard. As if for the first time, in a very long time, I was able to see how very much it mattered to me.

I looked down the hill, toward the wine cave. My mother was walking through the doorway, my father hoisting a case of wine over his shoulder, following her. I wanted to call out to them, but they were too far away to hear anything, let alone what I didn't know how to say.

Sebastopol, California. 2004

*I*t was the night before their child's wedding. It should have been a happy time, but Dan was worried about the wedding. He was worried about Bobby choosing Margaret. Dan loved Margaret and thought she'd be great for Bobby. That wasn't the problem. The problem was that he wasn't certain that Bobby thought Margaret would be great for Bobby. After Margaret lost the pregnancy, Bobby had expressed doubts to Dan as much as Bobby ever expressed things. He was young. And now that they weren't going to have the kid, what was the rush? Dan had asked him the simple question. *Why not wait, then?*

Bobby told him the truth. *Because I won't do it then and I think I should.*

Wasn't that the worst reason to do anything?

Dan drove into town to the brewery to see his kids, his daughter home from law school. She was like Bobby in this way. She thought she was supposed to take a certain path. She thought she should be in law school and, he knew, part of her wanted to be there, learning about torts. Tax law. She seemed happy, or she had convinced herself she was happy. That was often the same thing. Who was he to interfere?

When he got home, Jen was sitting on the front steps, making place cards for the reception: so everyone would know where they were sitting at the long farm table, lit by candles and lanterns, shining grape leaves.

She motioned toward Finn's room. "The bride is sleeping upstairs," Jen said.

"Margaret? Why?"

She shrugged. "Something about being here to help tomorrow. I sent her to Finn's room so she wouldn't see Bobby. Is that supposed to be bad luck? It's silly for me to think of that. But I do."

"Finn and Bobby are sleeping at Finn's place anyway, if they even leave The Brothers' Tavern. They were all drinking pretty heavily when I left them, your daughter included."

"That's comforting."

"Finn was in a mood. He was going on and on about how the barrel room looks ridiculous, but if worst comes to worst around here, we could rent it out for weddings. Call it the Great Barrel Room and charge fifty thousand to rent it for a week."

He walked up the stairs.

Jen smiled. "That's not a bad idea," she said.

He took a seat next to his wife. "I'm worried about them."

"All of them?"

"Yep."

"But I'm the one that worries. You're the one that says it's going to be okay."

"I thought we got to stop thinking about them so much, but this moment feels more important than even when they were young. They are becoming themselves."

She put more of the place cards in a stack.

"Your sons are good men. You raised them to take care of each other, and your daughter is getting where she wants to go."

He looked at her. "Are you finding it hard to talk to her?"

She shrugged. "She just likes saying *torts*. It'll pass."

He shook his head. "Bobby doesn't want to get married."

She took her husband's hands. "That will pass too."

He leaned in toward his wife and said it, what he'd never admitted before, even to himself.

"It makes me sad that none of them want the vineyard."

She looked up. "We raised them to want their own things."

He nodded. "I know, but . . ." He shook his head. "It's silly. I'm being silly. I'm glad that they're doing what they're doing. I'm glad for each of them. I'm just feeling nostalgic."

"I bet that you are," she said, but she moved closer to him.

"I was the one who discouraged her from staying here. I told her to go explore new worlds."

"And?"

"She seems like she isn't happy with the one she chose, not the way I've seen her happy."

"Then she'll find her way home."

They heard loud music coming from the guest bedroom, punk rock, blasting downward.

"What's wrong with Margaret tonight?"

"Bride's nerves?"

He looked up, deciding whether to throw a rock at the window or just run upstairs and ask his future daughter-in-law if she was going crazy too.

"I'm taking you somewhere," she said.

She took him down the vineyard, to Block 14, the small opening there, where she had a blanket and a bottle of wine and a small radio. They couldn't hear the music from here. They couldn't see anything but each other. Dan started kissing her, soft at first then harder, pulling up her dress from behind. She gripped his waist, his hip, bearing against him as he pushed himself into her. His hand holding her stomach.

He pushed her curls off her face. "Can this be the first time we're doing this?"

It was the first. It wasn't the last.

Have-to-Have

When I arrived at the house, the driveway was full of trucks, catering trucks and a florist truck, a van from a furniture company called Moving Up. The staff was in motion, setting up for the evening. They moved through the house and over the lawn, carrying candles and lanterns and flowers, lemons and grape leaves in glass vases, sofas on their backs.

"Hey there."

I looked up to see Suzannah standing behind me, in the middle of the driveway, wearing a long blouse like a dress, short booties. Eight months pregnant and gorgeous. Like she belonged there.

"I've arrived," she said.

She held out her arms to hug me, and I jumped in, so happy to see her it was crazy.

"What are you doing here?"

"What do you mean, *what am I doing here?* What do you think I'm doing here? I'm pawning off my work."

She squeezed me hard, then she let go.

"Um. How did you leave out that Michelle Carter was the baby mama? That is the craziest part of this whole thing."

"What does it change?"

"How I'm going to tell this story to everyone else." Her eyes went wide. "Is it true that she does a honey cleanse every January and the rest of the year lives on French fries and burgers?"

"Where did you hear that?"

"I read it somewhere. That's not the point."

"What is?"

"Can you find out how she does it exactly? I love French fries and burgers."

I tilted my head, looking at her. "Did you really drive all the way up here?"

"No. I flew and rented a car. For eight hundred dollars."

"That is crazy."

"For you, since you're insisting on paying me back."

I smiled. "You are amazing."

She rolled her eyes. "Can we avoid going over the obvious? There is a time crunch. I have fifty minutes until I have to catch a flight back to Los Angeles."

"You don't want to stay for the harvest party?"

She cradled her stomach. "Sweetie, if I can't drink, it may as well be the dentist."

~

Suzannah and I walked through the vineyard. "So let's start with what matters, okay?"

I nodded.

"What on earth are you wearing and why are you wearing it?"

I looked down at the jean shorts and peasant top I'd found in my closest, my hair in two loose buns. "This is how we dress in Sonoma County. It's casual."

She pointed at her own dress. "No, this is casual," she said. "That is circa 1971. Pull it together!"

I smiled. "Working on it."

"Good, because I have some advice for you, and it isn't easy."

"Okay."

"I know I said you should marry Ben, but I thought about it and you shouldn't marry Ben. You're doing the right thing walking away."

"What are you talking about?"

She linked her arm through mine. "I'm talking about how Charles cheated on me in high school. I'm talking about how that was its own form of betrayal I had to get over."

"But that was your evidence for why I should stay with Ben."

"I know, which is my point. I could forgive Charles because I knew I never would have to compete for him, not really." She shook her head. "I knew he really believes, as ridiculous as it is, that I'm the most beautiful woman in the world. That I'm his *have-to-have*."

She paused.

"I don't think Ben is yours."

That stopped me. "Why not?"

She squeezed my arm tighter. "I always thought Ben got you, that you guys got each other. That's why I've given him so much latitude with all of this, but . . I think if you came to that same conclusion, you'd know that you want to stay with Ben."

"I do."

"What do you mean you do?" she said.

"We're working things out."

She stopped walking. "What are you talking about, working things out?"

I shrugged, thinking about how to explain it to her, which was when she got there.

"He's your *have-to-have*?" she said.

I smiled, thinking about how I trusted that he was again. I was letting go enough to do it, to try to be happy.

"So you're all good?" she said.

"Well, apparently I'm throwing out these shorts, but yes."

"Good," she said. "That's good.

She looked in the direction of her rental car, realizing something else. "I got on a plane and drove from San Francisco for nothing? You're going to have to do a better job of keeping me posted."

The Harvest Party

It made me happy and sad at once, looking down over the party. From the upstairs bathroom, I could see people arriving, the bluegrass band playing them in. The tent was lit up with lanterns, tables inside lined with pizza and wine, gourmet pizza but pizza all the same—a tribute to the early harvest parties when that was all my parents could afford to serve. Tonight felt glamorous under the lanterns. Everyone was happy and excited to celebrate another harvest. My father's last harvest. It looked, I imagined, how my wedding might.

Ben had left a note on the mirror, fogged into the glass. COME DOWN SOON.

I touched it with my hand. Then I checked out my reflection, smoothing down my purple dress, my hair pulled back off my face in a low ponytail. After the chaos of the last few days, I was surprised to find that it hadn't taken me down. Maybe it was the break from the ninety-hour work weeks, but there was no denying it. I looked relaxed and happy.

I heard a soft knock and looked up to find my father standing in the bathroom doorway, looking handsome in his white button-down shirt and dark pants, holding out a sprig of lavender, like a bouquet.

"Here you go."

I smiled. "That's for me?"

He handed over the flower. "That's for you," he said. "If you'll escort me downstairs."

"I'd love that, but I should be asking you. How're you doing?"

He put his arm in mine. "Better now."

We headed downstairs and out onto the patio.

My father leaned in toward me as we headed into the tent. "A few days from now, I'll be walking you into a different party here."

My heart skipped a beat. "I guess you will."

A waiter walked by and handed us each a glass of sparkling wine from his tray, the only sparkling wine my father would be serving tonight. It was from Louise and Gary's small vineyard: a rosy, yummy mess of a California sparkling wine. Drier than it was sweet.

My father took one for me, one for himself, raising his glass in a toast.

"Thank you for trying to enjoin me. In an odd way, it's the nicest thing anyone has done for me in a while."

"You yelled at me, though."

He tiled his glass, smiling. "Well. It's also the meanest."

But before he could clink our glasses, I saw my mother walking on the patio, Henry by her side. He wore a suit, looking—as much as I hated to admit it—somewhat dapper. My mother, meanwhile, looked beautiful in a long, yellow dress. She also looked overwhelmed—perhaps by having Henry by her side, perhaps by the party itself, which was especially big this year. Perhaps by looking for my father, who maybe wasn't as okay with Henry being here as he might have suggested.

Then before my father could spot them, Gary and Louise walked up, Brian Queen behind them, and the three of them swept my father into the party. The beautiful party: tea lights and brown lanterns and flowers in jelly jars as far as the eye could see.

"I'll be right back," my father mouthed. "Is that okay?"

But he was already gone.

I closed my eyes, grateful for the opportunity to stay close to the tent's entrance, no one inside feeling like someone I wanted to talk to: not Henry and my mother, not Margaret and Bobby standing next to each other by the bar, looking miserable. Margaret was in a white dress, Bobby was in his designer suit—a twin in each of their arms, like blockers. Bobby was talking to Nick Braeburn—my father's California distributor—Margaret forcing a smile, looking down.

Then I saw them holed up at the far end of one of the farm tables, a box of crayons between them, large sheets of paper. Michelle and Maddie, coloring, Ben bending down beside them. It shocked me to see him with them. Even though I had wanted Michelle to come—to make a peace offering—it was different seeing her there with Ben. The two people who had made Maddie. Actually looking at them, together, it was a conversation I wasn't ready for. Especially when I saw who was standing by them, blocking people from getting too near to them. Deputy Sheriff Ethan Tropper, in a pinstripe suit.

I turned quickly and ran, champagne first, into Jacob. He jumped back, the champagne spilling all over him.

"Hello to you too," he said. He wasn't wearing a sweater vest, but a sports coat and jeans, looking handsome, Lee by his side. She was wearing a slinky shirt, and one of those rings that was also a bracelet. A chain running the length of her hand, from her finger to her wrist, looking sexy.

Jacob used one hand to dry the champagne off his shirt, keeping the other hand wrapped around Lee's waist.

"You could've just asked if I wanted a drink," he said.

I was focused on Lee. She put her hand to her face, the chain shiny against her cheek.

"I know you," she said. "How do I know you?" Her eyes got wide, making the connection. "We met yesterday at the Violet Café, didn't we?"

Jacob looked back and forth between us. "You did?"

Lee nodded. "Yes. We met and I met her stepdaughter. Pancake girl, yes?" She pointed at Jacob with that chain. "You guys know each other?" she said.

"We don't really," I said.

Jacob shot me a look. "Georgia is Dan and Jen's daughter."

"Oh . . ." Lee said, confused. And I could see her mind going. Hadn't she mentioned Jacob yesterday?

I gave her a smile. "I didn't make the connection that you were Jacob's fiancé."

She smiled back, but there was an edge to it, as if she didn't believe me. Which was fair—I had known who she was, I just hadn't wanted to. "Well, you made it now," Lee said.

Jacob took Lee's hand, looking increasingly uncomfortable. "Lee and I are going to grab a drink," Jacob said. "But I'm sure we'll catch up with you later. Or during the announcement."

"No," Lee said, her voice a little forceful.

Jacob looked at her, confused. "Why not?"

"I'll get us a drink," she said. "You guys catch up."

Jacob forced a smile, but Lee was already walking away from him. She was all legs and thin arms, glittering chain—a woman that you'd let leave you at the altar and then try to make things work with anyway.

Jacob turned to me. He turned to me and I could see him trying to decide what he wanted to yell about first.

"You filed an injunction against me?" he said. "You couldn't be a bigger pain in my ass."

"You weren't giving me much of a choice, were you?"

He shook his head. "You're making things difficult for your father here. No judge in his right mind is going to consider your case. You know that, right?"

I nodded, but a ruling wasn't what I was after. If the board disliked the headache of a lawsuit enough, they would stop Jacob from moving forward. Jacob knew that, which was why it was confusing, the grin he was wearing.

"Why are you smiling like that?"

He shrugged. "I appreciate your desire," he said. "Misplaced as it may be. I appreciate what you want to do for your family. Plus, you're kind of glad that I came tonight, which is nice to see. Especially after what a dick I was. Sorry about that."

"Really?"

"I'm a little sorry," he said. He paused. "Were you spying on my girlfriend?"

"No. I like her. She's lovely."

"That's not an answer. You were spying on my girlfriend. Why?"

"I don't really know. Can we leave it at that?"

Jacob looked at me, really looked at me. "Okay," he said.

Then he motioned to Michelle, the beautiful Michelle Carter. Ethan Tropper stood guard near her. Everyone was watching her every move and pretending they weren't. The Sebastopol housewives whispered to one another as they checked out her shoes, her skin, her legs. A group of teenage boys walked back and forth past the table, trying to get up the nerve to ask her for an autograph, or maybe just to touch her hair and run away. Who could blame them? She was mesmerizing.

"I didn't expect to see her here," Jacob said.

"Please don't say how pretty she is."

"How about sexy?"

He smiled and so did I. I couldn't help it.

"You decided that the way to go was to be a happy family?"

"I did."

"I didn't think you were going to do that." He nodded approvingly. "That's brave."

Jacob looked back at Ben and Michelle, and I followed his eyes as Ben hugged their daughter, Michelle standing close by, smiling at him. They looked like they belonged together.

Jacob leaned in toward me. He leaned in closer, pushing my hair out of the way, holding the back of my neck.

"What if I told you that Michelle Carter has nothing on you?" Jacob whispered.

I leaned in closer to him. "I'd say you're also the guy who predicted a rainstorm."

~

When I arrived at the corner table, they were laughing. Maddie was working ferociously on her coloring book—on a large drawing of a purple Cookie Monster—Ben and Michelle watching her, joining in.

Ben looked up and saw me before Michelle or Maddie did. Then he made room for me beside himself.

"Pull up a crayon!" Ben said.

"No!" Michelle patted the seat beside her. "Come sit here."

I forced a smile. "Great."

Michelle forced a smile too. I sat down beside her.

"Benjamin," Michelle said. "Shoo. Give us some girl time."

Ben looked at me nervously, but I nodded that it was okay. He smiled, patted Maddie's head. "I'm going to get this one a juice. Would you like something?"

I wasn't sure whom he was addressing, but Michelle answered. "The usual . . ."

We watched Ben walk away, holding Maddie, making her laugh as they moved through the party. Ben held her high over his shoulders so she could see every person, every pretty dress.

"My daughter loves him a lot, doesn't she?" Michelle said, looking sad, perhaps that she had kept them apart for so long when they so obviously were meant to be together. "Hard not to, I guess."

I wasn't sure how to react to that, but it didn't matter. She didn't wait for a reaction.

Michelle looked away again, something catching her eyes. "Jesus, is that Henry Morgan?"

She motioned with her eyes in Henry's direction. Henry was talking to a couple of party guests, the guests laughing at what he was saying, funny and confident Henry.

She shook her head. "I'm breathless. The inimitable Henry Morgan."

"How do you know him?"

"I don't know him personally, but I'm a huge fan. He was the guest conductor at La Scala when I was in Italy for the Venice Film Festival years ago. He is simply brilliant. That is to say, brilliant like Bernstein was brilliant. I've never seen anything like it. The passion he exudes up on the podium, conducting with his whole body . . ."

She was still staring, like she wanted to eat him. Why had I invited her again?

"Is he a friend of the family? Benjamin mentioned that your mother was a cellist. I would love to meet him if you don't mind introducing us, if it isn't an imposition, of course."

"Benjamin would be glad to do that," I said.

Michelle heard the edge in my voice. Then she smiled, returning to her mission, which apparently was to win me over. I wanted to give her a tip that complimenting my mother's special friend probably wasn't the best way to go.

"I didn't *really* have the chance to say it earlier," she said. "But I *really* appreciate being included tonight. It means a lot to me. And to Maddie. She has *really* taken to you."

I smiled, trying not to count the *really*s.

"Of course, I realize our first meeting did not go as well . . . but I'd like to fix that," she said.

"Being here tonight is all you need to do."

She cocked her head, and nodded, as if she appreciated that. "For what it's worth, your wedding dress is stunning. I don't think I've ever seen one quite as pretty as that." She shrugged. "At least not running down Sunset."

She gave me a sly smile. And I couldn't help it. I laughed. It was all she needed. Michelle threw her head back, laughing even louder. Which was when I looked around, noticing. People were staring at Michelle, basking in that laughter, wanting to know what she was laughing about.

Michelle leaned in. "Isn't this lovely? I'm sorry that it took so long for Benjamin to tell you about what was going on with Maddie and me," she said. "I would have come right out and told you myself, but I didn't think it was my place."

"It had to come from him, though I appreciate you saying that."

"Still, when we were in Shere last month? I certainly did push him. I told him that we absolutely had to get this all out in the open. That things really would be much better when you knew about us."

That stopped me. "Wait, where?"

She shook her head, confused. "Surrey. Benjamin came to take care of Maddie while I was filming reshoots for this horrible movie about a bakeshop owner who falls in love with a man who is allergic to gluten. That's what it's about. It's that bad. I play the underappreciated bake-shop owner, of course . . ."

Michelle was still talking, but I was stuck on the trip Ben had taken to London last month to finalize the purchase of our new home. I hadn't been able to reach him at the hotel, and he had felt badly about it, going on about how busy he was: telling me about a work dinner at our new neighborhood restaurant, telling me he had to stay a few extra days because the sellers were being difficult about the inspection. I didn't realize he had been telling me a slew of lies.

Ben had claimed to be setting up our home, but he was doing two things, and the other had to do with his other family. Maddie and Michelle, the center.

"He helped on the other side too," Michelle said.

I tapped back into what Michelle was saying.

"When we got back from Shere. I had a bunch of press to deal with, and Ben was able to help with Maddie then as well. You know, our house being a mere stone's throw away from where you'll be living. Isn't that grand?"

My heart started racing. "Ben didn't mention that you were nearby."

"Very. In fact, we have this lovely tree house in our backyard, this tall tree house that Maddie essentially lives in. She likes to have her tea parties there. Really, she likes to do everything there. I spent fifty thousand pounds on the damn thing, so that's probably good." She laughed. "Anyway, the last time Ben was visiting, she took him up into the tree house for one of her tea parties, and he showed her his house. Apparently, you can see it clear as day from up in her little tree. The red door and everything."

I felt like I was spinning, unable to get my bearings. Suddenly, I understood what she wanted me to know. My streets in London were never going to be my streets. My house, never going to be just my house. London wasn't going to be about Ben and me putting down roots in a new life. It was going to be, at least in part, about fitting around the roots that Michelle had planted.

Michelle jerked forward as if she realized what I realized, looking like she felt badly for saying the wrong thing. She smiled ruefully. "Ignore me, I'm just talking too much!" she said.

The transparency of Michelle's intention—pretending to be a friend, to deliver this information—was almost so cruel that I admired it. But I also realized it was a means to an end. What she really wanted, what she still wanted, was Ben.

It was the only thing she could see. The way it was the only thing Henry could see when he looked at my mother, the only thing Finn could see when he looked at Margaret. The only thing so many of us could see when we wanted something that we weren't supposed to have.

Michelle raised her hands in surrender. "I shouldn't have gotten into all of that. The important thing is that we're here now. I need to learn to keep my mouth shut! Now I've gone and made a mess of things, just when they seemed to be getting back on track for the two of you."

The tone in her voice was so sweet—but even her tone couldn't hide her eyes. Her urgency. There was urgency there for Michelle because this was her last chance too. Before the wedding, before Ben made me his permanently. It was her last chance to convince me that we shouldn't want that.

She leaned forward, performing. "I'm just such an honest person. It's very hard for me to keep secrets," she said.

"You kept Maddie from Ben."

Michelle gave me a wry smile, the gloves off. "Well. Sometimes it isn't."

This was when we were interrupted. Five of the older wine club members—seventy-five years old—unable to hold off any longer, surrounded us to ask Michelle for her autograph.

"For our grandchildren," their leader said.

Then, like a *whoosh*, Deputy Sheriff Tropper in his pinstripe suit was stepping in to run crowd control. He knocked the old women back. Drawing a two-foot barrier between them and Michelle.

"Ladies, you need to form a line. Ms. Carter only has two hands."

Michelle laughed, giving the old women a hearty shrug, smiling at Tropper gratefully. The mixed emotion she had been showing to me was gone from her face. Her winning smile back in its place.

A Few Good Men

*B*en held two glasses of scotch in one hand, Maddie's hand in his other, when I caught up to him. He gave me a smile, but I couldn't make myself smile back.

"We need to talk," I said.

Ben tilted his head. "Okay . . ." he said.

I took him in—tall and strong in his suit. Michelle could have any man in the world, and yet she was entirely fixated on this man—a man who wasn't available to her. Was it as simple as that? It would be easier to believe it was—Michelle wanting what she couldn't have, Michelle thinking she was entitled to it. Though she wanted him also because he was her child's father, the two things rolling around together, the generous and selfish parts of herself, to make Ben feel like he was her soul mate.

Ben sent Maddie back to Michelle and took my hand, walked us to the edge of the tent, the vineyard side, the moon and stars shooting out over the vineyard, shining over the vines.

"What's going on?" he said.

"I had a little talk with Michelle."

He looked at me anxiously. "I knew her coming was a bad idea."

"I'm just trying to understand if your visit to London was about our future there or your future there."

"Our future." He held my face in his hands. "Everything is about our future."

"Then why didn't you tell me about Surrey?"

"Surrey?" Ben looked at me, realizing what I now knew. "Georgia, come on."

"It was more than Maddie, wasn't it? You were trying to see if you could be a family. If you could be with her."

Ben shook his head. "Of course not. It was always about Maddie."

"What happened to no more secrets, Ben?"

"Nothing. Michelle tries to paint things in a light that she wants to see them in," he said. "I told you Michelle is complicated."

"Is she complicated or is she a liar?"

He pulled back, as if deciding how honest with me he needed to be. He picked his drink up, stalling.

"Look, when she came back, I had a moment, sure. I had a moment of thinking about this woman who broke me who was now the mother of my kid. Any man would have had the same moment of hesitation."

I looked away from him, my heart dropping. "You didn't tell me, though."

"How would it have been helpful to tell you that? To tell you I was having a moment? Do you share with me every guy that crosses your mind?"

I was too struck by what he said to fight back. How could I fight back? He was right—any man would consider the most beautiful woman in the world, if she wanted him, if she was the mother of his child.

"I know Michelle is throwing you, and throwing out your idea of our plan together. But don't let her."

He leaned in and put his face up to my ear, whispering.

"The important thing is what I decided. I decided to stay with you. It was the easiest decision I ever made."

I nodded and wrapped my arms around him, trying to trust his words. Still, something felt off in his explanation. It didn't feel like the whole story. The whole story was that Michelle had left Ben. Now she wanted him back. That seemed to be the story.

And here was the problem—it wasn't about Ben messing with our master plan—with my idea of what our ordered and lovely life was going to look like. It wasn't about knowing I was going to have to navigate Michelle.

It was about the fact that when Ben said it was the easiest decision he ever made, staying with me, he shielded his eyes. He shielded his eyes and, even if he wasn't saying it out loud, I knew he only wanted that to be true.

~

I told Ben I needed a minute alone and walked to the bar, pouring myself sparkling wine, downing a glass. The bartender stared at my speed, not saying anything, but wanting to say something. I gave him a look, daring him.

I took the bottle itself and moved away from the bar. I moved toward the corner, where I could watch Finn on his side of the party, Bobby on his. My mother looked back and forth between them as she stood there with Henry; Henry, who looked uncomfortable—not because he was there—I had learned enough about Henry to know there probably wasn't any room in the world he felt uncomfortable in. No, he was uncomfortable because he saw how agitated my mother was and he thought he was causing it. He was uncomfortable because he cared.

I poured more sparkling wine into my glass when Lee came up to me in the corner, like she belonged there too. "The bartender says you took the last of the good stuff. Care to hand some of it over?"

She took my glass out of my hands, making it her own. "You okay?" she said.

I nodded.

She took a long sip, my heart racing. "You don't seem it," she said. She looked at me, debating whether she knew me well enough to say it. She turned away, apparently deciding against it. Then, thinking again, she turned back.

"You shouldn't feel badly about it," she said.

"What's that?"

She motioned toward Michelle, back with her daughter and Ben. "It would be hard for anyone if Michelle Carter was their husband's ex," she said. "Even Michelle Carter."

Then she handed the glass back over. I smiled. "Thanks."

"You should feel badly about pretending not to know me when you met me yesterday. If you want to feel badly about something, feel badly about that. Why did you do that?"

"What?"

She took the bottle of champagne out of my hand, poured some more into our shared glass, taking another sip herself. "You heard me."

She shrugged, but she looked at me like she was playing way past that. I wasn't incredibly uncomfortable that Lee, computer genius, spoon and glass sharer, was a step ahead.

"Did Jacob tell you that I'm taking a job in Seattle?"

That stopped me. "You did? When?"

She nodded. "I just attended Foo Camp, which—do you know it from growing up here? Anyway, I was offered a job in Seattle at a start-up that deals with online privacy. I'll make software for them. Really cutting-edge stuff."

I remembered Jacob's suitcase in his trunk, the fight they must have had when Lee told him that was what she wanted.

She looked around the party, up toward the West County sky. "It's a little hard for Jacob to think about leaving here, but it's what's right for me. The job. Seattle." She shrugged, looking down. "Jacob says he's getting used to the idea . . . Murray Grant Wines has operation managers. More than they know what to do with. Jacob can oversee the production from Seattle."

"That's great," I said, trying to sound relaxed about it. Which was when it occurred to me how un-relaxed it made me feel: Jacob moving to Seattle, leaving here.

"Is it?"

Lee leaned in and motioned toward Jacob, where he was standing with my father toward the edge of the tent. And near them was Ben. So it was possible she was motioning toward him.

"Good men don't like to quit. Have you noticed that? I've noticed that. They don't give up, even when they should."

I nodded, wanting to agree with her, though I wasn't sure exactly what I was agreeing to, looking at Jacob, at Ben.

She met my eyes. "I would like to think that if I were staying here we would become friends. Don't you think so too?"

It was a strange thing to say and yet it was sincere. It warmed me to her. "Maybe we'll have another shot."

She smiled. "Maybe we will," she said.

Then she held up the champagne.

"Anyway, I'm going to find Jacob and drink the rest of this bottle," she said.

She started to move toward him where he was standing with my father. This was when she turned back.

"He is a good man," she said. "Jacob. He is a very good man."

"Why are you telling me that?"

"Because I know the reason that you didn't introduce yourself to me yesterday."

The Defrosting

Finn was hiding in the winemaker's cottage, defrosting the last frozen lasagna. He was stabbing at the thick noodles with a wooden spoon, but he wasn't making much headway.

He looked up. "I didn't do the best job defrosting this," he said.

"You can't just hide in here eating that, anyway," I said.

"Why not? Should I be out there chatting it up with Mom's new boyfriend? The guy walked over and introduced himself to me, said he's heard a lot about me. I was like, really? Because I've heard very little about you. That was my first mistake. I got like an hour on his seminal interpretation of Beethoven's Fifth. Reminded me of how much I've always hated classical music."

He stood up, turned on the burner. Then he dumped his bowl of lasagna into the saucepan, started stirring it back and forth.

"And I'm not just hiding," he said. "I'm planning."

"What are you talking about?"

He shrugged. "I told you I was going to change things. However I can. So I am. I'm doing it. I'm moving to New York."

"This wasn't what I meant."

"Well, beggars can't be choosers."

I shook my head, heartbroken. Heartbroken that he was leaving, but mostly because I didn't think that he was going to find what he was looking for there.

"Would you feel better if I told you I had some great photography opportunities waiting for me there?"

"A little."

"I have a great photography opportunity waiting for me there."

"Finn, you aren't going to find what you're looking for there. It doesn't work like that. Besides, you love it here. You belong here. What do you think somewhere else is going to give you?"

"Peace of mind. And joy."

I closed my eyes, unsure how to get through to him. He didn't want to listen, anyway—he was too busy shoving the wooden spoon into the frozen lasagna and getting nowhere with it. I stood up and took the spoon away from him, turned the burner up higher.

"Anyway, moving away worked out for you," he said.

"Less than you might think."

Finn sat down on the countertop. "Is a certain movie star slash ex-girlfriend ruining your night?"

"I think she loves him."

Finn tilted his head. "Are you sure? She's an actress. Isn't she supposed to pretend she loves everyone?"

I laughed.

"I don't want a lecture. And I don't want to give one. Though, I do think we could each use one on fighting a fight that we're not sure we want to win."

He paused.

"But I want other things more. Like hotter lasagna. Let's just agree to sit here quietly. If we sit here quietly, maybe we can get through the rest of the night without talking to anyone," he said.

I wanted to argue, but I couldn't argue—when Finn pulled the only card he had. When Finn reached over and took my hand.

"You lifted the lasagna?"

We turned to find our mother in the doorway, her arms crossed, looking pissed. Not just at Finn, but at me too. She looked pissed at me for not doing it, whatever she had come here to do.

"Oh, jeez," Finn said.

"That's right. Oh, jeez. Your father is looking for both of you. He wants to get started with the good-bye toast. He wants to introduce Jacob. And then he wants everyone to go home."

Finn stood, but she stood in front of him.

"He's your brother. Move on. However you can."

He nodded. "I am," he said. "I'm moving to New York."

"That's not moving on. That's moving away."

She started moving toward the doorway, done with the conversation. But Finn wasn't.

"Couldn't we say the same thing to you?" he said.

My mother put her hands up. "You can say whatever you want to me later. And maybe you should. Right now, I suggest you go outside before I lose my mind."

Then my mother hustled us both out of the kitchen, and back to the party, where our father was waiting to give the last harvest toast.

None of us stopping to do it. To take the lasagna from the stove.

Synchronization

My father held an unlabeled wine bottle in his hands. "Look at this crowd out here tonight," he said. "People in Sebastopol will go anywhere for some free wine, won't you?"

Everyone applauded, my father moving to the center of the stage, a small podium to speak behind.

The entire party was semicircled around him. My family stood together behind him but we weren't together. My mother stood by me, Finn next to him, trying not to look at Margaret, Bobby off to the side. The twins held on to their parents' legs. Exhausted. Exhausted from the party and maybe from taking care of their parents.

Henry stood on the edge of the tent, his eyes focused on my mother.

Ben was near him, Michelle and Maddie a few steps behind. He met my eyes and tried to give me a smile. I looked away.

Then I saw Jacob, Lee standing by his side. He was looking at my father, my father, who was staring at this party of two hundred people, my father, who was the reason so many of them were standing there. And tonight, because he could, my father put on his baseball cap, Cork Dork embroidered on the lid.

They laughed. My father turned the cap around, backward, and then he picked up the bottle of wine. "Jen is going to cork this, but I bet you guys are expecting a speech from me first."

"We are!" Gary called out.

"You ain't getting one," he said. "I have nothing to say to any of you."

Then he turned to my mother again.

"Except you."

He motioned for her to join him by the podium, which she did.

My father turned the microphone off. Then he whispered to my mother what she most needed to hear.

"What the hell are you saying, Dan?" Louise said. "Speak the fuck up, people."

But my father was looking only at my mother, waiting for her response.

My mother reached for my father, the way she had done a thousand times before, the way I'd taken for granted that she would do a thousand times more. My mother reached for my father and held him to her, everyone applauding. It took just a minute to realize what they were doing, which at first looked like huddling. My father's tapping foot giving it away, my mother's shoulders swaying. They were dancing. Terribly and wonderfully. And together.

Then Henry screamed from his place on the edge of the tent. Henry screamed loudly.

"Fire," he said.

Over the applause, it sounded like *liar*. So we didn't see it for a second, what was happening, where Henry was pointing.

He pointed toward a blast of smoke. It was coming from the winemaker's cottage, smoke and rising flames. A fire.

"Oh, shit," Bobby said.

We all started moving as fast as we could down the hill, toward the cottage. I was up front with Finn and Bobby and my parents, sheer terror driving us. Ben and Jacob were close behind, Jacob dialing 911 as he ran. The rest of the party—all two hundred of them—making their way down the hill to try and help. Lee and Henry, Margaret carrying the twins, Michelle holding Maddie.

"The fire department is on its way!" Jacob called out just as we reached the wine cottage, the smoke and heat from the fire hitting us, pushing us all back.

Ben put his arm in front of me, put his body in front.

"Jesus!" my mother called out, my father holding her back. She turned and saw Margaret and the twins, Michelle and Maddie, higher on the hill. It wasn't high enough for her.

"Get the kids out of here!" she said.

There was no arguing with that voice. They didn't want to argue. Margaret and Michelle were already steering the children away.

"Stand back," Finn said.

Bobby and Finn each triggered a fire extinguisher. Ben ran forward to stand by their sides.

My heart threatened to pound right out of my chest. In weather this dry, the cottage was like kindling—the wind blowing strong, the fire threatening to spread to the vineyard around it, if we didn't do something. Fast.

Finn aimed the fire extinguisher, high, getting as close to the porch as possible. But the fire extinguisher looked like it wasn't going to be able to take the fire down. It looked like it was flaming it.

Finn started coughing, still pushing forward.

My father moved forward. "It's enough."

I could hear the sirens, still far away.

Bobby stepped forward. "Get back, Dad," he said.

Then he aimed the fire extinguisher even higher, the wind catching the fire, pulling it toward the vineyard.

The wine cottage porch started to collapse.

"Let it go," my father called out.

Ben turned and looked at me, deep sorrow in his eyes.

I looked straight ahead at the wine cottage, the smoke wafting over it, moving toward the vineyard. I started to move forward, toward the fire, as if I could do what no one else had been able to do. As if I could stop it before it got to the vineyard.

I could feel a hand on my arm, stopping me. Jacob. I met his eyes.

"No," he said.

Then a bolt of thunder exploded in the sky. It came quickly: the rain following, splashing down, a waterfall. The thunder crashing onto the edge of the vineyard.

I looked up at the pouring rain, hard, deep pellets hitting my skin.

The rain heaped down, pushing through the cottage, the fire engines' sirens getting closer.

The water was taking care of the fire, the flames receding beneath the downpour. Relief seeped through me.

Synchronization. Wasn't this the definition? A fire hits a vineyard. And then, like a miracle, it starts to pour. It was overdue to pour but it starts then, pressing down at the fire.

And then I looked toward the vineyard and I realized. The rain. The rain that was saving the vineyard. It would ruin the grapes that were still on the vine—Block 14, my father's most valuable grapes. We had to get to them first. All of us realized it at once.

"Move!" Bobby said. "Move."

We took flight, me and Finn and Bobby, Jacob and Ben not far behind us, my mother and father not far behind them. The entire family ran through the vineyard to get to the rest of the grapes. The messy, wonderful business of getting the job done for each other when you most needed to.

We arrived at Block 14 and started pulling at the soaking grapes. We pulled at the clusters even without clippers, grabbing the available buckets from beneath the vines.

The fire trucks' sirens were loud and close, the firemen arriving to help with the fight.

It was why I didn't hear it at first, none of us heard it, through the rain, through the running.

My father was down on the ground.

Holding on to my mother.

Limp, listless. In her arms.

Part 4

The Last Harvest

The Waiting Room

*T*here was a moment before we were in the car racing to the hospital. There was a moment before we all stopped what we were doing and started moving toward our father. But that moment was blurred. By the rain, by the sound of my mother. What was clear was what came next. We were racing to the hospital, almost as soon as we saw my father there. Finn driving, me in the passenger seat, my mother holding my father in the back, Bobby and Margaret and Ben in the car behind. All of us were too scared to wait for the ambulance, needing to do something, leaving the kids behind with Michelle, all the kids staying with the movie star.

There was a moment before we were in the waiting room at Sonoma County Hospital, full of Fords, the mishmash of people they loved. All of them currently afraid of losing the person they loved the most: Margaret held on to Bobby, Finn stood with my mother, I was sitting with Ben on a bench. And Jacob. Jacob was standing off to the side.

Bobby started pacing. "We have been sitting here for hours, someone has to do something."

Finn shook his head. "What do you want us to do, Bobby?"

"Something."

I leaned in to Ben, Finn holding my mother. It was something when you lose your center. My father, in a way that we weren't willing to acknowledge, was that. And in the moment I saw him lying in the vineyard, I realized it wasn't the vineyard I feared losing. It was him. As long as he was working the land, I got to imagine it. That the day without him would never come.

My mother stood up. "That's him."

I turned, expecting to see my father, standing there with a hospital band on his wrist, telling us he was fine. But it was the doctor coming out to see us. The doctor giving my mother a hug, like they were old friends.

"Jen. He had another heart attack," he said.

"Another?" Bobby said.

"What does he mean another, Mom?" Finn said.

Which was when I realized what my father hadn't told me about the car accident, what must have happened. My father had had a heart attack while he was driving, causing that accident.

The vein popped in Bobby's neck. "What the hell is going on?" Bobby said.

My mother jumped in front of him, in front of all of us, her back to us, facing the doctor.

"What does that mean, exactly?" she asked him. "Is he okay?"

"It was a mild heart attack, though not as mild as last time. He's responding to a clot-dissolving agent, but he isn't out of the woods. I'm not pleased to see him back here. He has to take it easy, Jen. We have talked about this."

Bobby looked like he was going to explode. "When did you talk about this? Mom, how did you not tell us that Dad had a heart attack?"

"We didn't want to worry you," she said.

Finn stood behind his brother. "Why?" Finn said.

"Yeah, why?" Bobby said.

Bobby was yelling now, full-on yelling.

They both were.

My mother turned toward them, her voice the loudest of all. "We thought you'd overreact! Imagine that. We thought you'd make it about your own fear as opposed to, you know, what your father would need to actually get past it."

They both got quiet. Everyone got quiet, and the entire waiting room turned to look at my mother: the Ford family and Ben and Margaret and Jacob and an array of midnight strangers, crowding around. Everyone looked at my mother, who was done with all the nonsense, demanding that the rest of her family be done too.

"Now it's time for you to keep your father safe. To keep each other safe. Like you all didn't forget how." She moved toward the doctor. "So what does this mean for Dan?"

The doctor looked back and forth between my brothers to see if they were going to interrupt.

"He's resting now. We'll know more tomorrow, but you should get some rest."

Jacob looked down as if it was his fault.

"So he's going to be okay?" Finn said.

My mother caught his eye, trying to calm him.

"What you're saying means he's going to be okay?" Bobby said.

"It means we watch him until tomorrow. Run a few more tests. But assuming he is fine, he can go home then. Though he's going to have to take it easy. His body is not going to give him another warning call."

Bobby laughed. "Sure. That won't be an issue at all."

My mother put her hand on Bobby's shoulder. "Bobby . . ."

"What? Dad has never taken it easy. Ever."

The doctor turned and looked at him. Serious. "Until today."

My mother nodded and turned to us so we'd hear it, what she was saying in her silence, that it was time for everyone to think differently about our father. "Can we see him?"

"He said you had a long enough day and you should go home. I think that would be wise. Dan is groggy and could use his rest, and Jen, you need your rest too. He's right. You can see him first thing in the morning."

My mother nodded. "Sure. Okay," she said. "That makes sense."

She turned to me and squeezed my hand.

Then she walked right past the doctor, toward her husband.

Sebastopol, California. 2009

*O*en was furious with him and she was right to be. They were spending a month in Big Sur, in a beautiful house, large windows looking out over the ocean. She had told him what she needed. She needed a change and she had said that she'd go on her own. But he had insisted that he go with her.

That part was fine, but he wasn't really here. He knew that was what she was furious about. If he was going to barely be here with her, why had he come at all?

He wasn't making an effort. She loved everything about being in Big Sur and on the ocean. She had joined a musical theater group and she was playing in the band. It was beyond the fact that all of that made him feel threatened. It was this, if he was truthful. He felt neglected. He wasn't seeing her at all and he was being a child about it. He knew he was being a child about it. That was different from knowing how to stop.

"Is it because you're not feeling well?"

She asked him this all the time now, since the heart attack.

"I'm good. I'm really good."

"Then it just seems like you've forgotten how to do anything other than what you're doing." She shook her head. "And the thing is, that was why I fell in love with you. That vision, that passion. But you have to be able to do something else too. You don't know how to do anything but be at the vineyard."

"I know."

"And you haven't tried."

He nodded. "I know that too."

She was waiting to see what he'd say next.

"We can sell the vineyard," he said. "If that's what you want to do."

"No one is talking about selling the vineyard, Dan. Why is that all that you hear?"

She looked at him. And he saw it: The way she had looked at him at the beginning, all that love in her eyes—this looked like the opposite.

"What are we talking about, then?"

"Something else," she said.

She started walking away, but he held on to her arm. He didn't say anything, but he held on, hoping she would see what he didn't seem to know how to say. He was waiting for her to do it, the thing she would do when they were this angry with each other, the thing she was the one who knew how to do.

He was waiting for her to move back toward him.

The Details

*S*ynchronization.

A fire hit a vineyard. And then, like a miracle, it started to pour. It was overdue to pour but it started then, pressing down at the fire.

Synchronization. Your heart pumped blood to the necessary vessels. The vessels pumped the blood back to the heart muscle. Everything flowed through the coronary artery to the heart muscle. To where everything was needed.

An unspoken agreement.

~

Ben went back to the house to relieve Michelle. Margaret went with him to be with her twins. They needed her, and it was easier to be with them. She didn't expect Bobby to go with her. But he did. Bobby went to oversee the grape picking, to do the one thing for my father he felt he could do at that moment. Then Finn left to deal with the fire department, to see what was left of the winemaker's cottage. By the time my mother came out, there was only me, surrounded by empty seats.

My mother walked back into the waiting room, carrying an enormous care package.

"You all alone? How did that happen?"

"A little bit of luck."

She smiled. "Thanks for staying for me," she said.

She put the care package down on the seat next to me and took the seat on its other side, exhausted.

"What a night," she said.

"How is he?"

"He was irritated more than anything else, which seemed like a good sign."

"About what?"

She shrugged. "He wants to get to the grapes."

I started to tell her that it was taken care of, that Bobby was handling it, but that wouldn't have mattered to my father. He would need to be there himself to believe it.

"He tried to tell me yesterday about the heart attack. I only half-heard him."

"He probably only half-told you."

I looked down, still feeling guilty that I hadn't known intrinsically what was going on here. And also that I hadn't been here while it was happening.

"Don't do that."

I looked at her. "What?"

"Don't say this happened again because he's selling the vineyard," my mother said. "It's not. He wanted you to understand that. This is because he didn't sell it sooner."

I nodded. It seemed like she was right. My father had given everything he could to this land. He needed to give himself to something else now. I was done fighting him on that. I was done fighting him on anything, except what he said he wanted for himself.

My mother smiled. "He said it was a fitting ending."

"For the last harvest?"

"For the last harvest," my mother said.

She leaned toward me. "And that was before the fire inspector called. It seems someone left something on the stove in the winemaker's cottage."

She shook her head, laughing. What else was there to do? In the realm of disasters that night, the fire was lower on the list. Higher on the list was this: She looked happy. She looked happier than she should in a hospital waiting room. She looked happier than she had since I'd walked in the door in my wedding dress, her in her towel. Two different lifetimes.

And I saw it creep over her face, the rest of it, what she had to do. What was required of her. She needed to leave Henry, if she was going to reimagine her life with my father.

She looked down. "Henry is a good man," she said. "When I told you how Henry made me feel, how he made me feel seen, I left that part out." She shook her head. "One of these days, I'll tell you the whole story."

"How does it end, Mom?"

She paused. "With your father. It ends with your father."

I took a deep breath in. "The details don't matter, then."

She shook her head. "The details matter," she said. "It's the big picture that confuses us."

What were the details of today? What was the big picture? The big picture was that my mother made sacrifices. We all did, didn't we? Hers caught up. But now she was trying to let them go for what she had gotten in return.

My mother leaned forward. "Ben works hard to understand you," she said. "It doesn't mean he's good at it. But it's important that he tries. Sometimes all you need is a man to remind you he's doing the best he can."

My initial thought was that Ben did more than the best he could. He succeeded in knowing what I needed, often before I did. Except then I thought about the enormity of what he had kept from me, his daughter, her mother's feelings for him, his feelings for her. An entire other life he was living. If he really understood me, wouldn't he know that what I needed most—what I wanted in my new family—was what I had in my first family? What we still had? It was a mess and we fought and battled and lost it and made bad decisions for one another. But we put it on the table. We put one another first. Ben had done the opposite.

My mother pointed toward the care package. "Jacob dropped this. He left it outside your father's door. I don't know how he got back there. It doesn't matter. Jacob left this."

"He did?"

She opened the wrapping. "He wanted to make sure your father was okay. And, like a man, he brought everything we didn't exactly need." She held up a box of licorice as an example. "Doing the best he can."

She was quiet.

My mother put her arm around me. "Can we go home and go to sleep? I feel like I could sleep for five days straight. And I probably should. I should probably rest up so I can be back here in five hours."

I nodded. That I could do for my father. I could take his wife home and get her some rest.

"FYI. The last time I felt this shitty, I was pregnant with you."

I smiled. "Are you going to tell me what Dad said to you? When he whispered in your ear."

"Do you think that's what turned everything around? You think it's as simple as that?"

"I'm just nosy."

She pushed her hair behind her ears, considering what he said, whether she was going to share it. Then she smiled.

"Your father said the same thing he said when he got into my yellow buggy."

"What was that?"

She shrugged. "So, where are you taking me?"

She shook her head, taking a stick of licorice, taking a large bite. Then she stood up to go, care package in hand, my arm over her shoulder as we headed out the hospital door.

"It's not all a happy ending. We're going to have to get you a new tent," she said.

I looked at her, confused, at which point she rolled her eyes, like she couldn't believe she had to explain this.

"A new tent for your wedding. Rain damaged it. Rain and wind and everything else that a tent like that is supposed to stand up to, but doesn't."

She leaned in, as if listening to my heart, as if listening to how that made my heart feel.

"Not tonight, though." She shook her head. "Nothing is open tonight."

The First Contract

When I got back to the vineyard, I went down to the winemaker's cottage, the back of it burned off, Bobby sitting on the porch. He was sitting alone, drinking a beer. At 5:55 in the morning.

He didn't look at me, keeping his eyes on our vineyard, the sun not yet lighting it. The fog still dusting the vines, laminating them in frost and half-light.

Bobby stared straight ahead, glassy-eyed and confused, the stare of someone who had been up all night. "You may as well sit down," he said. "There's half a beer left, and I don't think anything is going to collapse."

He moved over and handed up the bottle of beer. I had a sip, taking a seat.

"Long night," he said. "We got half of the grapes. We can use half of them."

"It could have been worse, then," I said.

"It also could have been better," he said. He paused. "Mom back?"

"Yeah. She went upstairs to go to sleep."

"Good. She must be exhausted."

Then he took his beer back, even though I was mid-sip, which was when I noticed he had Band-Aids on his fingers, over the nails.

Bobby shrugged, looking down at them. "You've got to start somewhere, right?"

Then he took a sip, turning back to the vineyard. The morning glaze holding in the sky, intoxicating him. It was comforting, the way this place got more beautiful every day. Wasn't that the gift of a home? You looked at it the same way, but then when you needed it to, it showed you all over again the many ways you'd been during the time that you had been living there. The many ways it had brought you back to yourself. The many ways it still brought you back to yourself.

"Margaret went back to San Francisco with the twins just a few minutes ago. They were asleep but I helped her load them in the car. They didn't make a move. We're good at that. The two of us. You'd be surprised how much skill that takes."

I reached for the beer, took a small sip, mostly because I wasn't sure what to say, and I didn't want to upset him more than he had already been upset these past few days.

He took the beer back. "We talked before she went. We decided I would stay here for a minute with Mom and Dad. We decided to take a minute apart to see if that would help us remember how much we used to love being together. That's the plan at least."

He was holding the beer or I'd have handed it back to him, just so he could have something to do besides sitting there, telling me his family was falling apart before him.

"I made a mess of things," he said.

"I don't think you should be blaming yourself."

He laughed, a little angry. "What should I be doing?"

I shrugged. "Drinking?"

He smiled, took another sip. "She's not wrong. I stopped paying attention to her. I stopped doing the things that someone does for the person he loves. Because I was tired. Because other things always seemed to matter a little bit more."

He paused.

"That doesn't happen overnight, you know. It happens slowly. You should be careful of that. You should be careful not to take the person you love for granted. Not only because they'll notice. But you'll notice too. You'll think it means something it doesn't."

"Like what?"

"Like that's how much you care."

He looked like he had lost everything. If Margaret saw that, would it be enough? Bobby loved his wife in a way she couldn't feel, but he loved her all the same. Shouldn't that count for something? Shouldn't the effort, no matter how misinformed, be enough to keep people together—especially at the moment they might otherwise decide it was easier to be apart?

He took a swig. "I'm mad at her. It doesn't help, but I am mad at her and him."

"Me too."

"That really doesn't help."

I moved closer to him. "What are you going to do?"

"Make it up to her if I can. Forgive her if I can. Help her forgive me." He shook his head. "Something like that."

"That sounds like a plan."

"What choice do I have?"

He put down the beer, rubbed his hands together.

"You don't give up on a family. Not without trying to put it back together."

That stopped me. My brother, who always said the wrong thing, had said the most important thing of all.

His words vibrated in the place that had gone vacant the minute I'd seen Ben on the street in my wedding dress. With Maddie. With Michelle.

I hugged him. "Thank you."

He looked confused. "For what?"

"I wasn't sure what to do about Ben, and you just made it feel very clear. Thank you for that."

"You should marry him. You'd be an idiot not to."

And then there was that. I laughed, even though he wasn't kidding. And leaned forward, squeezing into my brother.

"Hey, guys. What's going on?"

We looked up, and Finn was there, holding a six-pack of beer. Finn stood there, Bobby stiffening at the sight of him. I made room anyway, for my good brother, who had behaved very badly.

Finn sat down on the other side of me, and maybe this was all that Bobby could do, but he did it. He didn't get up. I tried to reward him for that, handing him the beer.

Finn cleared his throat. Maybe so we would look at him.

Which was when I noticed that he was holding a paper in his hand: an entire folder, a blue folder, UCLA Law School's insignia on the front.

He handed it over.

"I stayed up looking for it. It wasn't easy to find. But there it is."

The contract. It was the contract we had signed saying we would never take this place over. I looked down at it. There were the signature lines I'd made. Bobby had signed the first one, Finn the third. But on the second line—saved for me—there was nothing.

"I never signed it?"

He shook his head. "You never signed it," Finn said.

Bobby looked over, as if to confirm it. He nodded. "No signature."

There was meaning to derive from that, probably that everyone is too busy in law school to do anything well. But maybe there was some other meaning too.

Finn put his arm over my shoulder. "You should frame that," he said. "It was like the younger you telling the older you something."

"But what?"

"But what? That is the question."

It was Bobby who answered.

"Maybe that you're a pretty crappy lawyer."

Then he took the contract and ripped it into a thousand pieces.

We sat there quietly, the early morning coming up over the vineyard, the fog moving away. Slowly but surely. Leaving a glistening in its wake. Leaving sunshine. From the half-burned winemaker's cottage, it couldn't have been more beautiful.

"I still don't want this place," Finn said.

"Me neither, I have no interest," Bobby said.

He didn't look at Finn when he did it, when he agreed with him, but he agreed with him all the same.

I looked at Finn, tempted to explain what had just happened, Bobby moving toward him, though I kept my mouth shut, in favor of trusting what I had learned this weekend, in the face of everything falling apart, and maybe coming together in a greater way than I could have hoped for. You couldn't always work so hard to fix it. Even if things didn't always go the way they should, sometimes they went exactly where they needed to.

Bobby took a sip of beer. "I don't want the responsibility," he said. "But it's more than that. I'm not really sure I would be good at it. I think you have to believe you'd be good at it."

"That might change," I said.

"Well, it only changed for you because it's too late," Bobby said.

Finn looked over.

"Maybe too late," Finn said. "Maybe not."

"Maybe not," Bobby said.

Then Finn reached over and held out his hand to Bobby.

Bobby took it.

And the three Ford children got drunk and watched the sun come up.

The Other Line

Ben was lying on my bed, awake. "Hey," he said. "You okay?"

I stayed in the doorway, not because I didn't want to go to him, but because it felt bizarre, looking at him in my childhood bedroom. This room, more than any place since, felt like my home.

"What are you smiling about?" he said.

I shook my head. "Can't answer that, at the moment."

He smiled. "I'm just glad you're smiling," he said. "Is she okay?"

I tilted my head. "Don't you mean *he*?"

"No, I mean *she*. Your mother. I knew your dad was going to be okay. He's the toughest bird I've ever met."

"They're both fine. They're going to be fine."

"Good. Then come here, already."

I sat down on the edge of the bed, and Ben put his arm on the small of my back.

"Maddie went to the hotel with Michelle," he said. "But she asked when she could come back. She asked if she could have pancakes with us in the morning. Isn't that cute?"

"That's nice."

"I told her we are working on keeping the vineyard, which she was thrilled about, but maybe because it's close to the pancakes. Fine by me if that's the reason. I feel good with her happy being in Sebastopol."

I smiled. Then I looked at him, really looked at him, trying to figure out how to say it. "You can't stay here, Ben."

"What are you talking about?"

"You can't stay here with me. Even temporarily. You need to go and start your life in London."

He looked at me, taking in those words. "And you're not coming?"

I shook my head, definitive. "I can't."

He paused as if considering how to fight this. "I thought we made a new plan."

"It doesn't work. You need to be with your kid. Down the street. To take her to soccer. To pick her up from school."

"She hates soccer."

I shrugged. "That's who you are."

He sat up. "You're who I am too . . ."

I leaned down toward him, tried to figure out how to explain it. "It isn't about Maddie. It's about the part of you that didn't tell me about Maddie when you could have fit us together."

He shook his head. "We're back to this?"

"That's why you kept them a secret from me, Ben. You didn't want me to see what I see when I look at you now."

"And what is that?" he said.

"That part of you wants to work things out with Michelle."

He was quiet, looking down at the pillow, trying to control his anger. He shook his head.

"Except I decided on us. Isn't that the important part?"

"Part of you wanted to go the other way. That doesn't seem like a problem?"

"That seems like reality." He paused. "We are presented with options and we either take them, or we remember why it isn't worth it to take them. Why what we're giving up is too much."

I nodded, knowing he believed that, and knowing he was wrong. Ben hadn't picked one option, which was why I sensed the intimacy between Michelle and Ben: They had been living a life together in which that intimacy was all there was.

Ben sighed. "I don't want to be with Michelle."

"No, but she is your *have-to-have*."

"Michelle isn't my *have-to-have* and what does that even mean?"

I didn't say anything. I didn't have to. He realized that I wasn't talking about Michelle. I was talking about Maddie.

He nodded, not arguing with that. It was the truth, after all. From the minute Maddie had walked into Ben's life, she was the only thing he could see, as she deserved to be. The rest—me, Michelle—was secondary. As we deserved to be. The problem was that if we were fighting for second place—and who wanted to fight for second place?—the tiebreaker was still to be determined, wedding or no wedding, London or no London. And maybe that was the bigger thing. Suddenly, I understood our life together—so far from my family, with someone who didn't feel like my family in the way he needed to—was my second place too.

Ben looked at me. He couldn't argue, so he said something else, which he knew to be true. "And you need to be here?"

I didn't answer.

"You need to be here," he said. No question attached. "And not temporarily."

He always got there, though this time I was there before him. I needed to be in Sonoma.

"What are you going to do?"

"I don't have a vineyard. I don't have a family intent on staying. They're working it out. My parents. My brothers." I shrugged. "I guess the reasons I want to stay are more complicated than I think they are."

"Or maybe they're simpler."

I pushed his hair out of his face. "I'm not trying to punish you. I'm not mad."

"I know," Ben said. "That makes it worse."

He reached for my hand, laying me down beside him.

"This still feels, in this moment, like where we belong. How do you account for that?"

Ben's face was so close to mine. He smiled at me, that smile I loved. Those lips, soft and sweet. And I agreed with him. There was a world in which we moved back toward each other, but I couldn't help but have another image locked in my mind. Another moment. Not tomorrow, but one day. Ben walking down the street with his daughter and her mother.

His wife, his hand on her back. An image like the one I had seen in Silver Lake.

But this time I'd be walking toward them. Michelle in town for work, Ben and Maddie tagging along. He'd complain that he still wasn't used to the cameras, to the scrutiny around their lives, and how much Michelle cared about those things. But he would complain in the way that showed that he was also amused by it, the way we got to be amused by the things we did for love. It would be good to see them. Hearing how Maddie was doing, how they all were doing together. Ben smiling, the charge gone, something kinder there. Something like friendship.

We lay back on the bed, hand in hand. My wedding dress was hanging on the door, still ready to be worn.

"Why do I feel like you're trying to do the right thing?" he said.

"Because I am," I said.

Ben turned toward me. "Who says there is a right thing?"

Synchronization. Everything lines up like a sign of where you are supposed to be. But what do you give up? Because you give something up. As simple—and complicated—as the other line, the other way your life could have been if you had taken a different path. If you had gotten into the right car. If you hadn't gotten out of the wrong one.

"Do not close your eyes. If we fall asleep, I won't be able to convince you," he said.

Then he did.

Everything Worth Doing

It was 9 A.M., so I went back to the hospital to see my father. He was sitting up in bed, his color back. He looked like himself, which was an enormous relief, the tears rushing to my eyes.

He stopped me with his arm, with a quick wave of it. My father had never liked tears and he didn't want to watch mine now, not on his watch, not when he didn't have the energy to stop them.

"I hate it in here," he said.

This instead of hello.

"I really hate it," he said.

"Then leave."

"Working on it. Your mother is getting me checked out as we speak. She's talking to the doctors and the administrators. Or at least, that's what she said she's doing."

"You think she's lying to you?"

"She could be running to get a sandwich."

I laughed and took a seat on the edge of the bed, took hold of my father's hand. Scare or no scare, I never wanted to be sitting there again.

"Are the brothers working?"

"Yes, the vineyard is all good."

"Good." He paused. "Do they still want to kill each other?"

"Yes, but the normal amount."

"Also good. Though it's really about the grapes. Remind them of that. If anyone loses perspective again, remind them that the most important things don't involve that much talking."

"Of course."

He closed his eyes. He was tired. There was no denying that. He needed rest. And all of this time, he'd had trouble asking for it. Now he was going to get it. "Thank you."

"For someone who says he doesn't care about that place anymore, you seem pretty concerned."

"Who said I didn't care? I'm just getting ready to care about something else."

That was the truth, wasn't it? We had so much space in our heart. My mother was tired of giving it all to our family, so she gave it to Henry. Until she realized that wasn't the answer either. My father realizing the same thing in time to save them.

"It's time for me to get out of here, kid," he said.

"You like to go out with a bang?"

He laughed.

He reached for my face, holding my cheek. "What happened?"

I shook my head without answering.

"You left Ben?"

I nodded, trying not to think about where Ben was now, what was happening with him. Maybe he was talking to Michelle, but probably he was letting it sink in for himself that he was going to London, that he was doing what he needed to do. We both were.

My father nodded. "It was the right thing," he said.

I smiled. "Now you tell me."

"You needed to get there yourself. Or it wouldn't have been. You get that?"

"Well, if you say so."

He smiled. "I think you're going to be okay, kid. He wasn't the person." He shook his head. "Or maybe that's just what I'm telling myself now so I don't feel responsible."

"Responsible for what?"

"Responsible for you. You don't understand your worth. That was my job."

I reached over and took his hand, my father, whom I loved more than anything in this world. My father. My mother.

"Daddy."

"Oh no, you're bringing out the big gun."

"I'm moving home, not because I'm scared, but because I'm not anymore. I want to be here."

He nodded because he could see that I meant it. Then he got sad, thinking about something else.

"It's too late, baby."

I nodded. "For our land, but I'll find new land. And I'll make Jacob give it back to me, the Last Straw name."

"He won't do it. He's not going to be allowed by his board, even if he wants to."

"Then I'll fight him to give me B-Minor, unless you don't want me using it."

"Then what?"

"Then I'll ask Mom."

He shook his head. "You're the most stubborn person that I've ever met. And if you think I mean that nicely, I don't. It's not a compliment, even if it sounds like one."

"Will you help me?"

"If you tell me why you want to be here so badly?"

My mother's words came to mind. *Be careful what you give up.* In a way, that was what I had done. I had focused on other things, on my relationship, on a life far from here. And I was glad I had. It had altered me in the ways that made it possible for me to want to be here. To know what that meant. I had given away a love that felt too dangerous, too risky, and being back here was the greatest reminder that it was real love. How I felt waking up here in the morning, and how I felt sitting on the winemaker's cottage porch at night. How the smells and sounds and people seemed to grab hold of me every time I let them in. How the wine still did.

The wine. And the fearless piece of me that wanted to be a part of it, even if I couldn't control it. The fearless part of me knowing that just maybe it was the way to build a life that I wasn't only good at, but that I loved.

He smiled. "You remember when you were a little kid, and you came into the winemaker's cottage and announced that you wanted to be a winemaker? I was relieved when you changed your mind."

"Why?"

"Because it's a life you have no control over. You do everything in your power and ultimately you have no control."

I moved in closer to him, trying to avoid sounding ironic when I said it, what I knew to be the truth. "Didn't you just describe everything worth doing?"

He smiled. "Not everything, wiseass."

"Give me the exception."

"Making clocks. That, you can control."

"Why does that sound familiar?"

"I tried to convince you to become a clockmaker. I even took you into San Francisco one afternoon to go to the oldest clock store in the city, to watch the clockmaker do his work."

"Seriously?"

He shrugged. "You had trouble telling time. I thought at the very least it would help."

"Did it?"

"Not really."

He closed his eyes. He was getting tired. I patted his hand, getting ready to leave him, to let him rest, to let my mother come inside and rest with him, the two of them quiet together, the way they belonged.

"So you're staying? And I'm going. I'm going boating. I'll hate every second of it, but I'm going."

I laughed. "Why are you doing that to yourself?"

"It's the only way to get where we want to be."

He looked at me, making sure I heard him. They weren't coming back to Sebastopol, or if they did, it wouldn't be on the terms I was imagining. The vineyard saved, my father's legacy, the way it had been, intact.

Then he smiled. "But you'll be okay. You're going to be a great winemaker for the same reason you're a terrible driver."

"Why is that?"

He shrugged, like it was the most obvious thing in the world. "No one else has a clue what you're doing, but at the end of the day, you get to where you want to go."

I smiled, leaning in toward him, starting to cry.

"Okay, let's not get dramatic. You really do have to work on the driving."

He motioned toward the doorway, where my mother was walking down the hall toward us. "Are we not going to talk about the other guy?" he said. "Before your mother gets here?"

"What guy?"

He tilted his head. "Your mother will make a big deal about it."

"Who?"

"Jacob. I'm talking about Jacob, of course."

I pointed at him. "Don't cause trouble."

He smiled. "Look, if you don't want to talk about it, just say that," he said. "Just say, 'Shut up, Dad.'"

"He's not the reason."

He shrugged. "In a way, he is. Actually, he's the reason for all of it. A guy decides to buy a vineyard from a winemaker. Weddings get cancelled. The daughter goes crazy."

"You're talking crazy."

"I'm not saying you're going to marry him or anything," he said. "Calm down."

"That's good."

"We do have that tent, though," he said.

I leaned in and hugged my father. I hugged him and felt it. The strength that came from him, that you couldn't get from anywhere else.

My father leaned in close. Then he smiled, pushed my hair back off of my face. "Can I tell you, you're my favorite kid."

"You say that to all of us."

"Well. That doesn't make it any less true," he said.

The Wedding

There was supposed to be a wedding at our vineyard. And in the end, there was.

Five days after my wedding was to take place, my parents stood there together under a homemade altar. My father wore a sports coat and jeans. My mother wore a blue beret, the blue beret she'd been wearing the day she'd met my father, the day he'd gotten into her car and never gotten out.

It wasn't an official ceremony. They were never officially divorced, but it felt official: Finn married them, and all their friends from town—from the life they'd built in Sebastopol—stood with them. All the local winemakers were there, Jacob included. Suzannah and Charles flew up to be there too.

I was by my mother's side. Bobby, my father's best man, stood by his. Margaret and the twins, eager flower boys, completed the circle.

"There is nothing for me to say that I haven't said," my father said, talking to everyone, his eyes held fast on my mother.

"Except *bon voyage*," my mother said.

He smiled. "Except *bon voyage*," he said.

With that, he kissed her. Everyone cheered. And we opened wine, more and more wine, as they spoke about leaving there, closing up the house. They told us they were going on a trip around the world, boating to the south of France and the Mediterranean, the gorgeous coast of South America. That part of the plan they kept: my father buying that wristband that he thought was going to stop the seasickness that he wasn't even worried about coming. There was no worry. Just excitement. The two of them were heading off to be together on a new adventure. Though this time instead of following, my mother was leading the way. My mother was leading him.

Suzannah and I walked away from the crowd, up to the top of the hill, the very top of the hill that looked out over the entire vineyard. The fifty acres that had taken my father his adult lifetime to accumulate: the original ten, the house and gardens he and my mother had built on them, the forty that followed.

How long ago had my father been the one standing here, looking over this land? How had he known what to do with it? How had I not figured out, before it was too late, how much that mattered?

"It's a good thing you listened to me and decided to stay here," she said.

I laughed.

"So is this your new look?"

She pointed at my curls falling over my shoulders, no makeup, none of my Los Angeles armor.

I smiled. "Much less refined?"

She shook her head. "Much more . . . happy."

She gave me a kind smile.

"What are you going to do now?"

"Apparently not return phone calls," Jacob said.

We turned around to see him behind us, his hands in his pockets, a button-down shirt on, wine running down the front of it.

"Am I interrupting?"

Suzannah smiled at him. "Of course you are," she said, irritated.

Suzannah walked away, turning back and making the so-so sign with her hands. I laughed, looking away from her, looking back at Jacob and his wine-covered shirt.

He shrugged apologetically, pulling on his shirt. "I'm a mess," he said.

"What happened?"

"The twins. They were fighting each other for my licorice."

I smiled. "Who won?"

"Not me," he said. "I had to take off my vest."

He moved closer so he was looking where I was looking, over the late-day vineyard. His vineyard now, The Last Straw, a subsidiary of Murray Grant Wines. And it was starting to feel like that was okay. I had lost that fight, which was hard to accept. But my parents were happy again, my brothers were on the mend. In the ways that mattered, I had won so much.

"They're leaving on their boat trip tomorrow?" he said.

I nodded. He knew the answer, but he was trying to ask me something else, maybe why I hadn't called him back. Maybe if it meant that I was staying here.

"You're okay with that?"

"As long as they're going together," I said.

"I told your father that the boat is a good idea," he said. "It will take them to the place they want to go next."

"How do you know?"

He shrugged. "I know some things."

I smiled, wanting that to be correct, that my parents would dock somewhere, call it Big Sur. Somewhere surrounded by water and trees. Somewhere they would make their home.

Jacob crossed his arms over his chest. "Lee's gone," he said.

"I heard something about that."

"I'm doing okay. Thanks for asking."

I laughed.

"She left the day after the harvest party," he said. "She moved to Seattle to take a job with Tim O'Reilly. And to get away from me. It was the right thing. She's happier there."

Jacob kicked the ground beneath him, soil rising up. Soft and damp. November soil, ready for a quiet winter, its well-earned rest.

"What about you?" he said. "What's next?"

He looked at me, held my eyes. It was too much, though, to meet his gaze. So I looked away, to the vineyard.

"I'm going to get a plot of land. I won't be able to afford much. But I'm going to start with a small plot of land. Five acres. See what I can do."

"Make some wine?"

I nodded. "That's the plan."

"You're going to need a winemaker to teach you," he said.

"Yes, and my father isn't available. He's so out of here."

He smiled. "You'll find someone good."

"Well, first I've got to get the land."

He pointed to the vineyard. "What if I told you I could help you with the land?"

This was when he did it. He handed me the deed. For The Last Straw Vineyard. My father's original deed. For the original ten acres.

I looked up at him. Then back down at the deed. Ten acres. That was where we were standing. It held the house and some of the gardens. And a half-burned wine cottage. And five beautiful acres of vineyard. Enough for me to get started.

"You're giving it back?"

"I'm not giving anything back." He shrugged. "We're going to have a contract and everything. A guy's got to eat."

I shook my head, not knowing what to do, thinking if I tried to do anything I might pass out.

"There is a caveat too. We still own the name The Last Straw Vineyard now, so you'll have to pick a new name for these ten acres, for what they produce. You'll have to start fresh."

I nodded, still staring at the deed.

"And if you flame out, you sell these ten acres back to me."

"Okay."

"Don't say *okay*. Think about it. Think about the fact that if this doesn't work, you're going to be the one selling the land back to the mean and mighty Murray Grant Wines because you're going to have to put that part in writing."

I started to say that wasn't going to happen, but he was looking at me. He knew that wasn't going to happen. It seemed like he knew too much. And it flashed before me: What if Ben and Michelle hadn't walked by the dress fitting? What if we'd walked down the aisle together in that beautiful tent and I hadn't met Jacob. Jacob, who was standing before me, offering me a future I hadn't known I wanted.

My father would call it synchronization. Not fate. Don't confuse it with fate. Because there was still the rest of it. The deed in my hand, the sense I was moving toward a place to build a home. The need I had—the hope I had—that I would do the right thing with these gifts now.

"You look like you might pass out," Jacob said. "FYI, I don't know CPR."

"You should know. I'm not ready to date anyone," I said.

Jacob nodded. "Me either," he said.

Then he kissed me.

Part 5

An Unnamed Vineyard

Sebastopol, California. Present day

*S*he takes a seat, cross-legged, and looks at the vineyard. It is her vineyard now. The gardens and the vines, rested from the winter. The winemaker's cottage—the new incarnation of it—painted a royal blue. Bobby helped with the painting. Bobby and Margaret both helped to paint. They had argued about the color. Bobby and Margaret had wanted to pick something more neutral, an ivory or a sand. Though she could only picture a bright blue greeting her in the early morning hours when she was supposed to be sleeping. And it's her winemaker's cottage. So she insisted.

Sitting here, she knows two things to be true. She shouldn't have insisted. The winemaker's cottage looks like a dollhouse. That is the first thing. It looks like a strange and impossible dollhouse. And she should be more nervous than she is. That is the second thing. She should be more nervous than this. But she isn't nervous, not looking over this land.

She has spent the winter quietly preparing for today. She painted the cottage and studied the compost patterns. She bent the ear of every winemaker who would spend time with her. She wandered the halls of her childhood home, her home now. She has turned it into something that feels like hers, slowly and surely, making better choices than that dollhouse blue.

She hears a loud honk and flips around. Jacob pulls down the driveway, Finn not too far behind him. They are stopping by on their way to work—Jacob heading to Napa Valley, Finn heading to a photo shoot in

San Francisco, then to lunch with his new friend Karen. But they wanted to stop by quickly to talk about the weather, to talk about her plan for the compost, to remind her that on the other side of today, they would be there to buy her a beer and for Jacob to cook some bad spaghetti.

That is the plan for tonight: Jacob's overcooked spaghetti, complete with a store-bought rich and creamy pesto sauce, which Jacob thinks masks the fact that he can't figure out how to boil water. She can hardly wait.

For another minute, she's alone in the vineyard. She will produce different wine than her father did, but she won't know what that means until she makes some decisions. So she turns toward the vines and bends down to touch the soil beneath the vine, the telling soil. To see where it is starting. Rubbing the soil between her fingers. Soft, lush. To see where she imagines it will go.

She is not twenty-five years old. She has a new boyfriend who has usurped her father's winery, a useless law degree, no money to speak of in the bank. And no backup plan if this vineyard goes bust. This unnamed vineyard, her whole beautiful future. Her past, her beautiful future. And something like the best thing that she could possibly do for herself.

She's been told that it takes ten years to figure out what you're doing. Ten years.

She takes a breath, smiles. She's ready to get started.

With the beginning of it. Her life.

Acknowledgments

I have to start with Suzanne Gluck, who not only encouraged me to write what I wanted, but was a dynamite partner while I did; and the brilliant Marysue Rucci, who made every page better. My deepest gratitude to you both. You are the dream team.

So many talented people gave their energy and expertise to this novel: Richard Rhorer, Cary Goldstein, Elizabeth Breeden, Andrea DeWerd, Sarah Reidy, Annemarie Blumenhagen, Clio Seraphim, and Kitty Dulin. My gratitude to you all—and to Carolyn Reidy and Jonathan Karp for a great publishing home.

I owe so much to the vintners and the gracious people of Sonoma County and Napa Valley who welcomed me into their world. A special thank-you to Shane Finley and Lynmar Estate Winery for your guidance—and for your Quail Hill Vineyard Pinot Noir, which takes my breath away. Thank you also to Helen Keplinger of Keplinger Wines. And to the good folks at Williams Selyem, Ampelos Cellars, and Littorai, who provided inspiration at critical junctures. I'm in awe of what you all do and how you do it. Any narrative liberties are mine.

I can't say thank you enough to Sylvie Rabineau, cherished friend and invaluable advisor, and Jonathan Tropper, whose guidance and friendship are irreplaceable. Many thanks also to Elizabeth Gabler, Greg Mooradian, Marty Bowen, Wyck Godfrey, and Jaclyn Huntling.

For insight and early reads, thank you to: Allison Winn Scotch, Dustin Thomason, Heather Thomason, Amanda O'Brien, Camrin Agin, Michael Fisher, Amy Cooper, Alisa Mall, Ben Tishler, Dahvi Waller, Johanna Tobel, Gary Belsky, Tom McCarthy, Wendy Merry, Shauna Seliy, and Dana Forman, who reads every story first.

A heartfelt thank-you to my parents, Rochelle and Andrew Dave, and the entire Dave and Singer families. And much love to my wonderful friends, who let me talk about titles and wine long after it was interesting.

Finally, my husband, Josh Singer. Despite five drafts and eighteen months of work on a mystery, he didn't blink when I put it aside. Thank you for not blinking. Thank you for never blinking. I love you with all my heart.

About the Author

Laura Dave is the author of the critically acclaimed novels *The First Husband*, *The Divorce Party*, and *London Is the Best City in America*. Her work has been published in fifteen countries, and three of her novels, including *Eight Hundred Grapes,* have been optioned as major motion pictures. She resides in Santa Monica, California.